Praise for

CHILI CON CARNAGE

OCT 14

"Maxie is an edgy firecracker of a main character, and I can't wait to see the trouble she gets into on the Showdown tour. I'm also anxious to meet her dad, the infamous Texas Jack Pierce. I've always found that chili gets better with time, and I predict that this fun new series is going to continue to get stronger and stronger!"
—*Mochas, Mysteries, and More*

"This is a fun mystery in a unique setting, and Maxie's dedication to finding her father promises that there will be an enjoyable future for readers in this new series."
—*Kings River Life Magazine*

"I am always excited when I find a new book by Kylie Logan. To not only find a new book but a new series is heaven. She draws you right into the story and you can't help but read the book to the very end . . . This is a fun, fast-paced read . . . If you like your mystery hot and spicy then you should be reading *Chili con Carnage*."
—*MyShelf.com*

"The mystery aspect of the novel was well thought out and planned. Maxie is a sort of no-nonsense character and her investigation proves that . . . I'm looking forward to the next book in the series as much for the family drama as I am for the mystery . . . A great first effort!"
—*Debbie's Book Bag*

DEATH BY DEVIL'S BREATH

KYLIE LOGAN

BERKLEY PRIME CRIME, NEW YORK

THE BERKLEY PUBLISHING GROUP
Published by the Penguin Group
Penguin Group (USA) LLC
375 Hudson Street, New York, New York 10014

USA • Canada • UK • Ireland • Australia • New Zealand • India • South Africa • China

penguin.com

A Penguin Random House Company

DEATH BY DEVIL'S BREATH

A Berkley Prime Crime Book / published by arrangement with the author

Berkley Prime Crime Books are published by The Berkley Publishing Group.
BERKLEY® PRIME CRIME and the PRIME CRIME logo are trademarks of
Penguin Group (USA) LLC.

For information, address: The Berkley Publishing Group,
a division of Penguin Group (USA) LLC,
375 Hudson Street, New York, New York 10014.

ISBN: 978-0-425-26242-9

PUBLISHING HISTORY
Berkley Prime Crime mass-market edition / August 2014

PRINTED IN THE UNITED STATES OF AMERICA

10 9 8 7 6 5 4 3 2 1

Cover illustration by Miles Hyman.
Cover design by Diana Kolsky.
Interior text design by Laura K. Corless.

For chili lovers everywhere!

Acknowledgments

Every book has its own story, and *Death by Devil's Breath* is no exception. The Las Vegas setting? I've visited Vegas a couple times, and I know it's the land of the weird and the wacky where anything can happen. Of course, it seemed like the perfect setting for a crazy hot chili contest and characters straight out of central casting. The spicy chili? Since my husband likes chili with far more heat than I do, discussing the wham-bam impact of one of his recipes is something that happens around here every time he puts a pot of chili on to cook.

    As always, my thanks to friends and family, who take the time to listen when I discuss ideas and to help out when I find I've written myself into a corner. Thanks to everyone at Berkley Prime Crime and, of course, to David for the recipe at the end of the book. He promises it's not too hot.

CHAPTER 1

The way I figured it, I had about three minutes.

The seconds tick, tick, ticked away, and before I could waste another one of them, I squirmed in my seat, cocked my leg at a funny angle, and stretched the toe of one stiletto toward the evening purse that was on the floor in front of the empty seat to my left.

Success! Or not.

My shoe snagged the sequin-covered purse, but my thigh muscle protested. I winced, morphed the expression into a smile when Jorge LaReyo, the man who ran the tamale stand at the Chili Showdown and who was sitting on my right, happened to glance my way, and counting on that smile to distract him, gave the purse a little nudge. Lucky for me, the floor in the theater of

Creosote Cal's Cactus Casino and Hoedown Hotel was
faux hardwood. The purse slipped, skittered, and slid
to a stop directly in front of me.

Head up and my gaze never leaving the stage three
rows ahead of me, I dipped and grabbed, then sat back,
unsnapped the little golden clasp at the top of the purse,
and dared a look down. That's when I grumbled a curse.
The stage was brightly lit, but out here in the theater
seats, the lights were dimmed. Teeth gritted, I pretended
to be interested in the proceedings up there in the spotlight at the same time as I slipped my hand into the
purse and felt around.

"It's an ordinary deck of cards!" Up onstage, the man
billed as The Great Osborn! waved a deck of cards still
in its box above his head, then showed it to my half
sister, Sylvia, who he'd called up from the audience to
help with the trick. "I'm going to take the cards out of
the box." He did. "And then I'm going to make one of
them magically disappear. But not until my lovely assis-
tant here . . ." He wiggled his eyebrows at Sylvia and
got a laugh from the audience. "Not until she chooses
five cards and, without looking at them, places them
facedown on the table."

The Great Osborn was middle-aged, and his belly
hung over the royal blue cummerbund he wore with a
black tux that was a little threadbare at the elbows.
When he looked from the brightly painted prop table to
Sylvia, his eyes gleamed.

But then, Sylvia is known to have that sort of effect
on weak-minded men.

It's her fairy tale–princess looks that do them in, of course. The honey-colored hair she had pinned into a knot at her nape, the elegant line of her neck, the high cheekbones, and perfectly bowed lips. The pink dress dusted with sequins didn't hurt, either.

Of course, the sparkly dress was exactly why she'd been invited to help The Great Osborn with this particular trick in the first place. From the magician's vantage point onstage, it was impossible to miss a woman in the audience who twinkled like a drag queen on steroids.

Lucky for me.

Sylvia's moment in the spotlight gave me the three minutes I needed.

Three minutes that were quickly slipping away.

"Lose something?"

I didn't have to glance to my left to know when Nick Falcone slid into the seat next to mine. But then, the temperature in the auditorium shot up a couple dozen degrees at the same time an army of goose bumps popped up on my arms and a shiver cascaded through my body.

Ex-cop. Now head of Showdown security.

Deliciousness personified.

Attitude.

How could a girl have any other reaction?

This girl, it should be noted, kept her cool in spite of it all.

Hand in purse, I cast an oh-so-casual glance in Nick's direction, biting back my disappointment when all I felt inside the purse were the usual essentials: wallet, tissues, contact case.

"Just looking for my lipstick," I told Nick, then I pretended to be interested when The Great Osborn looked at each of the cards on the table and asked a man sitting in the front row to write down their names as he called them out. "Ace of diamonds. Three of hearts. Queen of spades. Seven of hearts. Six of clubs."

Finished, he slipped the cards back in the deck and had Sylvia take the list and search through the deck for the original five cards she'd chosen.

"But there are only . . ." No one could do wide-eyed wonder like Sylvia. How she made herself blush a color that perfectly matched her outfit—and on cue—was anybody's guess. She went through the entire deck one more time before she surrendered and put a hand to one cheek. "Only four of my cards are in the deck! The six of clubs is missing!" she gasped.

"That's because . ." With a ta-da sort of motion, The Great Osborn opened the box the cards had come out of and extracted the missing six. "It's here!" he said, and smiled and bowed when everyone applauded.

Except for me, of course. But then, clapping would have been a little hard since one of my hands was still in the purse.

And Nick. He didn't clap because he was too busy leaning in nice and close. His hot breath brushed my ear when he whispered, "It might help you find your lipstick if you looked in your own purse."

He never had a chance to notice the frigid smile I shot his way in response. That's because the trick was over, and The Great Osborn kissed Sylvia's hand and shooed her back to her seat.

Nick got up and sidled out of the row. Sylvia waited until he'd exited, and flush from her triumphant stage appearance, she sashayed back to her seat.

That left just enough time for me to replace her evening bag exactly where she'd left it.

"So?" Funny how she could twinkle even when the lights weren't trained on her. "What did you think? How did I do?"

"Shhh!" I said, even though it didn't matter. The Great Osborn took his final bows, and Creosote Cal himself strolled to the center of the stage and told everyone it was time for intermission.

"But don't you go far," he said, his pseudo-cowboy twang in keeping with the boots, the jeans, and the ten-gallon hat that fit in with the Wild West theme of Cal's hotel in Vegas, where the next day we'd be opening another Chili Showdown. "Y'all are gonna get your booth assignments in a few minutes, and then, we've got a real treat in store for you. Hang on to your funny bones, pardners, because Dickie Dunkin is up next."

I popped out of my chair, but dang, I couldn't get away from Sylvia fast enough. Not when Jorge and the other folks to my right were being slowpokes about getting out to the aisle.

She knew I was stuck, and Sylvia pounced on the moment. "The Great Osborn said I was a natural," she purred.

I'm not a big believer in batting my eyelashes, but this seemed as good a moment as any to give it a try. "A natural what?" I asked her.

I guess the way she puckered her lips made them need freshening up, because she got her lipstick out of the purse that only moments before had been in my hot little hands.

From the other side of the aisle, I saw Nick raise his eyebrows.

I ignored him.

I was getting pretty good at it. The ignoring part, that is. In spite of his deliciousness and all. Nick and I had actually been thrown together a time or two only a short while before when a Showdown roadie was murdered and I (yes, that's right, little ol' me) solved the crime. Nick wasn't happy. About me investigating, and especially about me taking credit where credit was certainly due. But then, if there was one thing I'd learned about Nick in the weeks since I'd joined the Showdown to take over my missing father's chili and spice truck, it was that Nick was never happy.

Far be it from me to try and be the one to bring some sunshine into his life.

"There's my two favorite girls!"

Tumbleweed Ballew was one of only two people in the world I'd let get away with that kind of happy-family horse hockey when it came to talking about me and Sylvia. The other was his missus, Ruth Ann, and when they closed in on us, they were both grinning like prom queens.

Tumbleweed and Ruth Ann were the administrative heart and soul of the Showdown, and they'd been family friends for years, ever since back before I was even thought of when my mom showed up looking for work at Texas Jack Pierce's Hot-Cha Chili Seasoning Palace and stole the job—and Jack's heart—from Sylvia's mother.

"We've got booth assignments!" Ruth Ann and Tumbleweed wore matching outfits: jeans, denim shirts, vests with long leather fringe on them. Ruth Ann had an envelope in her hand, and she waved it in front of me. "Bet you can't wait. You checked out Deadeye when you got here, didn't you? Isn't it a hoot?"

The simpering smile that I'd thought was a permanent fixture on Sylvia's face melted around the edges. Her lower lip protruded. "I think *tacky* is a much better word. Honestly, Tumbleweed"—she turned to the seventy-year-old—"how did you get talked into this whole fake Western thing? It's going to make us look—"

"Like we can actually get into the spirit of things and have a little fun?" I refused to wilt beneath the acid stare that came from my half sister. That didn't mean I ignored her. It was plenty fun to goad Sylvia. In fact, it was one of the joys of my life. "Get with the program! This is Vegas! Everything's supposed to be over the top. And it's all for fun!"

"Fun." She rolled her baby blues. "A wing of the building that's meant to look like a Western town."

"Yeah, the town of Deadeye," I reminded her.

A shiver snaked over Sylvia's slim shoulders. "Sweet.

And what's the point of Deadeye anyway, except to make more work for us? If we've got to move all our merchandise and supplies out of our trucks and into one of those hokey little booths—"

"There's a sheriff's office, a blacksmith shop, a general store. Even an undertaker." When Tumbleweed chuckled, his belly shook. "These next few days are going to be more fun than a pillow fight! Visitors will get to walk down the main street and stop into each of the little shops to do business with our vendors."

"And this . . ." Once again, Ruth Ann waved the envelope in her hands. "Here's your assignment."

In Sylvia's world, time was money, and she didn't like to waste either. She plucked the envelope out of Ruth Ann's hands and opened it. When she read the single piece of paper inside, her jaw dropped. "The bordello? You've actually assigned Texas Jack's stand to the bor . . . the bor . . ."

"Now, now, honey." Tumbleweed put a hand on her shoulder. "It ain't like we're casting you two girls in a bad light or anything. It's just that we looked the place over. You know, earlier in the week when we got here." He leaned closer. "It's the biggest space in Deadeye," he confided. "And the nicest. We convinced Creosote Cal to assign it to you gals because we wanted to make sure you got the best spot."

"Well, I think it's hilarious and who knows . . ." Because I knew it would annoy her, I poked Sylvia in the ribs with one elbow. "Maybe we'll end up getting a little action. Hey, what happens in Vegas—"

I didn't get the chance to finish; Sylvia had already walked away.

"Seriously." I shook off the bad vibes of Sylvia's annoying Sylvia-ness. "We appreciate the plum spot. I can't wait to see it."

"There's a bar along one wall where you can set up your spices," Tumbleweed said.

"And even a red velvet fainting couch!" Ruth Ann grinned. "You're going to love it, Maxie, honey. And Sylvia . . ." She looked toward where Sylvia made her way toward the ladies' room. "She'll come around."

"Yeah, like in about a million years." This didn't bother me especially. After all, it wasn't news. Sylvia was and always had been a stick-in-the-mud. You'd think a woman who had been arrested for murder back in Taos and owed her freedom to me finding the real killer would relax a little and get over herself. But then, we were talking about Sylvia.

I decided right then and there that it didn't matter. The night before the opening of every Showdown was always a party, and I wasn't going to let thoughts of Miss Tighter Than a Tick spoil my evening. Especially not in Vegas. "You ready for tomorrow morning?" I asked Tumbleweed.

His grin traveled ear to ear. "Devil's Breath chili judging first thing in the morning! I've got to admit, having it be event numero uno was a stroke of genius."

"And your idea!" Ruth Ann wound an arm through her husband's and smiled up at him. She was a dozen years younger than Tumbleweed and as stick-thin as he was beefy. When I was a kid and fantasized about the perfect family that I did not have, I always thought of Ruth Ann and Tumbleweed. Unlike my own parents—divorced going on twenty years—they'd stayed together through thick and thin. I always thought they were the perfect couple, and over the years nothing had made me change my mind.

"Karl Sinclair is here, you know," Ruth Ann purred. "That ought to attract plenty of attention to the Showdown."

Sinclair was a showman extraordinaire. He billed himself as the champion of hot chili and had a legion of followers from all over the world. Well, tomorrow's event ought to prove if he had the chops to go along with his reputation. Four regional winners coming together to earn a national title that was as hot as . . .

Well, as hot as Devil's Breath.

See, in the chili community, Devil's Breath is an all-encompassing name for the hottest of the hot. I, for one, was thrilled that this special category had been added to the cook-off for the weekend show along with the usual divisions: traditional red chili (made with any meat and red chili peppers but absolutely no beans or pasta), chili verde (made with any meat and green chili peppers but absolutely no beans or pasta), salsa, and homestyle (made with any combination of ingredients including beans and pasta). The Devil's Breath contest was garnering us plenty of publicity and putting us on the map here in Vegas, where, let's face it, you have to be over the top to get noticed. And since I love chili—the hotter the better—and after the contest, attendees could donate money for charity and get a taste of each of the finalists' recipes, I couldn't wait.

"What a weekend it's going to be!" Tumbleweed beamed. "Why, we're even going to have a wedding."

"You mean *weddings*," his wife corrected him. "And speaking of that . . . oh, Reverend!" Ruth Ann waved toward a woman who made her way through the crowd toward us. "Reverend Linda Love," she told me as an aside while we waited for the minister to come over. "She owns the largest wedding chapel in Vegas, and on Sunday, she's going to officiate at a ceremony that will get her in the record books. The largest mass wedding ceremony—"

"Ever performed in Nevada at a Western-themed hotel on a Sunday afternoon."

I had to give Reverend Love credit. When she finished the sentence for Ruth Ann, she smiled in a way that told me that even she knew how crazy it sounded. But like I said, this was Vegas, and you didn't get to be the proprietor of the most mega of the wedding chapels in the town that wild and crazy built without having a little bit of attitude, and a lot of circus ringmaster going for you.

I could tell Reverend Love had plenty of both.

She was a tall woman of sixty, slim, and she wore her chin-length blond hair stylishly mussy. The hairdo added a casual little bit of pizzazz to what might otherwise have been a forbidding persona: black power suit, sparkling diamonds at neck and wrists, a watch that no doubt cost more than the worth of Texas Jack's entire enterprise.

She shook hands all around. "I hope you'll all be here for the ceremony," she said, taking each of us in with a glance. "Tumbleweed and Ruth, like I told you when we made the arrangements, you could always renew your vows."

"That's a great idea!" I said.

That made Reverend Love turn her attention to me. "And how about you?" she asked. "If you've got a special someone in your life, Sunday would be the perfect day to make it official."

"Oh no!" My hands out flat, I backed away, both from the woman and the thought of such a thing. "Been there, done that," I told her, which wasn't technically true because Edik and I were never married. "Not going to make the mistake again."

The reverend's smile never wavered. "Love is never a mistake," she said. "No matter the outcome. It's that moment of commitment that matters. The way it shines through the universe and touches the world with love."

Maybe.

Or maybe Linda Love had never had her credit cards scammed and her bank account emptied by a rock band lead guitarist she thought she loved.

The old memories came crashing down, and a shiver snaked over my shoulders. I twitched it away and changed the subject as much as I was able, scrambling to remember any little bit of info I'd heard about the weekend ceremony. "One of the performers from here at the casino is going to assist you, right?"

"Absolutely!" Reverend Love glanced around at the crowd, obviously looking for the performers. Like The Great Osborn, each of them—except for Dickie Dunkin, who was slated to be up onstage next—had already done an abbreviated show for the gathered vendors. "Each of the regulars here is going to perform one more show this weekend, and whoever sells the most tickets, well, that's the performer who will help me out with the ceremony and be immortalized along with me in the record books."

"I hope it's that magician fellow we just saw perform," Tumbleweed said, rocking back on his heels. "He was mighty good. Did you see the way right there at the end, he made that card magically move from the table back into the box?"

I didn't have the heart to point out that even I could have gotten away with that trick. That six of clubs had never left the box to begin with.

"Or that wonderful singer, Hermosa," Ruth Ann piped up.

Again, I kept my mouth firmly shut. Hermosa (just Hermosa, one name, like Cher but without the looks or the talent) had treated us (and oh, how I use those words in the broadest sense) to a medley of songs right before the magician came onstage.

"Or Yancy. Don't forget Yancy. He's a perennial favorite here at Creosote Cal's." With a nod, the reverend indicated the elderly African-American man who chatted with a group of people on the other side of the room. I'd come in late and had missed Yancy Harris's performance, but I remembered seeing the poster that advertised his act when Sylvia and I checked in. Yancy was blind, had been all his life, and according to what I'd heard about him, he could wail on the piano keyboard like no other man around.

"And then there's Dickie, of course," Tumbleweed reminded us.

Was it possible? Did I actually see the reverend's eternally pleasant expression droop at the mention of the comedian's name? It sure didn't last long. But then, a middle-aged balding guy in an orange-and-brown-plaid sport coat came up behind the reverend and wound an arm around her waist, and whatever expression had been on her face, it was lost in a tiny screech of surprise.

"Talking about me, aren't you, sweetie?" Dickie Dunkin himself, I recognized him from the posters out in the lobby. His publicity photos had obviously been taken by a skilled professional—or thirty years before. They didn't show the bags under Dickie's eyes, or the blubbery jowls. They definitely weren't scratch and sniff, either, because if they were, I would have caught wind of the musky aftershave Dickie must have applied with a soup ladle.

"You are going to stay around for my act, aren't you, Reverend?" Dickie asked, then gave me a broad wink.

"She'll stay. I know she'll stay. Reverend Love here, she's a real doll!"

One more squeeze and Dickie hurried onto the stage. It was our cue to get back to our seats.

I slipped into mine just as Sylvia came to hers from the other aisle.

She smoothed her skirt. "Busy mingling, I see."

"Maybe." We'd just gotten off the road a couple hours before and parked our RV and the food truck we hauled behind it, and I hadn't bothered to get dolled up like Sylvia had. I was wearing skinny jeans and a skin-hugging top that was nearly as dark as my short, spiky hair. Vegas, remember, and I wasn't about to be intimidated by the likes of Sylvia because I went for casual (and pretty sexy, if I did say so myself) rather than for her sober good taste.

I smoothed my hand over the legs of my jeans. "Mingling is good for business."

"Business is good for business," Sylvia shot back and I braced myself. If she started into another lecture about price points and profit margins, somebody was going to have to call the Vegas boys in blue because I was going to go off on her.

Good thing she didn't have the chance.

The stage lights dimmed, and a single spotlight turned on Dickie Dunkin.

We clapped politely.

And I settled back, all set to enjoy a little comedy.

At least until Dickie opened his mouth.

"Hey, did you see who's here? It's the Lee family!" The comedian pointed down toward the front row, and like everyone else in the audience, I craned my neck to see who he was talking about. Turns out it was Tumbleweed and Ruth Ann.

"Ug and Home!" Dickie announced with a flourish. "Get it? Ug Lee and Home Lee."

A couple people actually had the nerve to laugh.

I was not one of them.

"Not here." Just as I was about to jump out of my seat, Sylvia's hand came down on my arm. "You'll embarrass us," she said.

"I'll pop that idiot in the nose."

As if this was exactly what she expected, Sylvia was ready with an answer. "That's what he wants. It's how he gets attention. Dickie picks on everyone and everything in the room during his shows, and the madder they get, the more he picks. Look, Tumbleweed's laughing."

He was, but not with a whole lot of enthusiasm.

Ruth Ann, it should be noted, was not.

"And that Reverend Linda Love!" Both hands to his heart, Dickie went into a pretend swoon. "Have you heard about the big wedding on Sunday here at Creosote Cal's? That's going to be something, huh? And I'll let you in on a little secret . . ." As if it was actually what he was going to do, he leaned toward the audience. "You know, the one who sells the most tickets to his show in the next couple days is going to help out Reverend Love with her ceremony. Come on, folks! You know where you're going to be on Saturday night. My show. My show!" He pointed a finger at his own chest. "If you're not, you're idiots. Or you've got lousy taste. But then, I'm guessing you must not be the brightest bulbs in the box anyway. Otherwise you wouldn't be traveling around with this crazy cook-off show! I don't even think any of you are Americans. I think you must all be from Chile. Chile! Get it?"

Somebody must have; there were a few laughs.

"Hey, as long as you're all here." Dickie glanced around the audience. "I figure you're all experts, and I've been meaning to ask you, where do you find chili beans?"

Someone in the back row thought Dickie was serious and called out the name of his own stand, to which Dickie replied, "Idiot. You find chilly beans at the North Pole."

He actually got a couple laughs out of that one.

"So, back to that wedding ceremony. You know, the one Reverend Love is going to perform. Reverend Love, she's a real doll." He put a hand to his eyes and scanned the audience. "Where are you, Reverend Love?" he asked and waved when he saw her. "A doll," he said. "A real doll. And since I'll be selling the most tickets this weekend, I'll be helping her out with the ceremony. She's going to be marrying a whole bunch of people, all at the same time. Hey, Osborn!" He leaned back and looked into the wings. From where I was sitting, I could see that The Great Osborn was watching the show. "Bet you're not gonna be one of them, huh?"

It was an inside joke so it was no wonder nobody laughed. Especially not Osborn, who threw a look at Dickie that could have incinerated asbestos.

Water off a duck's back. This time, Dickie aimed his sights on Yancy Harris.

"You see who's over here." From the stage, he pointed down to where Harris sat all the way at the end of the same row I was in, sunglasses on and a white-tipped cane in one hand. "Hey, Yancy, you see what I mean by all this, don't you? I mean, you *see* what I mean, don't you?"

Yancy shook his head and I couldn't hear him, but I saw a muscle bunch at the base of his jaw at the same time his lips moved. Something told me the words weren't a glowing review of Dickie's shtick.

"And then there's Hermosa! You all saw her here earlier this evening, didn't you, folks?" Dickie pointed to the back of the theater, and we all turned in our seats when he waved Hermosa toward the stage. It took a moment for the spotlight to find her, but when it did, it followed along. She was a chesty woman with a big head of bleached hair, and she was squeezed into a green dress that fanned out at the bottom, like a mermaid tail. She took tiny, mincing steps up to the front of the theater.

"She's something, isn't she, folks?" Dickie clapped and the audience joined in. "Hermosa has an unforgettable voice. And have you seen the way she sways left and right when she really gets into a song?" Dickie swung his hips back and forth. "You know why she does that, don't you? It's harder to hit a moving target!"

I didn't even bother to groan. But then, I was pretty busy watching Hermosa curl her lip, toss her head, and turn on her heels to march out of the theater.

Me? I was pretty much with Hermosa. I'd had enough of Dickie Dunkin. I got up out of my seat to leave.

"Hey, where you going, sweetheart?" Dickie called after me and checked his watch. "We had it all planned. You're not supposed to meet me in my dressing room for another fifteen minutes. Hey, that would be something, wouldn't it? That little chickie and me." He whistled low. "Talk about a hot tamale! And believe me, when it's all over, I'm going to talk about it plenty!"

By the time I punched open the door and walked out, I wasn't even mad, just disgusted by stupid Dickie and his stupid jokes.

Come to think of it, I guess I wasn't the only one. There hadn't been very many laughs packed into Dickie's performance, but there had been plenty of people—Tumbleweed and Ruth Ann, Hermosa, The Great Osborn, Yancy Harris—who looked like they would have liked nothing better than to commit murder.

CHAPTER 2

We moved into the bordello that night.

We carried boxes and arranged merchandise, and Sylvia grumbled the entire time. I, it should be noted in the interest of fairness, didn't let that get to me. Yes, the Deadeye house of ill repute was as corny as can be with its fake red velvet, its grainy photographs on the walls of women in various stages of undress, and its faux bar (complete with bottles of colored water to look like liquor), but Tumbleweed was right. It was the biggest spot in Deadeye, and there was plenty of shelf space for us to display the spices and chili mixes and peppers we sold. It was also immediately to the right when folks walked in from the casino. Primo. And with me out front all weekend dancing and waving people inside dressed in the giant red Chili Chick costume I wore at every Showdown, I predicted our profits for the weekend would be primo, too.

The next day was Thursday, and walking into Dead-eye, I decided life was good and Deadeye . . . Deadeye smelled like hot-enough-to-self-combust chili heaven!

I took a deep breath, savoring every bit of the aroma that wafted out of the auditorium at the far end of the "street" between the rows of shops. The general store was next door, and the night before, after I was done setting up Texas Jack's Hot-Cha Chili Seasoning Palace in our spot and before I moseyed into the casino to lose twenty bucks at video poker, I helped Gert Wilson put her crockery and pot holders and cookbooks on display there. Next to her was the bakery shop, where the bean guy who'd taken over for the late (not so great) Puff sold his dried beans and, beyond that, the sheriff's office. As if the Universe was conspiring to get my goat, just as I looked that way, Nick walked out. Sheriff's office. Secu-rity. Get it? I bet Creosote Cal thought he was one hilar-ious guy.

Just so Nick didn't get any ideas about lecturing me for the purse-stealing incident the night before, I turned my back on him, and while I was at it, I closed my eyes and tilted back my head, too. The fragrance of hot spices didn't just tickle my senses, it punched me right in the nose, and from there, it tingled its way into my lungs. My eyes watered just a little. My breath caught. My stomach growled.

I couldn't wait until after the judging, when I could get my hands on a couple bowls of Devil's Breath.

I was so busy indulging my chili fantasies and dreaming about the butt-kicking good times my taste buds were in for, I would have completely missed the tapping noise if it wasn't followed by the polite sound of someone clearing his throat.

"Didn't mean to bother you."

I opened my eyes to find Yancy Harris, white-tipped cane in hand, sunglasses in place, and a smile on his face. Yancy wore a black suit that was a little too big for his slim frame and a fedora with a jaunty red-and-gray feather in the band. He lifted his hat in greeting. "I asked at the front entrance and I was told Miss Maxie Pierce was the woman to see."

"Well, you've got the right person," I told him. "What can I do for you?"

As if he could actually see and make sure we were alone, Yancy looked around before he stepped nearer. "I've got a problem of a delicate sort of nature," he confessed.

I was already shaking my head before I remembered it was a waste of time. "I'm not exactly a delicate sort of person," I told him.

Yancy laughed. "This, I have also heard. That's why the guy out front said you could help. You see, my problem is a chili problem."

"Chili." The word escaped me on the end of a sigh. "Chili problems I can handle. What do you need?"

"It's more like what *don't* I need. You heard about the contest judging this morning, right?"

I stopped myself on the brink of a nod. "Devil's Breath. Yeah, it's going to be fabulous."

"Well, I'm one of the judges."

This was not news. I knew that Yancy would be judging along with Reverend Love, Hermosa, The Great Osborn, and Dickie Dunkin.

"A celebrity panel of judges," I said, repeating the words on the posters I'd seen plastered all over the hotel. Even though I was pretty sure *celebrity* wasn't completely accurate, I had to admit it was good publicity. "It's going to be a blast."

"Exactly what I'm afraid of." Yancy patted his stomach. "See, from what I hear, this Devil's Breath is hotter than a two-dollar pistol. And my stomach . . . whew!" Yancy blew out a breath that smelled like peppermint. "Now this isn't something I want to get around," he confided. "Can't have people thinking I'm just an old man who can't handle his food. But I'll tell you what, I'm not as young as I used to be and I'm not sure my stomach can take it. Not if this Devil's Breath stuff is as hot as everybody says it is. When I asked out front, the man said you might know what to do. You know, to tone down the spiciness so that I don't sit up there at that judges' table and go up in smoke."

"I get it." I did. Though I was a lover of all things hot (the aforementioned Edik being the perfect example), I understood people who liked less fire with their chili. I would never want to be one of them, but I understood. Honest.

"There's baking soda," I told Yancy. "You can mix a teaspoonful of that into the chili to tone down the heat. I'm pretty sure I don't have any of that in the RV, but there are limes!" I'd already taken a few steps toward the exit (disguised as a livery stable door) that led to the parking lot and the RV where Sylvia and I lived on the road when I remembered this surefire remedy. "I know I've got some limes in the fridge. A couple squeezes of that ought to help."

A smile made Yancy's face fold into a thousand crinkles. "Much obliged," he said and added a little bow. "You don't think this will get us in trouble, do you? I mean, I understand these cook-off contestants are a serious bunch. If they think I'm messin' with the flavors of their chili—"

I waved away his objection with one hand, then grumbled to myself. The man was blind. I had to be more aware and more considerate. "It's not like this is a part of the official contest," I told Yancy. "This Devil's Breath championship is pretty much just for bragging rights, not some big prize. And besides, a squirt of lime juice isn't going to change the taste of any of the entries all that much. It's just going to tone down the heat."

I promised Yancy I'd meet him back in the auditorium, and a few minutes before the judging was scheduled to start, I had a tiny Tupperware container of lime juice in my pocket, and I squeezed (pun intended because that's what I'd just done with the limes) my way through the throng of spicy-chili lovers who waited outside for a chance to watch the judging and grab a bowl of fiery goodness.

The air inside the auditorium wasn't just filled with anticipation; it was peppery and perfect. Inside the door, I paused so I could take a moment to bask in the spiciness, my gaze roving over the stage. To my left was the long table where the judges would taste and score the entries. To my right and directly opposite, the four regional winners were busy cooking.

See, that's how the chili categories of cook-offs work. In the salsa category, contestants can make their mixtures and bring them along to the contest finished. But for the chili categories, everything has to be cooked on-site. Oh, not things like canned tomatoes or tomato sauce or pepper sauce or the beer that many competitors use in their chilies. But the meat and anything else they throw in, yup. That has to be prepared at the event, and contestants usually have between three and four hours to do it all. Which means these contestants had been here chopping and mixing and working their magic since before the sun came up.

Curious as to how it was going, I watched the first contestant stir his pot. I have to admit, it was a little strange to see a man in monk's robes at a chili cook-off, but from what I'd heard, Brother William had all the right reasons. His monastery back in Minnesota was looking to make some extra cash, and they'd decided a chili mix was just the ticket. In fact, I'd heard they'd already chosen a name for their mix: Devil's Breath with an Angel's Touch. Cute marketing. We'd see if his recipe lived up to it.

The second man at the table was Karl Sinclair, he of the giant touring motor home with his picture painted on the side of it. Karl was a perennial Showdown contestant, and he'd won a few titles in his day. My opinion? The hype got him further than his cooking ever would. But then, Karl was pretty good at hype.

The third man was someone I didn't recognize from the circuit, a young guy with golden hair that gleamed in the stage lights. In fact, everything about this guy was shiny, from his perfect setup to his glistening chili pot. He wore khakis and a pristine white shirt, the sleeves rolled above the elbows, all topped with a white (how did he keep it so clean?) apron. I watched him mix, sniff, and add a little salt to the chili pot, thinking that he looked more like a model in a cooking magazine than a contestant at a cook-off.

But hey, who was I to judge? I'd had people tell me I looked more like a bartender at a biker spot than a woman who sold chili spices.

The fourth and final contestant . . .

My gaze swung toward the woman who chopped peppers down at the far end of the table. Tall and in her forties, she moved with ease, like she was perfectly at home with a knife in her hands. For a couple seconds, I watched her graceful movements: the quick, efficient way she diced the peppers and the way she swept them off the cutting board and into her chili pot. She blew a curl of dark hair out of her eyes, put a hand to the small of her back, and stepped back for a moment's rest.

That's when she looked up and her eyes met mine.

What was that I said about her being good with a knife? Well, she was plenty good with daggers, too, because that's exactly what she shot in my direction. If looks could kill, I wouldn't just be dead, I would have been drawn, quartered, and buried deep.

I sucked in a breath and glanced over my shoulder, sure she must be aiming that death ray look at someone behind me, but there was no one else around.

No one but me in the crosshairs of a perfect stranger. Or was she?

My eyes narrowed, I exchanged her look for look, thinking there was something vaguely familiar about the set of her shoulders and the tilt of her nose. She was taller than me, I could tell that all the way from over where I stood, and quickly, I rummaged through my mental Rolodex. Tall, middle-aged women. Tall, middle-aged women with dark eyes and hair. Tall, middle-aged women with dark eyes and hair who looked like they would like nothing better than to see me go up in flames.

Just like her pot of chili was just about to do.

The woman realized her pot had boiled over just a second after I did, and she snapped to attention to take care of it and released me from the tractor-beam hold of her Evil Eye.

Fine by me. I didn't have a clue who she was, but believe me, I intended to find out.

I would have done it right then and there, too, if just

as I stepped toward the stage, I didn't hear The Great Osborn's voice ring through the auditorium.

"You really should mind your own business, Dickie." Osborn and Dickie Dunkin stood toe to toe, and hey, I was never one to miss out on any excitement. Anxious to find out what the beef was, I scooted toward the stage, where just the night before, they had both performed for the Showdown crowd. "And while you're at it, why don't you take those stupid jokes of yours and stick 'em where the sun don't shine!"

"That would be at my Saturday night show," Dickie countered. This morning he was dressed in khakis and an oatmeal-colored golf shirt that made his face look pastier than ever. He propped his fists on his hips. "There won't be room for sunshine in here on Saturday," he purred. "Because my show is going to be sold out. Unlike the shows of the rest of you losers."

This time, he wasn't just talking to The Great Osborn. Hermosa was there in a flowy purple caftan and Dickie shot a look her way as well as one toward Yancy, who was already seated at the judges' table.

"Not talking about you, Reverend!" Dickie called out when Linda Love walked onto the stage and slipped into her seat. "You, you're not a loser like the rest of 'em. You're a real doll!"

Reverend Love smiled in the polite sort of way people do when they're not sure what they've gotten themselves into.

Hermosa, it should be noted, did not. In fact, she marched around to the front of the table, shot one look at the reverend, and poked a finger into Dickie's stomach. "Watch it, Dickie." Another poke for good measure. "If you're going to call anybody a doll—"

"It's you, honey lamb!" Dickie smacked a big, wet kiss on her cheek. "You're my one and only."

"And you're a real big mouth," The Great Osborn growled. He put his hands on Hermosa's shoulders and stepped her to the side so he could face Dickie. "How about minding your own business for a change?"

"How about you keeping your mouth shut, and your hands off my girl," Dickie shot back.

"Oh yeah?" Osborn took a step toward him and after that . . .

Well, I wouldn't exactly call it a melee. It was more like a little pushing and shoving, like kids on a schoolyard who are afraid to take a couple real swings and, instead, opt for trying to look like tough guys instead of actually acting like them.

Osborn threw a punch that missed Dickie by a mile.

Dickie ducked out of the way, tripped over his own feet, and stumbled back against the judges' table. Styrofoam bowls and plastic silverware went flying.

By the time Dickie righted himself, his face was an ugly shade of purple. He curled his fingers and raised his hands toward Osborn's throat.

That is, until Nick hopped onto the stage and stepped between the two men.

"That's it. To your seats." Talk about looks that could flash-freeze a perp at twenty paces! His shoulders steady and every muscle tensed, Nick glanced back and forth between the two men. "Now!" he barked.

Turned out Dickie and Osborn could move pretty fast for a couple middle-aged guys.

A few more seconds and it was all over. Osborn took his seat at the far end of the table closest to the audience; Dickie took his seat on the other end, next to Reverend Love, who along with Hermosa was already putting the place settings back where they belonged.

Excitement over, Tumbleweed stepped to the center of the stage, rubbed his hands together, and glanced from contestants to judges, and when he realized everyone was where they were supposed to be and no blood had been shed, he heaved a sigh of relief. "It's time to start," he said. "We'll get the auditorium doors open and get folks in here."

I scampered up to the stage, set down the little container I'd brought with me, and whispered in Yancy's ear that the lime juice was near his right hand, where he could easily grab it, then I ducked backstage before anybody could point out that I was somebody who didn't belong there.

From there, I stepped back to watch visitors file into their seats. A few minutes later, the judging officially began.

So here's the thing about a chili cook-off. The way it works—or at least the way the Showdown contests always work—is that the person in charge of the contest (in this case, Tumbleweed) takes a bowl from each judge over to the contestants, one at a time. Each contestant ladles one scoop of their chili into a bowl and that chili is then delivered to the judge for tasting. As for what they're supposed to be judging, according to the orientation Tumbleweed gives the judges before each contest, they are supposed to look for things like good flavor, the texture of the chili, the aroma, and how skillfully the spices are blended. Of course, for this special Devil's Breath category, heat mattered, too.

When everyone was settled, Tumbleweed got the first scoop from Brother William, delivered it to The Great Osborn, went back for another, and so on.

"They're not actually going to eat that stuff, are they?"

Since I knew Nick was a philistine when it came to chili, I tried to be understanding. That didn't mean I didn't throw a look over my shoulder when he came up behind me. "Spicy is what chili is all about."

"The only thing spicy is good for is burning your lips and scalding your insides."

Like I could miss an opening as good as that?

I looked up into Nick's eyes. Even all the neon in Vegas couldn't compete with that vivid blue. "What's wrong with burning your lips?" I asked him.

He looked down at me. "It all depends if you're talking a little burning or too much."

I leaned back. Just a little. Just a hairsbreadth closer to his chest. "Is there such a thing as too much?"

Nick barked out a laugh. It was the first I realized his gaze had moved up the stage, where The Great Osborn had just swallowed his first spoonful of Brother William's brew and his lips puckered and the tips of his ears turned red.

Nick laughed. "Guess that's my answer."

And here I thought we were talking about something other than chili.

I crossed my arms over my chest and turned my attention back to the contest, watching as Hermosa swallowed a taste of chili, coughed, and pounded her chest.

Yancy was next. He popped a spoonful of chili in his mouth, let it sit on his tongue for a couple seconds, swallowed, and smiled when he looked into the wings. If I didn't know better, I'd say he knew exactly where I was standing when he sent that silent thank-you for the lime juice.

Next up, Reverend Love, and it seemed she was not one to take chances. She put a tiny bit of chili on the tip of her spoon and carefully touched it to the tip of her tongue. She let it settle in, flicked her tongue toward the spoon again, and her mouth fell open with surprise. As soon as she was done writing down a few comments on the score sheet next to her, she took a drink of water.

"Amateur," I grumbled. "Water doesn't help."

"So now you're a chemist?"

This time, I didn't dignify Nick's question with so much as a glance. "You don't have to be a chemist to know spices. The capsaicin in peppers is what's hot, and when you taste it, then drink water, all the water does is spread the hotness all around your mouth."

"So now you know about hot lips and hot mouths?"

This time, I wasn't going to rise to the bait. But then,

I was pretty busy watching Dickie, who spooned up a mouthful of chili and called out, "You guys are wimps! No wonder none of you are going to be up there with me and the reverend when she makes Vegas history on Sunday. You have to be bold to make it in this town. You have to be daring!" And with that, he swallowed down two more big gulps of Devil's Breath.

Dickie's cheeks turned fire-engine red.

His shoulders stiffened.

He took another taste.

So, okay, the guy was a total jackass, but I had to give him credit; he knew how to handle his Devil's Breath.

And so it went.

Karl Sinclair's chili elicited much the same responses except from The Great Osborn, who after one taste, had to excuse himself from the table so he could stand backstage, pound his chest, and cough.

The shiny guy with the pristine apron got a thumbs-up from Yancy, and the woman contestant . . . well, she caught sight of me, and after that, I'm not sure what was hotter, the looks she shot my way or her chili.

No matter. Like all the other chilies before hers, she got pretty much the same responses, a little choking, a little gagging, a whole lot of red faces.

"You guys are lightweights," Dickie called out and took another taste of the woman's chili. "You think this stuff is hot? You don't know hot! Hermosa, now there's one hot chick! And hot—" Another bite and Dickie sat back in his chair. "There's a restaurant here in town that

serves only hot food. It's got three seating sections: daring, wild, and downright crazy."

He hauled in a breath. "And then there's the place
where all the chili is free." Dickie pulled a handkerchief
out of his pocket and mopped his brow. "This place . . .
and the chili is free and . . ." There was a glass of water
nearby and he glugged it down so fast, the water dribbled
over his chin. "All the chili you can eat is free, but . . ."
His shoulders dropped, his arms fell to his sides.

"Water is ten dollars a glass."

It was the last thing Dickie said before he fell, facedown, into his bowl of chili, and the last bad joke he'd
ever tell.

CHAPTER 3

So much for selling bowls of Devil's Breath for charity.

Within a couple minutes, hotel security showed up. The local cops weren't far behind. They interviewed the folks in the audience, and I watched as, one by one, they were told they could go and the cops turned to one another and mumbled, "That one didn't see anything, either."

As for the judges, the contestants, Ruth Ann, Tumbleweed, Nick, and I (the one who didn't belong, but luckily, no one had noticed that yet), we were herded backstage and told to stay put and wait.

"This has got to stop happening." Tumbleweed plopped into a chair and dropped his head into his hands. "People dying left and right. The Showdown's gonna get a bad name!"

He was right, and he didn't need me to tell him so. I left Ruth Ann holding her husband's hand and closed in on Nick.

"You were out there with the security guys. What are they saying? What do you think?" I asked him.

He toed the line between what was considered onstage and what was technically off, stepping closer little by little to where a team from the Clark County coroner/medical examiner's office studied the bowl of chili at the end of the judges' table. Dickie, it should be noted, had been removed from the abovementioned chili by Nick, who hurried onstage the moment he realized there was trouble and tried CPR to no avail. Dickie's body was sprawled on the floor, his arms splayed at his sides, his face red and greasy, his eyes open, glazed, and staring up at the chandelier that looked like a wagon wheel.

"I wish I could hear what they were saying," Nick grumbled.

"Who cares what they're saying! You got a nice, close look at Dickie. What do you think?"

He shot me a look. "You don't want to know."

"Because you think there's something fishy going on."

"I think that Devil's Breath chili was strong enough to take paint off walls."

"Maybe, but I don't care how hot they are, peppers can't kill you. Not even Trinidad moruga scorpions and those are the hottest peppers in the world. I mean, not unless you sat down and ate a whole lot of them all at one time. Admit it, Nick. You're thinking what I'm thinking. And I'm thinking Dickie was poisoned."

Nick's grunt was all the answer I needed.

I tossed a look over my shoulder to where Yancy and Osborn had their heads together and Hermosa sobbed in Reverend Love's arms. The whole female bonding thing actually might have been a touching scene if the good reverend wasn't trying to flag down a passing cop. When that officer ignored her, Reverend Love rolled her eyes, gave Hermosa three quick pats on the back, and did her best to attract the attention of another cop.

"They all hated him," I said, watching as that cop, too, ignored the reverend. "And who can blame them? You heard Dickie at the show last night. He made fun of each and every one of them, and this morning, Dickie and Osborn, they got into a scuffle. You saw it. You stopped it."

Nick spun to face me. It was the first I saw that his efforts at first aid had cost him—at least when it came to his wardrobe. Like he'd been shot, there was a wide streak of tomato on his charcoal gray suit that started at his heart and smeared all the way across his ribs. As far as I was concerned, his tie was no big loss. It was a way-too-conservative maroon-and-charcoal stripe that now included dots of red, bits of pepper, and dashes of grease that gave me a glossy wink when the light hit them. There was a smutch of peppery sauce on Nick's chin, right above the spot where a muscle jumped at the base of his jaw.

"Don't," he said, and whether he was referring to the delicate subject of murder I'd brought up or the fact that I yanked my green long-sleeved T-shirt down over my hand and swiped at the gunk on his face, I wasn't sure. I kept on wiping, even when he did his best to duck out of the way.

"It's going to burn," I told him, then realized it probably already did. Even after I got rid of the chili, Nick's jawline was red and inflamed. Don't ask me how I thought I had a snowball's chance in hell of finding any right then and there, but I looked around for a remedy. "We need alcohol. Or hand sanitizer." I barked out a laugh. "If Sylvia was here, we'd be all set. She always has it with her. Hand sanitizer, that is, not alcohol. Germs, you know. They're lurking everywhere."

But I don't think Nick did know. Or if he did, I'm pretty sure he didn't care. Then again, his mouth pulled tight and his eyes watered. When I took another swipe at his face, he winced.

That's when I noticed that one of the paramedics had left his first aid kit open behind where he and a couple other guys were looking over Dickie's body. I darted out to the stage, and just as I suspected, there were packets of disposable alcohol pads in the kit. I grabbed a couple, tore one open, and as soon as I was in range, I slapped it on Nick's face.

He batted my hands away but don't think I didn't notice that he held on to the wipe. "Don't."

I pretended I didn't know what he was talking about, and just to prove it, I pulled out the batted-eyelash arsenal. It's not like I thought Nick would find this especially attractive. In fact, I'd think less of him if he did. But I knew it would annoy the heck out of him. Which was precisely why I did it.

"Don't what?" I asked. I ripped into another packet with my teeth and handed a fresh wipe to Nick.

He dabbed his skin. "Don't start seeing bad guys where there aren't any, and don't start assuming a crime has been committed. We don't know that. And while you're at it, don't start coming up with half-baked theories and don't—"

I opened my mouth to defend myself and snapped it shut again when he stepped into my personal space and glared at me. Any other guy would have looked pitiful and a little pathetic with that patch of inflamed skin outlining the angle of his jawline. But then as I'd come to find out in the weeks I'd been with the Showdown, Nick wasn't any other guy.

"Don't," he said.

I crossed my arms over my chest. "There's nothing wrong with being curious. Besides, you must have had a few suspicions of your own. I see you didn't do mouth-to-mouth on Dickie."

It was true, and it proved he was thinking exactly what I was thinking, and what I was thinking was that since there had been no violence done to Dickie, the culprit just might be poison; Nick touched the alcohol wipe to his lips. "What I do and don't do has nothing to do with you. If you think you can go around and investigate—"

I twitched away his criticism with a lift of one shoulder. "You mean, just like I did last time?"

"Last time, you were lucky."

Arms uncrossed, pressed to my sides. Fists clenched. Chin up. "I was smart."

"You took too many stupid chances."

"And found out who the killer was."

"Well, I don't care what happened here, there's no way I'm going to stand by and watch you try to do it again."

"So you admit it! You *do* think Dickie was poisoned!" Poking a finger at Nick's nose to emphasize my point probably wasn't the best idea. Since he ground his teeth together as if he might bite it right off, I moved fast and tucked my hand behind my back. I was just about to ask what kind of poison Nick thought it might have been when one of the cops onstage waved him over.

I would have followed if he hadn't thrown me a look as dangerous as a pot full of ghost peppers.

I kept in my place and watched him talk to the cops, and since I couldn't hear anything, I got bored. I gave Sylvia a quick call, not so much because I thought she was worried, but to tell her what was going on and remind her that I'd be a little busy from now until I-didn't-know-when and she'd have to work the brothel alone. Big points for me—I did not mention that if it had been a real house of ill repute and Sylvia had been the only one there, chances are there wouldn't have been much business.

That taken care of, I strolled over to where the Devil's Breath contestants waited. Yes, I admit it, I wouldn't have had the nerve if the nasty, dark-haired woman hadn't been busy being interviewed by a detective, and I figured I didn't have to worry about going up in flames thanks to her dirty looks.

I took the chair next to Brother William, whose lips

moved over a silent prayer while he fingered the beads of a rosary.

"So what do you think?"

Brother William's lips froze. "I think it's terrible," he said. He was a young man with short-cropped, rusty-colored hair and his cheeks were stained with tears. "Terrible for that poor man, and terrible for us. The monastery, that is. We hoped a contest win would lead to getting some publicity for our chili mix, and that would boost sales. The added income would help with the monastery's expenses. We may be men of God, but we still have utility bills. I suppose that's the lesson to be learned. If you put your trust in material things . . ." His thoughts faded along with his voice, and he went back to his prayer.

It wasn't hard to decide on a next move. Karl Sinclair stood over near the red stage curtain. He was on a phone call, and even though I couldn't hear the words distinctly, there was no doubt that Karl was not a happy camper. His baritone rumbled like a freight train. I know an opportunity when I see it; his back was to me, so I closed in.

"Son of a—" Sinclair swallowed the rest of what he was going to say to the person on the other end of the phone. "You can't let them pull the endorsement, Fritz. Not just because some fool of a comedian happened to pick the wrong time to keel over dead. I would have won the Devil's Breath contest. You know it and I know it. Nobody makes chili as hot and as good as mine."

His head bent, he listened to whatever it was Fritz had to say. "Yeah, well, I'd like to see you take that to the bank," Sinclair spit out. "If you can't talk them into continuing the negotiations, then it looks like I'm going to need to find another agent. What's that?" Sinclair's shoulders shot back. "Yeah, well, same to you," he growled and ended the call.

When he spun around, Sinclair's expression went blank. "Oh." He gulped in a calming breath, shoved his phone back in his pocket, and looked past me toward the activity going on out front. He even managed a quick smile designed, no doubt, to make me think everything was hunky-dory. Yeah, just in case I didn't hear the shouting match on the phone. "Are the cops saying anything? They're going to let us continue on with the contest, right? When can we get started again?"

"Really?" I crinkled my nose and stuck out an arm, pointing to the stage. "There's a guy out there who's dead and all you can think about is you?"

"About me. About the title. About the big, fat endorsement deal my agent has been working on with one of the major canned chili companies. Damn!" There was only so long he could hold it together. Sinclair paced out the area between the curtain and a painted backdrop of Creosote Cal's Saloon complete with whiskey bottles, a lady of the evening in a gown with a plunging neckline, and a bald fat guy wearing an apron behind the bar. Mumbling, he came back in my direction. "Thanks to that stupid fool of a comedian—"

"Something tells me Dickie's having a worse day than you are."

"You think?" Sinclair didn't look convinced, and honestly, I wasn't surprised. Any guy who billed himself as the World's Greatest Chili Cook (which was clearly not true since Jack made the best chili on earth) had to have the ego to go along with the hype. "Tell that to the bank that approved my new mortgage on the basis of that promised endorsement. I was a shoo-in for the title and you know it. Everyone knows it. Karl Sinclair is the greatest . . ."

My stomach might be able to tolerate hot chili, but there was only so much Karl Sinclair I could take. He was still singing his own praises when I turned my back on him and looked around for Shiny Guy.

I found him sitting by himself in a quiet corner, texting away.

"Hey."

His fingers flew over the keyboard, and he barely spared me a glance.

"We haven't met. I'm Maxie."

He tapped out a few more words. "Tyler York."

I thought about Brother William's and Karl Sinclair's reactions to the tragedy. "You must be pretty bummed, huh?"

"Bummed?" He finished his message and finally gave me his full attention. "About . . ." Somebody called for a stretcher, and Tyler's gaze moved beyond me to the commotion onstage. "Oh, you mean about the dead guy."

"Not something you see happen every day. Guy. Chili. Dead. Pretty nasty stuff."

His shrug pretty much said it all. "It happens."

"Not so much."

"Well, it did today."

"And ruined the contest."

"The contest, sure." He stood in all his unsullied, untouched by tomato sauce, unspattered with grease glory, and the smile Tyler shot my way was as blinding as his white apron. "There's always next time," he said.

Part of me admired the incredibly adult way he handled the disappointment. But I'd spent my whole life around chili cook-offs and chili cooks, remember, and if there's one thing I've learned, it's that chili is the center of their universe. Cooking chili, eating chili, dreaming up new ways to serve chili and new things they can add to make their chili just a little different and just a little better . . . that's what chili cook-off contestants are all about.

Yup, there's an unalienable truth about chili cooks and chili eaters—they are a passionate bunch.

And Tyler was as blasé as I'd seen Sylvia when the Showdown vendors got into a really heated discussion about if real chili had beans in it.

Fishy?

Plenty.

Don't think I didn't notice.

"So . . ." If I do say so myself, I did a pretty good job of pretending that I was just passing the time. "Since the contest is going to be canceled, how about sharing your cooking secrets? You're a regional Devil's Breath winner, and that must mean you make really good, really hot chili. What kind of poison do you put in yours?"

I didn't actually expect him to cop to the crime right then and there, but hey, it would have been nice. When all I got back from Tyler was a blank look, I burbled out a laugh. "Poison! What am I talking about? I mean peppers, of course. What kind of peppers do you put in your chili to kick up the heat? Devil's tongue? Yucatan white? Or are you a habanero kind of guy?"

Tyler's smile was as stiff as meringue. "Peppers? I use hot ones."

The joke was pretty lame, but I didn't let on. "No, I mean it. Seriously. Not Trinidad scorpions. Nobody in their right mind would put those in a contest chili. Unless you add just a tad for kick and flavor."

"Maybe."

"Oh, come on! I was looking forward to tasting the Devil's Breath. The least you can do is share."

He gave me a wink. "My recipe is a secret," he said, and he turned around and walked away.

Me? I vowed to keep an eye on Tyler York. Anybody that perfect had to have plenty to hide.

I considered my next move, and when I saw that the woman contestant was finished with the detective and her fiery gaze lit on me (and likely would have lit me up if I stayed in one spot too long), I spun around and headed back the way I'd come. I cozied up next to Ruth Ann and slipped my arm through hers just as Tumbleweed started talking to one of the cops.

"There's no way a whole pot of chili could be poisoned," I heard him tell the cop. "All the judges' samples come from the same pot. And if one of them was poisoned . . ."

Tumbleweed didn't need to finish the thought. The cop scratched a line in a small notebook. "You're saying they'd all be poisoned."

Tumbleweed nodded so hard, his jowls flapped. "They'd have to be, see. The scoops, they all come out of the pot at the same time. Which means the scoop Dickie got from that last contestant . . ."

He went on explaining, but I was too busy thinking to listen. That last contestant he talked about was the woman who'd decided for some strange reason that she didn't like me, and wondering about her, I looked over to where I'd last seen her. Didn't it figure, now that I was interested, she was nowhere around.

"Maxie will tell you." Tumbleweed's words snapped me out of my thoughts. "She'll tell you that's how a cook-off works. Always has, always will. No way one judge can get a taste of something another judge can't. It's all mixed. It's all stirred. It all comes from the same pot at the same time."

I nodded my agreement and took another thought for a spin. "That could mean what happened to Dickie . . ." At that particular moment, the guys from the medical examiner's office were taking Dickie away, and we all watched as they lifted his body into a big black bag, set it on a stretcher, and strapped it on so it wouldn't take a tumble. I am not a particularly queasy person, but the sound of the bag zipping closed sent shivers over my shoulders.

"Dickie wasn't exactly a spring chicken and he was overweight, and I bet you anything he was a smoker, too." Believe me, this was not a criticism on my part.

Until a couple months before, I, too, had been a smoker, and there were days I wished I'd never quit. "Maybe Dickie died of natural causes."

"Maybe." The cop got our contact information down and flipped closed his notebook. "Maybe not."

I guess The Great Osborn had been eavesdropping, because he darted forward, looking a little less great and a lot more panicked. "We should go to the hospital," he told the cop. "We should all get checked out. We all ate from the same pots of chili. We could be ticking time bombs."

Hermosa rolled her eyes. "If there was poison in your chili, you'd be dead by now, Osborn. Although if memory serves, the last time we went to bed together, you were already pretty dead."

Osborn's smile was acid.

Hermosa turned her back on him.

"Tumbleweed's right," I told the cop though he certainly hadn't asked for my opinion. "The judges' bowls are all filled at once. If the whole pot was poisoned, everyone would have gotten some. I'm going with natural causes." I nodded, and so did Ruth Ann and Tumbleweed, not because they thought my announcement carried any weight, but because I knew what they were thinking: a death from natural causes was much easier to deal with than the thought that someone wanted Dickie dead and took the opportunity to help him along with a little Devil's Breath.

"It's possible." The cop took pity on us. He even patted Ruth Ann's shoulder. "Don't you worry. We'll get to the bottom of it."

"Well, you could get to the bottom of it right now if you'd pay a little more attention." Her eyes gleaming, Reverend Love stepped forward. "I've been trying to talk to someone but—"

"We'll get around to interviewing everyone," the cop assured her.

Reverend Love stepped back, her weight against one foot. "Do you know who I am?" she asked, but she didn't wait for an answer. "I'll tell you what, sonny, you will once I talk to your superiors." She clapped her hands to get everyone's attention. "If you'd all stop running around like chickens with your heads cut off, I could put an end to the questions right here and now. I know who killed Dickie!"

Like everyone else, I pulled in a breath and leaned toward her, hanging on her every word.

Now that she was the center of attention, Reverend Love stood tall and threw back her shoulders. She also threw out an arm and arced it slowly across the circle of gathered judges and contestants.

"I saw it. I saw it all," she announced. "Right when Osborn and Dickie went at each other and everyone was watching them and he didn't think anyone would notice, I saw him pour some kind of powder into one of the judges' bowls. Well?" When no one moved fast enough to suit her, Reverend Love sent a laser look at the detective in charge. "Don't just stand there. Arrest him. Yancy Harris poisoned Dickie Dunkin!"

CHAPTER 4

In a town where over-the-top is never over-the-top enough, chili poisoning was so over-the-top, folks couldn't resist.

By that afternoon word was out, and the dusty main street of Deadeye (which also happened to be the only street of Deadeye) was packed.

It said something about people's love of the weird, the offbeat, and the just plain disturbed, but I will admit, it was also good for business. Never one to shy away from a sale, a sales pitch, or a chance to sell more product and maybe catch up on the bills, I took full advantage. As soon as I got back to the bordello, I put on my Chili Chick costume, which covered me from the top of my head to below my hips, my fishnet stockings, and my stilettos, and got to work out front.

"I don't suppose you could see anything really interesting from here." Even though I was mid–dance step and obviously busy, a middle-aged woman with a big belly who shouldn't have been caught dead wearing the tiny pink tube top she was wearing walked out of the bordello and stopped to chat. She craned her neck to look beyond the crowd toward the far end of Deadeye, and the doors to the auditorium that were now crisscrossed with yellow crime scene tape. "Have they arrested anybody yet?"

I was tempted to tell her I'd make sure she got arrested if she stepped any farther away from the door while she was hanging on to the unpaid-for bags of peppers she had in her hands. Instead, I opted for a little of the chili-palace-proprietor charm that usually eluded me.

"I haven't heard a word about an official arrest," I said, and it was the absolute truth. While I thought about it, I did a couple quick dance steps and waved my arms in the hopes of attracting the attention of a group of men who walked by, and even though they couldn't see my face behind the red mesh insert at the front of the costume, I grinned a welcome when they stepped into the bordello to look around and (hopefully) buy. "I do know they're questioning a suspect."

A suspect.

Yancy Harris.

The very thought made my stomach turn, and I would have pressed one hand to it if I wasn't incased in the giant red chili. I liked Yancy, and I couldn't see him as a killer, yet if what Reverend Love said was true . . .

"Questioning isn't the same as arresting," Tube Top Woman said. "I watch enough TV to know that. If they thought the person they're questioning did it, they'd already have him in jail by now. Isn't that how it works? Can't they find out who really did it in like an hour? I mean, with all the science and DNA and stuff they have now?"

I would have mentioned that counting commercials, it probably actually takes something like forty-five minutes for the cops to find the bad guys on TV, but something told me she wouldn't have picked up on the sarcasm.

"Maybe nobody killed Dickie," the woman suggested. "Maybe it was the hot peppers that did him in." She looked at the bags of dried scotch bonnet and datil chilies in her hands. "Because you know, if hot peppers really can stop somebody's heart, I've got this real loser I'm married to. You think these will do the trick?"

I would have laughed if I didn't think she was serious. Instead, I mumbled something about how all hot peppers need to be used with caution, waved her toward Sylvia, who was behind the cash register, and got back to my dancing.

For about three seconds.

That was when Ruth Ann showed up.

"Oh, Maxie!" She grabbed on to my hand, and for a small, bony woman, she had the grip of a WrestleMania superstar. A couple seconds in and I had to yank my hand away and shake it to get the circulation going again.

Not such a bad move as it turned out. A guy walking out of Gert's place next door thought I was waving to him and came on over to check out our wares. Right after he checked out my legs.

"We've got to talk, honey," Ruth Ann said.

One look at the tears that shimmered in her eyes, and I grabbed on to Ruth Ann and tugged her out of the walkway and closer to the building.

"What's wrong?" I asked.

A single tear slipped down Ruth Ann's cheek. The last time I'd seen her cry was when Gingerboy, her nineteen-year-old cat, kicked the bucket, and now, like then, my throat clutched and my heart beat a little too fast. "Something happened . . ." Like I could help it if I hiccuped over the words? "Did something happen to Tumbleweed?"

"Oh, no, honey." I'm pretty sure she needed the comfort more than I did, but Ruth Ann patted my hand. "Nothing's happened to Tumbleweed. Not yet. But it's . . ." She drew in a shaky breath. "It's gonna, Maxie, I just know it in my heart. Something's gonna happen to my Tumbleweed. People dying at the Showdown! He's so worried about what it's going to do to our reputation, it's got his stomach in knots."

A group of guys with badges around their necks that said they were part of an insurance company convention walked by, and one of them knocked into the Chili Chick but didn't bother to apologize. At the same time I sent him a death ray look he was probably too drunk to notice even if I weren't hidden inside the costume. I steadied myself. "Tumbleweed shouldn't be worried.

Obviously, Dickie's murder isn't hurting us at all," I told Ruth Ann. "Look around. The place is packed."

"Oh, sure. Here. In Vegas. People here are always looking for the sensational. But what's going to happen at the next Showdown when we're in San Antonio? Or the cook-off after that? Or the one after that?" Ruth Ann dug a tissue out of the pocket of her yellow shorts and wiped her eyes. "Most places aren't so free and easy about things as Vegas is. Including murder. Tumbleweed, he's afraid this is going to be . . ." Ruth Ann's throat clogged. She coughed. "He's afraid it's going to be the end of us."

"Well, it isn't." I did not know this for a fact, but I made it sound like I did. "The last person who's going to put us out of business is a jerk like Dickie Dunkin. Besides, the cops found the killer, right? Yancy Harris." Even though Ruth Ann couldn't see me, I shook my head at the thought. "I just can't believe it. Yancy seems like such a nice guy."

Ruth Ann took ahold of my arm. "You haven't heard? The cops took Yancy away, all right, because Reverend Love, she said she'd seen him sprinkling something in one of the judges' bowls. Turns out it was Yancy's own bowl and what he was sprinkling—"

I would have slapped my forehead if the Chili Chick had a forehead to slap. "Baking soda! I'm the one who suggested it to him. He wanted something to cut down on the heat of the chili. I didn't have any baking soda so I gave him some lime juice."

"He got baking soda from the kitchen." Ruth Ann laughed. "You should have seen the looks on the cops' faces when one of the cooks back in the kitchen confirmed it. They thought they had their man."

"Well, I'm glad it wasn't Yancy," I admitted. "As to who it could be . . ."

"Well, that's just what I wanted to talk to you about." Ruth Ann scooted closer. She was even shorter than I am, and since I had the added advantage of stilettos with four-inch heels, I had to bend over to see her out of the red mesh panel that covered my face. "You need to investigate," she said.

Not what I was expecting, though what I was expecting, I couldn't say. "Nick says I need to mind my own business."

"Nick." Ruth Ann flicked away the thought with the snap of her fingers. "The man's hotter than a habanero. You being the beautiful young woman you are, I bet you've noticed. But he obviously doesn't have a brain in that gorgeous head of his. If he did, he'd know what I know. You're the one who cleared things up back in Taos, Maxie. You're the one who found the murderer and got your sister—" She couldn't see me open my mouth, but she knew exactly what I was going to say and corrected herself before I could. "Half sister. Yes, I know. You're the one who got your half sister out of jail. You'd think Nick would just admit it and admit that the cops couldn't have done it without you."

"Well, he won't. And he says I shouldn't stick my nose where it doesn't belong."

"Except that we're talking Tumbleweed here."

The waterworks started again, but three cheers for me, I stayed strong.

"You found the killer last time," Ruth Ann whimpered.

"I hoped last time was the last time," I reminded her.

She clutched my arm. "We all did. But that's not how things worked out."

"But a crazy artist came after me with a chainsaw!" I reminded her. "And I had to break into a dead guy's apartment. And there was the dead guy's girlfriend, the one who was gunning for me and—"

"And this is Tumbleweed."

Did she hear the sigh of surrender from inside the Chili Chick?

That would explain why Ruth Ann's expression brightened just a bit. "Oh, Maxie, honey, I knew I could depend on you."

"I didn't say I was going to do it."

"You didn't have to. All you had to do is think about Tumbleweed. Just like I did. He's no spring chicken anymore. And the stress . . . Oh, Maxie!" Even though there was a smile on her face, there were tears on Ruth Ann's cheeks. "We've got to leave town with a clean reputation. That will make Tumbleweed feel better. We can't . . ." She gulped down a breath. "We can't let anything happen to him."

Inside the Chick costume, my shoulders drooped, but Ruth Ann couldn't see that, not with the infrastructure of wires and mesh that allowed the red canvas to hold its chili shape. "I can't promise anything," I said.

Her fingers dug into my arm. "Just knowing you were trying would cheer me right up."

"I don't know any of the players."

"That doesn't matter. If I know you're out there talking to people and looking for motives and digging for the truth, that would make me feel so much better!"

"I can't let Nick find out."

Ruth Ann could be as sweet as spring roses, but that didn't mean she wasn't a cagey ol' girl. Her mouth pulled into a smile and she narrowed her eyes to give me the sort of penetrating look she used to aim my way back when I was a teenager and she suspected I'd pinched a can or two of the beer in her fridge (which I usually had). "You're not afraid of Nick, are you?"

The very thought felt like a kick from a mule. My shoulders shot back and my chin went up. "No, I'm not afraid of him, but—"

Ruth Ann didn't wait to hear what was bound to be a pretty wimpy defense anyway. She gave me a wink. "You can handle him, Maxie. I know you can. I mean, when it comes to investigating. And other things."

Oh, I was pretty sure I knew what other things she was referring to, but before I could squelch the sudden heat that boiled through my blood or ask for confirmation, Ruth Ann sauntered away.

"Great, you just promised Ruth Ann you'd investigate." Good thing I was encased in the chili so nobody could hear me mumble to myself. "Now what are you going to do?"

I wasn't sure, but whatever it was, I knew I couldn't do it at the bordello.

To make it look like I was actually working the job I was supposed to be working, I ducked into the bordello ard grabbed a stack of Texas Jack Pierce's Hot-Cha Chili Seasoning Palace flyers, then I headed down the dusty main street of Deadeye, handing flyers left and right to everyone who happened to so much as glance at the giant chili. I knew the auditorium was off-limits—at least through the main doors—so when I got over there, I looked around for what might be another way in. I found it in the form of a door painted to look like the entrance to a mine shaft with a sign hanging from it that declared, *Do Not Enter.*

Just as I hoped, the door opened directly backstage.

I closed it behind me and took a couple cautious steps forward.

As far as I could see, there was no one around and, now that Dickie's body had been removed and the cops were gone, no one out front, either.

I headed for the stage.

And stopped in an instant.

The moment anyone heard the sounds of my stilettos rapping against the wooden floor, Security was bound to come running.

And Security, I didn't need.

I slipped off my shoes and, dangling them from one hand, slid across the floor in fishnet-stockinged feet.

Except for the fact that Dickie's body was gone and all the chili—including the bowls the judges had been sampling—had been packed up and carted away to be tested, nothing looked different than it had when I waited backstage for the cops to talk to me. Now, I stood in the center of the stage, imagining what I'd seen earlier that day, before the cops arrived, before Dickie took a header into the Devil's Breath.

"The Great Osborn, Hermosa, Yancy . . ." Standing in front of the judges' table, I let my gaze move left to right, picturing where each judge had been seated. "Reverend Love, Dickie. And the scuffle between Dickie and The Great Osborn . . ."

That had taken place right at center stage, between the judges' table and the tables where the contestants did their cooking.

My stockings sliding against the slick floor, I made my way over to the cooking space, but like the judges' table, nothing looked different to me. Brother William's cooking area was neat and well organized. Karl Sinclair's included a life-sized poster of him hanging from the front of the table. Tyler York's makeshift kitchen was as shiny as Tyler himself, and still curious about him, I gave it a closer look. Every pot looked brand-new. Every pan, like it had just come out of the box. Every spoon and spatula and knife gleamed. Shiny. Like Tyler.

Finally I looked at the space that belonged to the woman with the dark hair. Unlike Tyler's, her area was dotted with grease and spotted with tomato sauce. Her spoons looked as if they'd put in years of service. And the smell . . .

I stopped in my stocking-foot tracks, sniffing the air around the woman's cooking space.

"Blackstrap molasses and . . ." I pivoted, carefully

taking another whiff, and breathed the words "Jack Daniel's."

I darted to the other side of the table and looked through the woman's stored supplies and found exactly what I knew I'd find—a bottle of tequila.

"Tequila, molasses, Jack Daniel's." I really didn't need to review the evidence, but I couldn't help myself. In all my years on the chili circuit, I'd known only one person who used all three of those ingredients in his chili—my dad, Texas Jack Pierce.

And eight weeks earlier, Texas Jack Pierce had fallen off the face of the earth.

Don't ask me what I was looking for, but even that little bit of a shaky connection made something that felt like hope blossom in my heart. I riffled through the rest of the woman's supplies and, in the end, found myself right back where I started. There was no sign that she knew Jack, and nothing that indicated that the woman might know anything about his disappearance.

Annoyed at myself for getting carried away, I gave an empty pot under the table a little kick.

And stopped cold.

A thump from backstage told me I wasn't the only one poking around.

Careful not to make a sound, I headed that way.

There was a hallway behind the stage, and I peered around the corner, only to find a man looking into the open door of one of the dressing rooms.

It was Dickie's, and while he was still busy carefully

poking his head past the crime scene tape strung over the doorway, I closed in on him.

"Can I help you?" I asked.

The man jumped and spun to face me, his back to the wall outside the dressing room.

He was fifty or so with hair that must have once been sandy and now was a washed-out shade of mouse. He had a wide nose, a weak chin, and very small hands. I noticed them right away because they flew around him like butterflies on a caffeine high.

"Um . . . what . . . hey, how are you?" He must have realized he was way too jumpy because the man hooked his thumbs into his belt buckle. It was big and silver and there were turquoise chips in it. The Southwestern theme went along with his jeans and his black shirt with red stitching.

"Who are you?" I asked him.

The man scratched a hand behind one ear, and call me crazy, but I would swear he didn't think it was all that unusual to have a conversation with a giant red chili. Then again, we were in Vegas.

"George," he said. "George Jarret. I was just looking for . . ." His gaze darted to the dressing room. "I was just checking to see if Dickie was around."

If George Jarret hadn't heard the news, he was the only one in Vegas. "Are you a friend?" I asked. "Or maybe a fan?"

"Fan. Definitely. I'm a fan." Jarret ran his tongue over his lips. "I mean, the guy's a comic genius, right? I see his show every time I'm in Vegas, and I thought if I stopped by, I might catch him when he was rehearsing. I thought . . . well, I thought maybe Dickie would give me an autographed picture of something."

"Or you figured nobody would be around and you could pick up a little souvenir now that the news about Dickie is out," I suggested.

Jarret stepped away from the wall and backed a few steps down the hallway. "News? I hope nothing bad has happened to Dickie."

I wondered if he could pick up on my nonchalance, I mean what with the costume and all. "I'd say murder qualifies as something bad."

"Murder?" Another couple steps and Jarret was almost all the way to the door opposite the one I'd come in. "Dickie's . . . Dickie's dead?"

"As a doornail."

"Oh. That's too . . ." And before he could say what it was too much of, Jarret turned and raced out the door.

Curious, I took a moment to peep into Dickie's dressing room, too, and I have to admit it wouldn't have bothered me—I mean even knowing the guy who'd recently used it to don the tasteless clothing for his tasteless shows was dead—if not for the fact that there was a stack of eight-by-ten photographs of Dickie looking up at me from a nearby table.

He was smiling, and the autograph scrawled on the top picture said, "Keep up the laughs."

Poor Dickie sure wasn't laughing now.

Convinced there was nothing of any interest in Dickie's dressing room, I went the other way, and as it turned out, my timing was pretty bad. Just as I got backstage, the main door of the auditorium swung open and a couple uniformed cops walked in with the chili contest contestants. Something told me they wouldn't be happy that I'd been poking around, and I ducked behind the curtain.

"It's all been checked and dusted for prints," one of the cops told them. "So you can go ahead and pack up and get your stuff out of here."

Karl Sinclair walked in first. "Which means no contest," he grumbled.

His sentiment wasn't echoed by either Tyler York or Brother William, who followed behind. The dark-haired woman, I noticed, never moved a muscle. She toed the line between the outside entrance and the auditorium like she'd been flash-frozen, and her eyes wide, she glanced around.

"You can come in," the cop said and waved an arm. "It's time to clean up your stuff and clear out."

I'm pretty sure the woman wasn't listening. Her gaze landed on the spot onstage that was still sprinkled with Devil's Breath chili, and her skin paled.

"Come on, miss," the cop said, louder this time, and when she still didn't move, he raised his voice. "Bernadette, are you listening? You can come in now, Miss Kromski!"

The name slammed into me like an out-of-control cement truck, and it was my turn to freeze. Well, except for my heart, which started a cha-cha of epic proportions inside my chest, and my brain, which whirled with the possibilities (all of them bad) of this sudden turn of events.

Now everything made sense! The death ray looks. The woman's knowledge of the basic ingredients in one of Jack's all-time best recipes.

The last time I'd seen Bernadette Kromski was at a Showdown when I was thirteen or fourteen years old, and since I hadn't put on an inch since and I'd always worn my dark hair short and spiked, I suppose it was easy for her to identify me.

But it was no wonder I hadn't recognized her from the get-go. Back then, she was a big-breasted, long-legged goddess, and though she was still plenty tall, the years had added a few pounds and rounded her shoulders. I'd bet anything her chestnut hair was natural and the golden tresses I remembered her with came straight out of a bottle.

Bernadette Kromski!

When I gulped, I hoped the cops didn't hear me.

See, I suddenly knew why she looked like she wanted me to go up in a puff of smoke—Bernadette Kromski hadn't forgotten and neither had I. We were archenemies!

CHAPTER 5

Bernadette Kromski is Evil Incarnate.

I do not use those capital letters lightly.

She is devious. She is underhanded. She is nasty.

And I knew if I was going to look into Dickie Dunkin's murder, I'd have to start with her.

After all, it was her chili that Dickie had been eating when he went from alive to deceased.

And then, of course, there is the whole Evil Incarnate thing.

Finding Bernadette once she'd packed up her cooking pots and left Creosote Cal's wasn't all that tough. A little shmoozing in the admin building (aka the blacksmith shop) with Ruth Ann and I had my hot little hands on the contestants' info. According to her entry application,

Bernadette lived right there in Vegas and worked at a little place not too far away known as Bibi's Bump and Grind.

Like I expected anything else?

I lied through my teeth and told Sylvia I was going to get something to eat, peeled out of the chili costume, and headed out to streets as hot as a Naga Viper pepper. Bibi's was pretty much what I expected, a low-slung brick building with a neon sign above the door where a bouncer read the newspaper and didn't look like he was too particular about who he let in.

Until I walked up.

The guy was six-six and at least three hundred pounds. The muscles that bulged on his arms had muscles. I wasn't just another of the middle-aged men who'd walked into Bibi's before me, and that sent up enough of a red flag for him to give me a quick once-over.

"They're not hiring," he said, and before I could tell him that wasn't why I was there, he added, "And you're too short anyway."

I had long ago come to terms with my lack of height so I did not take this personally. At least not too personally.

Which was why I was able to give him a dazzling smile. "You should see me in my stilettos."

His eyes lit. "Stilettos, huh?" I guess I warranted a second glance because his gaze skimmed my black shorts and the sleeveless purple top I wore with them. "I'd like to see that."

"So maybe you'll get the chance." I patted the gigantic

denim hobo bag I had slung over my shoulder. In truth, my stilettos were back at the bordello along with the rest of my Chili Chick costume, but this guy didn't have to know that. "When I'm done inside."

Another once-over. "Done doing what?"

I couldn't think of a lie that was anywhere near convincing so I opted for the truth. "I need to talk to Bernadette. We're old"—I nearly choked on the word—"friends."

The bouncer checked his watch. "She goes on in a few minutes."

"So I'll only talk to her for a few minutes. Then if you have time and you want to see me in my stilettos . . ."

Since I didn't finish the thought, I didn't exactly promise anything, right?

The bouncer waved me inside.

A minute later, I was in the backstage dressing room, where six women in various stages of dress, undress, and OMG-you're-really-going-to-wear-that-leopard-print-unitard-in-public were just heading out for their next turn in the spotlight.

Bernadette was down at the end of the long, narrow room cramming her dark tresses into a blond wig. She wasn't wearing much of anything else except a neon blue bikini and a garter belt, and though I'm certainly not passing judgment, I could say without a doubt that the years had not been kind to her. The Bernadette I remembered was leggy and lean. Today's Bernadette had a bit of a belly, and the skin on the underside of her arms flapped. There was a tattoo on her left thigh. Before she could notice me and call in the bouncer to toss me out on my keister, I flattened myself against the door to let the other dancers leave and closed in on her.

"Hey, Bernadette, long time no see."

She froze, but just for a second. Then she went right back to adjusting the wig. It had two long braids, and once she made sure the golden curls sat just right on her head, she flipped one braid over each of her breasts.

"What the hell do you want?"

It was pretty much the welcome I'd expected, but then, the way I remembered it, Bernadette wasn't much for being polite. Fine by me. The way I remembered it, I never had been, either.

"Just thought I'd pop in and say hello. You didn't bother to stop to chat at the Showdown this morning. I thought that maybe you didn't remember me."

Her top lip curled, she gave me a quick look. "You're hard to forget."

I pretended this was the compliment I was sure it was not meant to be. "A lot of people say that. The bouncer at the door is already looking forward to seeing me later."

"He's a first-class idiot." Bernadette did not bother to mention if she'd always thought this of the bouncer or if his interest in me was what qualified him for the title.

"I would have come right over and said hello. At the Showdown, I mean. But I didn't recognize you." That was the truth, though I didn't bother to mention the belly or the flabby arms. "It's been a long time."

She slathered on dark red lipstick and smacked her lips together. "Not nearly long enough."

I have a thick skin so none of this bothered me.

Especially since I didn't give a hoot about Bernadette or her opinions. I was tempted to tell her that the feeling was more than mutual, but I had an alternative motive for being there, remember. I mean an alternative to just making Bernadette's life miserable. As far as I was concerned, that was noble work and would have been reason enough if I didn't have poor, dead Dickie to think about, and poor, stressed-out Tumbleweed to consider and poor, worried Ruth Ann to care about.

Hoping not to look too anxious, I took a moment to study my surroundings.

There were dressing tables lining both sides of the room, each with a bare, anemic lightbulb hanging above it and a chair pulled up in front of it. The dancers I'd waded through on my way over to visit Bernadette were all far younger than she was, and that would explain why their tables were heaped with lipstick and mascara, and Bernadette's included those things as well as under-eye concealer, a heavy-duty foundation, and a couple sets of false eyelashes. Still, I guess age had its privileges because Bernadette's costumes weren't strewn over the back of her chair like the other dancers' were. In addition to the last dressing table in the farthest corner of the room, Bernadette also had her very own closet. Even as I watched, she ducked in there and came out holding a blue-and-white gingham gown that looked like something straight out of an old Western.

"You must be disappointed," I said, when she closed the closet door and pulled the dress over her head. "I mean, about the Devil's Breath contest being canceled."

She barely bothered with a shrug. Instead, she adjusted the cotton petticoats under the wide skirt of her dress, and for just a second, she allowed her gaze to brush mine. "I'm disappointed I didn't see Jack at the Showdown. I was sure as soon as he saw my name on the list of regional winners, he'd come running."

It was an interesting theory considering that my dad had been missing for something like eight weeks and no one had a clue where he'd gone. I guess Bernadette hadn't heard the news.

"You think?" I asked her.

There was a cigarette burning in a nearby ashtray and Bernadette grabbed it and took a puff. In the close confines of the dressing room, the smoke trailed toward me and I hauled in a long breath, hoping to catch a bit of it without looking too desperate. I'd given up my pack-a-day habit even before I joined the Showdown in Taos, but there were times—this was one of them—when I was dying to slip back to my old ways.

The breath lodged in my throat when Bernadette said, "Maybe that's why you're here. You know Jack is going to come running and you wanted to get here before he did. What are you going to do this time, little girl?" Her eyes were wide and her mouth pulled open to expose teeth yellowed from years of smoking. Suddenly, I wasn't missing my bad habit so much anymore.

Bernadette leaned closer. "Do you think you can scare me away?"

"I think I was surprised to find out you live right here in Vegas. So did Dickie."

"Dickie." She rolled her dark eyes.

"You knew him?"

Bernadette shot me a look. "Who says?"

This was one of those questions better left unanswered. "I'll bet the cops asked you the same thing."

"You didn't see them haul me away, did you? Not like they did Yancy Harris."

"He didn't do it," I told her.

"Good. He's good people. Not that you would understand what that means. I like Yancy."

"But you didn't like Dickie."

"You're trying to put words in my mouth."

"Your chili was in his mouth when he died."

Bernadette checked her reflection in the mirror. "If my chili was poisoned, all the judges would be dead."

This, I knew, so there was no use acknowledging the obvious. "Why did you hate him?"

"Who says I did?" Apparently, Bernadette didn't really care. She twitched away the question with a lift of her shoulders and shot me a smile I imagined she usually saved for the guys in the front row who were ready, willing, and able to stuff ten-dollar bills in her G-string. "Everybody who ever met him hated Dickie. Just like everyone who ever met you."

"Except Jack."

She tried to pretend this didn't sting, but don't think I didn't notice the way her jaw stiffened. She covered up the reaction by bending closer to the mirror to check her makeup. "You didn't come over here to tell me all about how you're daddy's little girl. Admit it." She whirled to face me. "Jack sent you."

"You think?"

"I think that after all this time, he didn't want to walk right up to me at the Showdown this morning. He didn't know what to say." She touched up her mascara. "It's sweet, really. He's a little shy."

Not hardly. Jack could be a lot of things, including flashy, as charming as hell, and as unreliable as getting an Internet signal in the RV that Sylvia and I used to travel the Showdown circuit. What he'd never been was shy.

"You know Jack," I said, as noncommittal as can be. "If there's one thing he loves even more than chili—"

"It's a beautiful woman. Yes." Admiring her reflection in the mirror, Bernadette smoothed her hands over her hokey gown. "Some things never change. Some men never change."

"I thought we were talking about chili. And about how Dickie died."

"I had no reason to kill him."

"I'm sure that's what you told the cops."

She touched a comb to the blond wig. "You were there, too."

"Yeah, but I never even knew Dickie existed until we got to Vegas."

Her smile was sleek. "I heard that during his show last night, Dickie made fun of your precious Tumbleweed. A girl with your temper and your psychotic tendencies . . . well, I imagine that just sent you right over the edge."

"Except Dickie wasn't eating my chili when he kicked the bucket."

"You're accusing me of killing him!"

"If the shoe fits . . ."

She barked out a laugh. "Not a chance! Except for the fact that he used to come in here once in a while, I never knew Dickie. And when he did come in . . ." As if she was remembering the scene and not liking it at all, she narrowed her eyes. "Cheap bastard never tipped more than a dollar or two. Even for a lap dance."

"That must have made you mad."

"It made me poorer than I should have been."

"And that made you mad."

"That made me send one of the other girls over when he asked for a private dance. Sorry." She tossed her comb down on the dressing table. "I'm sure you'd love to see me led away in handcuffs, but it's just not going to happen. If the cops thought I did anything wrong, they would have brought me in for more questioning by now."

"So who do you think could have done it?"

Her gaze shot to mine. "You're asking me for an opinion?"

"I'm saying you were right there onstage, not twenty feet from where Dickie ate the laced chili. You might have seen something."

"And if I did, I'd be sure to tell you all about it."

Believe me, I did not fail to catch the not-so-subtle

cynicism in her voice. "I don't really care," I told her with a casual shrug of my shoulders. "Like I said, I never met Dickie so it's not like it matters to me who offed the guy. But Jack and I were talking and—"

"Jack?" Her eyes lit. Yeah, like a hyena's do before it chomps into some poor crippled wildebeest. "He wants to know what I saw? What I heard? That's why he sent you here?" Her dark brows dipped over her eyes. "But why doesn't he come around himself and ask?"

Why, indeed.

I shrugged like it went without saying. "He didn't want to muddy the waters. You know, with a bunch of emotion. He thought if I talked to you first—"

"Then he could get the basic information before he came and saw me himself!"

By now, Bernadette's eyes weren't just gleaming, they were as bright as the searchlights that raked the night sky over Vegas. She pulled her chair out from the dressing table, turned it, and plunked down, her elbows on her knees. "Tell me, what did he say? Tell me everything he said."

"About Dickie."

"About Dickie, about the murder." Bernadette giggled like a schoolgirl. "About me."

Since I didn't know what to say, it was a good thing she didn't give me a chance to say anything. Her cheeks flaming, Bernadette reached for a pair of stockings studded with silver sparkles and pulled up her skirt.

This close, I saw that the tattoo on her thigh was a frilly heart with the name *Jack* written in the center of it.

My stomach swooped. My brain froze. Or at least it

would have if it wasn't so busy gyrating over the fact that the woman seemed to have an unhealthy obsession with my father.

She slipped on her stockings, then snapped them onto the garters. "When will he be coming by?"

He.

Jack.

The father who'd fallen off the face of the earth when I was still back in Chicago and he was in Abilene with the Showdown.

Obviously, Bernadette didn't know that. Just as obviously, I knew it was a weakness and jumped to take advantage.

"He didn't exactly say when he'd be here," I told her.

"But he was there. At the Showdown." She stuck out her bottom lip. "I didn't see him."

"Jack's a busy guy."

"Yes. Of course he is. Busy." She popped out of her chair. "Always so very busy. Even so, I know he adores hot peppers. Oh yes, I haven't forgotten that. I thought for sure he'd be there for the Devil's Breath judging."

"Which is why you decided to enter one of his old recipes."

Bernadette stopped mid-gush. Her dark eyebrows rose just a fraction of an inch. "You were poking around my cooking table."

"I've got a nose for tequila and Jack Daniel's."

She wrapped her hands around the high back of the wooden chair. When she pushed the chair back under the dressing table, her knuckles were white. "You always did."

"Jack's recipe, the one with the molasses and the tequila in it, it's good stuff," I told her. "But Karl Sinclair is a pro, and Brother William has God on his side. And then there's Tyler York. I don't know what his deal is, but he could have won big-time just for being the shiniest contestant. You think you actually had a chance to win?"

"I won the regionals, didn't I?" Like electricity, her question crackled in the air between us.

"But maybe you didn't care if you won the national title. Maybe all you cared about was being at the Show-down. About seeing Jack again."

The dressing area next to Bernadette's was empty, and I leaned back against the table and crossed my arms over my chest. "Maybe you were hoping Jack would get a taste of the chili and then he'd notice you."

A tiny smile playing around her mouth, she slid me a look. "But now he doesn't have to taste my chili to notice me. He's already noticed me. Of course he noticed me! That's why he sent you around to see me."

"Sure. Of course. And to find out if you saw anything as far as the murder, of course."

Before she had a chance to reply, a guy with a cigar hanging out of one corner of his mouth stuck his head into the room. "Two minutes, Bernie," he said, and I knew I was going to lose her if I didn't act fast.

"He knows you didn't do it, of course," I said, stepping into her path when she pushed away from the dressing table. "Jack says he knows there's no way you'd ever kill anyone."

"He knows that if my chili was poisoned, all the judges would have gotten some of it."

"Exactly what I . . . what Jack was saying," I said, and I bit the inside of my mouth to keep myself from thinking how much I hated to agree with her about anything.

"And if my chili was poisoned . . ." Bernadette laughed. "Hell, if there was poison in my chili, I would have had a great big serving of it delivered right to you." Still chuckling, she reached into the corner and grabbed a long pole with a bent top.

"You're Little Bo Peep!" I said.

Bernadette's smile was sleek. "Oh, you always were a smart one."

My smile equaled hers. "I still am."

"And I—"

"Come on, Bernie," the man with the cigar called out. "Your music's starting and the regulars are waiting."

When she whipped by me with that pole in her hand, she made sure it banged into my shoulder.

I would say I didn't take any of this personally, but of course, I did. What I didn't do was waste any time. As soon as Bernadette was out of the room, I closed in on her dressing table.

I'm not sure what I thought I'd find, but when I didn't find anything, I was disappointed anyway. My arms crossed over my chest, I spun around, and leaned back against the table, considering my options.

As far as I could see, Bernadette hadn't left a purse for me to look through. Or a phone lying around so I could check her calls. In fact, the only other thing there was to check . . .

My eyes landed on the closed closet door, and with one more look toward the main door of the dressing room to make sure none of the dancers was on her way back in, I pushed away from the table and headed that way.

I opened the door, flicked on the switch on the wall to the left—

And just about swallowed my tongue.

Sure, there were costumes in Bernadette's closet. Sparkly, trashy costumes of all sorts. They were hung from a pole on the wall to my left. But there was also a shelf built into the wall opposite the door, and on it, three small battery-operated candles flickered in red glass holders. There was a bunch of flowers there, too, fresh enough that I imagined she replaced them every day, along with a cheap gold bracelet, what looked to be some kind of herbs wrapped in cheesecloth, and—

My legs felt as if they'd been weighed down with lead, and I forced myself to take a step forward.

And seven photographs, all framed.

Big photographs, little photographs, some that were good quality and others that looked as if they'd been printed off the Internet.

Each and every one of them was of my dad, Texas Jack Pierce.

CHAPTER 6

"But you've got to help, Nick. Don't you see?"

I don't know why I bothered to ask; it was obvious he didn't.

And just as obvious that it was my job to make sure he did.

I was back at the Showdown. Behind the cash register of the Chili Palace/bordello while Sylvia went out to grab a late afternoon lunch. Lucky for me, I'd seen Nick walk by just a minute before. Not so lucky for him, he noticed me jumping up and down and windmilling my arms and came inside to see what was up.

I had already told him once, but he obviously didn't get it so I repeated myself. "She's got an altar in her closet, Nick. An altar to my dad!"

When he strolled by, Nick had been busy (catch the irony, please) sipping a cup of coffee and he set the cup on the counter, where Sylvia had arranged an artsy display of dried peppers, alternating small, round, red tepin peppers and Thai chilies with orangy Bird's Eyes and nearly black Aji Pancas.

"So?" Nick asked.

"So?" I was glad there were no customers around. It was probably best for business if they didn't see the look I aimed in Nick's direction. "Candles? Flowers? Pictures? You think that's normal?"

Nick had changed out of the charcoal gray suit that had been stained by the Devil's Breath that morning. He was dressed in a killer navy suit, a white shirt, and a tie that featured splashes of navy and red against a background that reminded me of waves on a stormy sea. Yes, he looked delicious. More like a *GQ* cover model than head of security for a traveling chili cook-off show. That didn't mean he wasn't the most boneheaded man this side of the Mississippi.

"Okay, so it's not exactly normal," he said with a lift of those Greek god shoulders. "That doesn't mean—"

"But it might." I emphasized my point by hopping up and down. "Don't you get it? The woman's crazy! She's obsessed! She's a crazy woman who's obsessed and she's obsessed with my missing father. She's so obsessed, I'm thinking she might have had something to do with it!"

"It?" His eyebrows rose just a tad. "And the 'it' you're referring to is—"

"Is Jack missing. Is Jack kidnapped. Is Jack—"

No, I wouldn't say the word. I wouldn't even think it.

"She's obsessed," I repeated instead, and slapped a hand against the counter to emphasize my point. "Hey, I see the news. I know people who are obsessed with people sometimes do weird things to the people they're obsessed with."

"Except that your dad was in Abilene when he disappeared and this Bernadette lives here in Vegas."

"And there aren't any roads between here and Abilene." This, it should be pointed out, was a shrewd bit of logic.

One Nick ignored.

I screeched my opinion while I went to the back of the room and scooped up the Chili Chick costume I'd left on a chair when I ducked out to talk to Bernadette. As soon as Sylvia came back from lunch, I'd get into the costume and start dancing again. But until then . . .

Well, until then, I had the Palace to mind.

A group of middle-aged women trooped in, *ooh*ing and *ahh*ing, looking around, and asking questions. Big points for Nick. While I took care of them and rang up their sales, he didn't take the opportunity to run.

In fact, once the ladies were gone—shopping bags with Jack's face on them in hand—he said, "So tell me about Jack and Bernadette. What's the connection?"

I refused to let him see how relieved I was that he'd finally seen the light and come to the realization of how important this might be. I'd been looking for Jack since the moment Tumbleweed called and told me I had to get to the Showdown because Jack was missing. And I'd gotten absolutely . . .

My shoulders drooped.

Nowhere.

No one had seen Jack. No one had talked to him. The cops back in Abilene insisted there was no sign of foul play, and though Gert, she of the too-cute dishtowels and crockery at the shop next door, had thrown out a couple tantalizing hints that she might know something, she wasn't talking. In fact, she insisted she couldn't.

Now—finally—I felt as if we might be on the verge of finding out something, and just imagining that Bernadette might be the break I was looking for made me feel as if I'd pop right out of my skin.

So Nick wouldn't notice and accuse me of being too imaginative or too optimistic or just too plain stupid to know not to get all excited about something it might not be any use getting excited about, I reorganized the bags of peppers and jars of chili powder the women had messed up in their buying enthusiasm. "Bernadette worked at the Showdown. A long time ago. That should be some kind of clue right there. It was a long time ago." I looked at Nick over the bottles of cumin, paprika, and oregano I'd stacked in a Sylvia-worthy tower. "Anybody who holds a torch for a guy that long—"

"Oh, come on." Nick leaned a forearm on the counter and smiled at me over a display of Thermal Conversion. It's one of our most popular chili powders simply because it's a middle-of-the-road sort of spice. Not too wimpy, not too hot.

That is, until that smile zipped through the air between us. I swear, the SHU (that's Scoville Heat Units, the scale used to measure the spiciness of a chili pepper) went up a couple thousand points in every single jar of Thermal Conversion.

"Are you telling me there are guys you forget?" he asked. "Just like that?"

I wasn't sure where the conversation was headed; I only knew it was a direction I didn't want to go. Heat or no heat—and believe me, when Nick looked at me that way, there was plenty of heat—we were talking about Jack. About finding Jack. And finding Jack was the main reason I was traveling the chili circuit. Well, that, and getting away from the creditors who were all over me like ants at a picnic once Edik drained my bank account and maxed out my credit cards.

"I don't think fifteen years qualifies as just like that. And it's been about fifteen years. You think she would have moved on by now, don't you?"

"Like you would."

I grabbed a bag of tepin peppers and winged it at him. Too bad Nick had such good reflexes. I aimed for his stomach, but he caught it in midair. "We're not talking about me," I reminded him. I shouldn't have had to. "We're talking about a woman who knew my dad fifteen years ago and still has pictures of him surrounded by candles." Remembering the altar in the closet, I shivered.

"Sheesh! Some of the pictures looked like they'd been taken back in the day. But some of them looked like they'd been printed off our website. Come on, Nick, admit it. That's downright creepy."

Nick tossed the bag of tepins back to me, and I caught it and set it where it belonged. "So back in the day . . . Bernadette and Jack were an item?"

I didn't like the way the tepins were stacked so I removed the bag I'd just put there, rearranged the ones below it, and set the last bag on top. "Bernadette was nuts about Jack back then," I told Nick. "Obviously, she's still nuts about him."

"And he . . .?"

When that group of customers came in, I'd been forced to lay the Chili Chick costume on the counter so I could take care of them. Now I picked it up again and cradled it in my arms. "Well, he's not nuts about her. I can tell you that. How can he be when he hasn't seen her in fifteen years? And when he's missing?"

"Not what I meant and you know it. I meant back when she worked at the Showdown. Was Jack as crazy about Bernadette as she was about him?"

"No one's as crazy as Bernadette." I scooted to the back of the bordello. If Sylvia was punctual—and believe me, Sylvia is always punctual—she'd be back in just a couple minutes, and I wanted to be ready when she arrived. I sidestepped into a tiny storage room behind the bar to slip on my fishnet stockings, then reached out to grab the chili. I stepped into the costume, hauled it up and over my head, and walked over to Nick so he could do up the zipper at the back of the chili.

"Maxie." After he zipped, Nick leaned in close and I caught a whiff of his aftershave. I've never been to a tropical island, but if I had been, I imagined this was what it smelled like, all sun-kissed and rummy and dripping with undertones of hot night air and cool sea breezes. "You know what I mean," he said. "And you're avoiding my question. When Bernadette worked for the Showdown, how did Jack feel about her?"

"Jack was Jack!" I threw my hands in the air. No easy thing now that my arms were sticking out of the chili. "Jack was . . ."

I twitched my shoulders. I shivered. My back itched, and didn't it figure, now that I was encased in red chili, that itch was impossible to scratch.

"Jack was . . ." Nick did his best to lead me back into the conversation.

I moaned. And believe me, it had nothing to do with what we were talking about. A feeling like a thousand little pinpricks scooted up my back. The costume had never chafed me before, and I danced a little circle pattern, and when I ended up facing the way I'd been facing when I started, I saw Nick watching me, the left side of his mouth pulled into an expression I wouldn't exactly call a grin.

"You can't expect my help if you refuse to talk about it," he grumbled.

"It's not that." I jumped around and tried to slap at my back, but with the way the costume came down to just below my hips, it was nearly impossible. Desperate to relieve the prickling, I scooted over to the wall and rubbed my back against it, but that didn't work, either. In fact, it only made the itching worse.

I squealed and hurried back over to Nick. "Take it off!" I demanded.

He glanced down at his suit. "Take it—"

"Oh, stop being such a goof!" I gave him a *boof* on the arm. By now the itchiness had spread down my stomach and over my hips. My eyes watered. My voice burbled when I turned my back on Nick. "Unzip the costume and get it off! Hurry! I'm dying in here!"

He unzipped, and I shot forward and peeled out of the chili. When I did, a shower of powder hit the wooden floor.

"What the hell!" Nick looked from where I was hopping like a jumping bean on a hot sidewalk to the sprinkle of brownish dust on the floor. He dipped a finger into the powder, then instantly brushed it off. "It's itching powder. I saw bags of it down in the gift shop. You know, gag gifts. I was looking for something I could send my nephews."

"Well, it's no gift!" I waved my arms up and down.

"You'd better not." Nick put a hand on my shoulder when I started to scratch. "Your skin is red and irritated." He lifted the back of my purple shirt and peeked. "It's even worse on your back and your neck. Something tells me scratching it will only make it worse."

"Well, I've got to do something!" I wailed. Tears streamed down my cheeks and mixed with the itching powder on my face. "Nick, it hurts!"

"Right." He kicked the costume to the back of the

bordello, but just as he went up front to shut the door and put out the *Closed* sign, Sylvia walked in. She had a bag from one of the hotel shops in one hand and an iced green tea in the other.

"Hi, Nick!" Didn't it figure, she noticed the gorgeous hunk and completely ignored her half sister, fidgeting and crying in the corner. "What brings you here?"

"Maxie needs help." Nick zigzagged around Sylvia and headed in my direction. "Someone's—"

"Someone?" Sure there were tears streaming down my face, and my skin felt like it was on fire. That didn't stop me from pointing a finger at Sylvia. "That was a sick prank."

Sylvia clicked her tongue. "I have no idea what you're talking about. But why . . ." She gave me a careful look. "Why are you so red?"

I jumped up and down and waved my arms. "I'm itching to death!" I wailed. "Because you . . ." Another pointed finger that she completely ignored. "You're a sneak, Sylvia. And I won't let you get away with this. I'll get even."

She closed in on me, her golden brows low over her eyes and her gaze on the welts on my neck. "You think I did that to you?" Sylvia tsked her opinion. "You don't know me very well."

"I do know you very well. That's just—" The itching on my back intensified and I screeched. "The costume was right there." I swung my finger away from Sylvia and toward the back of the bordello. "You had all morning to mess with it."

"Because you were gone all morning, and most of

the afternoon doing I don't know what." The way she nodded made her golden hair gleam in the overhead lights. "I may have been justified wanting to get even since you abandoned me and left me to do all the work all day, but I didn't do it, Maxie, I swear."

Nick stepped between us. "And right about now, none of it matters. You . . ." He looked at Sylvia, then at the front door, where a group of loud-talking women had just stepped in. "You have customers. And you . . ." Before I had a clue what he was about to do so I could make sure he didn't, Nick twirled me around and shooed me toward the door. "The only thing that's going to help you is a long shower. I'm taking you back to the RV. Now."

Don't ask me how Nick knew I needed a little pick-me-up, but when I got out of the shower, I found him sitting on the bench behind the driver's seat of the RV. There was a can of Coke open on the table in front of him, and when he saw me, he poured it over ice and told me to sit down and drink.

"Better?" he asked.

I took a long glug of soda. The bubbles tickled my throat, and I nodded. Just like Nick had instructed me before I showered, I'd put the clothes I'd been wearing into a garbage bag and I swept the bathroom floor and rinsed down the shower really well to make sure that none of the itching powder still lingered. I'd hauled the garbage bag out of the bathroom with me, and I pointed to it.

"You going to take it and collect evidence?"

I guess the way he raised his eyebrows should have told me everything I needed to know.

"Come on, Nick." I slapped the table. "That's got to be a crime. Sylvia—"

"It wasn't Sylvia. She was clueless."

"In case you haven't noticed, Sylvia's always clueless."

"Well, this time, clueless in a good way. I don't think she's the one who put the itching powder inside your costume."

"Then who—"

His shrug said it all. "The costume was out all day, right? While you were . . ."

I timed my next glug of soda just right so that I didn't have to answer him, but when I was done and he still waited, I grumbled. "Doing stuff," I said. It was all he needed to know. "Like talking to Bernadette and finding that creepy altar."

"But you haven't explained why you were talking to Bernadette."

He was bound to ask sooner or later. Good thing I realized that and had already come up with an answer. "Like I said, she used to work at the Showdown. We're old friends." It was the second time that day that I'd allowed the lie to slip past my lips. This time, I washed it away with caffeine, cola, and bubbles. "I saw her at the contest, but what with Dickie dropping over dead and all, I didn't have time to say hello. So I went to find her."

"Uh-huh." He didn't say it like he believed it.

I pretended he did.

While I'd showered, Nick had found the bag of Chips

Ahoy! I saved for chocolate emergencies and he grabbed one cookie for himself and pushed the package across the table toward me. "I decided not to get that itching powder for my nephews," he said.

"You think?" I grabbed two cookies and chomped them down. "That stuff should be illegal. I still . . ." I jiggled my shoulders. "I feel like I've got a sunburn."

"No worries." Apparently while I was washing away somebody's idea of a sick joke, Nick had been a busy boy. He'd ducked out and gone to Creosote Cal's gift shop, and now he grabbed a plastic bag from the seat next to him and reached inside for a bottle of aloe lotion. He handed it across the table to me.

"Thanks." I popped open the bottle and smoothed the lotion over my arms and legs, sighing as it soaked in and relieved the sting.

"The rest of you, too." Nick grabbed the bottle, then crooked a finger to tell me to come over to his side of the bench.

"You're not going to—"

"Stop being a baby!" He grabbed my hand and tugged me nearer, and I had no choice but to slide across the bench, get up, and sit down next to him. It was that or lose my fingers. "Turn around," he ordered.

I twirled on my butt so that I was at a right angle to the table. When I got out of the shower, I'd put on a fresh pair of khaki shorts and one of the T-shirts we sold at the Palace. It was the green of an unripe habanero and there was a caricature of Jack on the front, a wide grin on his face and a halo of colorful chili peppers circling his head.

"Come on." Nick poked me in the back. "Pull it up."

I'm not a prude. I mean, not like Sylvia. And I'm certainly no stranger to guys' attempts (sometimes successful, sometimes not) to get me into bed. That didn't explain the sudden knot of emotion that blocked my breathing. Or the way my heart pounded against my ribs.

"You shy?" Nick asked.

"No." I couldn't talk the talk and not walk the walk, so I pulled my T-shirt up to my armpits.

And waited.

One heartbeat. Two. Three.

When I finally looked over my shoulder to see what he was up to, I saw Nick staring at my bare back, the bottle of lotion in one hand.

"Well, are you going to do it or aren't you?" I asked him.

He snapped out of his daze. "You're not wearing—"

Too bad he was looking at my back or he would have seen the way I rolled my eyes.

"You try putting on a bra when your skin's red and itchy. And since I'm red and itchy . . ."

"Oh yeah. Sure." He opened the bottle, and I heard the burping noise it made when he squirted lotion on his hand. "It might sting," he warned.

It did.

The second the lotion touched my skin, I winced and I would have moved away if Nick's other hand didn't settle on my shoulder to hold me in place.

"It will only take a minute," he assured me, and I guess he was probably right, but in that minute when his fingers smoothed the lotion over my irritated skin and his hand slipped over my ribs and down to my waist, I thought I'd died and gone to heaven.

Although according to Sylvia, that's not where I'm going when I die.

For all I knew, Sylvia was right. About how I'd spent my life wasting my talents and my time. About how I always chose the wrong guys to fall in love with and how I did whatever I could to dodge work and how I didn't listen to her when she was generous enough to offer advice.

Right about then, I honestly didn't care.

Not about anything but the cool touch of the lotion against my irritated skin.

And the smooth sweep of Nick's hand.

And the heat that built inside me like the lava in some Pacific island volcano.

"Done." Nick's voice snapped me out of my stupor. "I'll let you . . ."

When I sat up and turned, he pointed to the front of my T-shirt with the bottle of lotion.

"Yeah. Sure." I snatched the bottle out of his hand and stood, and like it was on fire, Nick popped off the vinyl-covered bench and raced for the door.

"I'll take . . ." He grabbed the garbage bag with the Chick costume in it. "And I'll see you later and . . ."

And what, I'd never know.

Nick hotfooted it out of the RV as if that devil Sylvia said was waiting down below for me was right on his heels.

CHAPTER 7

The Chili Chick was trashed.

Well, the costume was, anyway, although with the way the day was going, the wearer of the costume was thinking it might not be a bad idea.

On the plus side, the nice folks in the hotel who took care of things like the blackjack dealers' cowboy outfits and the waitresses' pseudo-Western leather shorts and vests said they'd clean up the costume for me.

On the downside, they promised they'd have the Chick back in business in no time.

No time too soon, I hoped.

Firmly holding on to the excuse that I could not possibly work because the Chick was out of commission, I neglected to return to the Palace and instead headed out to find Yancy Harris.

The why was a no-brainer. Back when Reverend Love announced that she'd seen Yancy sprinkling a mysterious white powder into a bowl, nobody seemed all that surprised to think he'd put poison in Dickie's chili.

And that made me plenty curious.

Both about Yancy and about the people who were all too eager to point an accusatory finger in his direction.

As it turned out, though, Yancy was not scheduled to appear at Creosote Cal's that Thursday night so I had no choice but to put on my saddest face and stop in at the HR Department. I had, after all, I told the receptionist with tears in my eyes, been there for Dickie's sudden and unfortunate demise and Yancy and I planned to get together to share our feelings about the traumatic event. Just as I hoped, the receptionist was a softie and only too glad to help.

Yancy's home address clutched in my hot little hands, I headed out to a neighborhood of single-story homes, rock-and-sand front yards, and scrubby landscaping.

Not exactly what I pictured when I thought of a Vegas headliner.

Then again, Yancy wasn't exactly a Sin City legend.

I knocked on the security bars on Yancy's front door and gave him plenty of time to answer. The guy was blind, after all, and I figured it would take him longer than most folks to get around. No answer, and after a couple minutes of standing there tapping my foot, I tried again.

Still no answer, and I grumbled a curse for letting my cab leave and dug my phone out of my purse to call for a pickup.

I put it right away again when I realized that I still heard tapping. This time, it wasn't my foot.

I bent my head and followed the sound, along the front of Yancy's white adobe and to the side, where a fence far taller than me ringed his backyard.

Again, I heard the sound, a tap, and from here, I could also hear that it was followed by a gentle swish.

Then another tap. Another swish. Another tap.

Curious, I tried to look through the slats in the fence, but they were positioned in a way that made that impossible. My only solution was to pull over a nearby planter and climb. One foot on either side of a long-dead geranium, I stretched and squinted and craned my neck.

Yancy, sans dark glasses, stood at the far end of the yard putting golf balls into a little plastic cup.

Tap, and the golf ball sped toward the cup, where it landed with another tap.

Again. And again. And again.

The supply of balls gone, Yancy spun the club like a drum major's baton and sauntered across the yard, gathered up the balls, and tossed them in a pile. His back to me, he lined up to hit the balls back in the other direction.

For a few seconds, I was paralyzed with surprise. That is, until I decided my eyes must surely be deceiving me. The only way to find out for sure was to see more—better. I braced my forearms on the top of the fence and pulled my weight up. I am not by anyone's definition a big woman, but let's face it, hauling bags of chili peppers doesn't exactly qualify as manual labor and I have never been one to waste my time working out. Maybe I should have. Maybe then my muscles would be toned, and I wouldn't have gotten a cramp in my arm that made me wince. All it took was that one moment of relaxing my grip on the fence. I slipped.

In the second before my chin slammed into the fence and starbursts exploded behind my eyes, I screeched my surprise. Stunned and hurting, I didn't even realize I'd let go of my hold on the fence until I looked down and saw the ground heading way too fast in my direction.

I couldn't dance without the Chili Chick costume? Well, I was pretty sure I couldn't dance with broken legs, either. At the thought, my stomach flipped. I clawed at the fence to slow my fall, and for a moment it worked. The world settled back into place and I let go a breath, at least until gravity took over and the inevitable happened. I squeezed my eyes shut, bracing myself for the impact.

That is, before out of nowhere like a superhero on a mission, Yancy showed up. He was up in years, remember, a small and wiry guy, and there was no way he could actually catch me. In all fairness, I think what he tried to do was steady me. Instead, it was more of a slam. Caught between Yancy and the fence, my feet dangled just above the ground.

"You okay? You get hurt?" Yancy couldn't hold on for long. His arms gave out and the second he loosened his hold, I flumped down on that geranium. Good thing it was already dead.

It took me a moment to catch my breath and another few before I could think clearly enough to check my arms and my legs and make sure there were no bones sticking out anywhere they shouldn't be. My chin hurt like hell, and when I touched it, there was blood on my fingers.

Yancy to the rescue again. He pressed a white hand-kerchief into my hand, and when I looked from it to him, I found him fumbling for the sunglasses in the pocket of his blue-and-white-striped golf shirt.

I waved my unbloodied hand, hauled myself to my feet, and brushed dead geranium off my butt. "Forget it. It's too late for the sunglasses."

I guess he realized it, too. With a sigh, Yancy walked over to the gate in the fence and shooed me into the yard. There was a table and chairs on the cement patio under a canvas awning, and he went over there, grabbed ice cubes out of a cooler near the back door, and wrapped them in a paper napkin. He handed me the impromptu cold pack along with another wet napkin to wipe up the blood.

I did, and flinched.

Yancy took the wet paper towel out of my hand and cleaned up the wound, then pressed my other hand and the ice in it to my chin. "It won't stop bleeding until you stop squirming. Head back."

"It hurts." It wasn't exactly easy talking, I mean what with my head tilted back and a sack of ice just above my

windpipe. Still, I felt obligated. After all, Yancy might
not have saved my life, but he sure kept it from being a
whole lot more painful. "Can I just get . . ." I ducked
away from Yancy's ministering hands and darted over
to the table, where there were other paper napkins piled
next to a bottle of beer and a bag of Fritos. "A dry paper
napkin," I said, holding up the one I'd plucked from the
pile, then touched to my chin. "Look," I said, showing
the almost-unstained napkin to him. "Better already."

"Won't be for long if you don't take it easy." He
pointed me toward a chair. Truth be told, I was a little
shaky from the near-bone-crushing experience and I
gladly sat down.

"So . . ." Yancy handed the bottle of beer to me and
got another one out of the cooler for himself, then sat
down across from me. "Now you know."

It had been an exciting couple minutes, and my heartbeat was still ratcheted up way past what was healthy
or normal. I can be excused for not thinking clearly for
a moment or two.

The truth that had been niggling in my head when I
watched Yancy fumble for his glasses dawned, and the
words whooshed out of me. "You can see! You're not . . .
you're not really blind!"

"Shhh!" There was no one around, but that didn't
keep Yancy from looking over his shoulder. "The neighbors don't know."

"But . . ." Words failed me. A not-so-common occur-
rence. I flapped my arms at my sides, which did the
double duty of expressing my amazement and keeping

the ice off my chin because, really, the cold on my raw skin hurt like hell. "Why would anyone . . .?"

Yancy took a long drink of beer and, with a crook of one finger, urged me to do the same. Who was I to ignore the hospitality of my host? Even the icy beer wasn't enough to cool the heat of my curiosity. It took a long time of staring at Yancy before he finally gave up with a toss of his hands.

"Don't you get it?" he asked. "I'm just a guy who plays the piano, and I play the piano really, really good. But in Nashville, or Memphis or Las Vegas, there are about a million guys who play the piano really, really good."

I thought this through. "So you pretend that you're blind so you can stand out in the crowd?"

He shrugged. "It works for Stevie. And it worked for Ray."

"Except Stevie really is . . . and Ray really was . . . they're both really blind."

He made a face. "A technicality! And now . . ." One corner of Yancy's mouth pulled into a frown, and he scrubbed a finger under his nose. "You gonna tell?"

Was I?

I turned the thought over in my head, but right from the start, I knew my answer was a no-brainer.

"It gets you more gigs?" I asked him.

"Got me a permanent spot at Creosote Cal's, and I guarantee, that wouldn't have happened if I was just another guy who knew his way around the ivories."

"And everybody thinks . . .?"

"Like I said, the neighbors don't even know. I mean,

I can't let them, can I? Cal would hear about it, and I'll tell you what, he'd get all bent out of shape. I've seen it happen before. Back a couple years ago he hired what he thought was a drag queen. Turned out she was a woman just pretending to be a man pretending to be a woman, and Cal, he might not have the best sense when it comes to business, but he's got good connections in this town, and they go deep. I hear that woman's waiting tables at some local diner now. She's never appeared onstage again."

I raised my beer bottle in a toast to Yancy. "It's brilliant!"

His slim shoulders shot back and a smile tickled his lips. "You think?"

"I know a thing or two about promotion, and this . . . well . . ." I wrinkled my nose. "Isn't it a pain in the neck, though?"

"You mean acting blind? Sometimes, yeah. But hey, it keeps a roof over my head and beer . . ." He clinked his bottle against mine. "Beer in the fridge. Life might not be perfect, but it's plenty good and that's good enough for me."

We settled back and finished our beers, and when Yancy pushed the open bag of Fritos toward me, I grabbed a handful.

"So I guess I can ask now . . ." I brushed corn chip crumbs from my hands. "About the murder this morning. What did you see?"

Whatever Yancy had been expecting me to say to

explain my appearance at his home, it obviously wasn't this. He pursed his lips. "Cops send you?" he asked.

"Nope. Ruth Ann did."

"She believe that horse hockey about me poisoning Dickie?"

Now that I thought about it, I hadn't had lunch, and when Yancy got up to grab a couple more beers, I scooped up another handful of Fritos. "Reverend Love and Hermosa and Osborn sure did."

Yancy opened my beer and sat back down. "And you wonder why one of them didn't jump right up and tell the cops that there's no way good ol' Yancy Harris would ever poison Dickie Dunkin."

"It crossed my mind."

With his fingertips, Yancy tapped out a beat on the metal tabletop. "Truth?" He didn't wait for me to answer; he knew that's exactly what I was looking for. "I think we were all in shock so none of us could be expected to be thinking straight. The good reverend, she proposed a solution to the problem, and nobody had the good sense to jump in and say it couldn't possibly be right. But after we had a couple minutes to come to our senses . . . well . . ." He tipped back the bottle and drank some of his beer. "I think each of them—I mean, the reverend and Hermosa and Norman, that's Osborn's real name, you know—I think each of them knew they didn't do it, so naturally when Reverend Love thought it was me . . ." A shrug finished the thought and said all he needed to say.

"But if each of them knew they didn't do it and you know you didn't do it . . ." I let the thought hang in the air between us for a while before I asked, "So who do you think did do it?"

Another shrug was his only answer.

It was my turn to rap out a beat on the table. Mine wasn't nearly as rhythmic as Yancy's. But then, I was starting to get frustrated. "Do you think this has anything to do with Reverend Love's big wedding ceremony on Sunday?" I asked him. "You and Hermosa and Dickie and Osborn, you were all fighting about who was going to sell the most tickets and participate in the ceremony. Osborn and Dickie went at each other before the judging started, remember."

"Osborn and Dickie going at each other had nothing at all to do with that silly contest Cal came up with. Mark my words about that. Come on, Maxie, you're a smart girl. Two guys jawing at each other, puffing out their chests, and acting like big macho men. What do you think it was really all about?"

"A woman."

Yancy laughed. "A woman who was right there to watch it all."

"Reverend Love?"

This time he didn't just laugh, he roared. "Now there's a visual! Reverend Love with either Norman or Dickie! No, no, not the reverend. Hermosa. Norman and Dickie, they are—well, they were—both in love with Hermosa."

Maybe another drink of beer would help this make

sense. I sat back and sipped and thought it over. "But last night, Dickie made fun of Hermosa's singing."

"It was his thing. His shtick. You know? My guess is that Hermosa knew it was coming and played along. After all, it gave her a couple extra moments in the spotlight. And I'll tell you what, Hermosa loves her time in the spotlight."

"So The Great Osborn and Dickie and Hermosa . . ." When it came to middle-aged people, it was hard for me to wrap my head around these sorts of passions. "Who was with who?"

"Well, Hermosa and Osborn used to be a couple. Lived together for a while. Then a couple weeks ago when I got to work one night, I heard all this yelling and carrying on. Turns out Hermosa dumped Osborn. Right before he was set to go onstage. Told him that she was in love with Dickie and he was moving in with her."

I whistled low under my breath. "That might give Osborn . . . er, Norman . . . that might give him a motive to want Dickie dead."

"Yeah." Yancy made a face. "If you thought Hermosa was worth fighting for!"

I made a mental note of it. "And then there's the ticket sales, too," I reminded Yancy. "All of you were competing to sell the most. Do you think—"

"That somebody would kill Dickie over something like that?" Yancy shook his head. "Besides, I always sell out my shows. And the others, they hardly ever do. Especially Dickie. There was a time folks thought his teasing people in the audience was funny, but not so much anymore. Kindler, gentler. You know, all that. So it just goes to figure, if anyone was going to get poisoned because of the contest, it should have been me."

"But you and Dickie weren't even sitting next to each other. So it's not like somebody could have meant to poison you and poisoned him by mistake."

I think the way Yancy screwed up his mouth said that even though he'd proposed the idea, he'd never actually thought it was a possibility. Now that he thought about it, he realized it was pretty darned scary. "Anybody who would kill anybody because of how many show tickets they sold, well, that's just crazy."

"As crazy as poisoning a bowl of chili?"

He scrubbed a hand over his face. "That's not crazy, it's evil. Imagine doing that to another human being."

"It happens all the time."

He was about to take another drink, and he shot me a look over his beer bottle. "People have their reasons, I suppose. So I guess the thing we should be asking is, did any of the people at the contest have a reason to kill Dickie? I mean, other than Osborn because he might have been jealous about Dickie and Hermosa. For instance, those other contestants—"

I cut him off with a shake of my head. "I don't think so. Whoever killed Dickie must have known that the murder was going to put an end to the Devil's Breath contest. Karl Sinclair, he lost some big canned chili endorsement because of it. The way that man believes his own hype, if he did kill Dickie—and I don't see any reason why he would—he would have waited until after the contest was over. Then there's Brother William. Why would he kill Dickie? He's a holy guy, and besides, no contest means no chance of winning and he's convinced that means the sales of his monastery's chili mix are doomed."

"And that woman?" Yancy asked.

I tsked my opinion and that should have told him all he needed to know, but he still waited for more. "The jury's out on her," I told him. "I knew Bernadette a long time ago, and I know she's a sneaky, sly, nasty individual." I thought about the altar with Jack's pictures on it. "I'm for sure not counting her out."

"She's a good looker."

I would not go so far as to agree with him on that.

"And then there's Tyler York," I reminded him. "He's too good to be true."

Yancy laughed. "And that makes you suspicious of him right off the bat."

"You got that right." I laughed, too. After I got more Fritos. "The only other people in that room were me and Nick and Ruth Ann and Tumbleweed."

"Those two, Dickie made fun of them at the show the night before." Yancy didn't need to remind me.

"Maybe, but that's not a reason to kill somebody. Then again, at the show last night . . ." I sat back, letting my memory linger over everything that happened when Dickie took the stage. "He pointed you out in the audience. He said something to you, something like, 'You see what I mean, Yancy. You *see* what I mean.'" I sat up like I'd been zapped with an electrical current.

"Dickie knew, didn't he? Dickie found out your secret, just like I did."

Yancy glanced away. "I told you, nobody knew. Nobody knows now. Nobody but you and me."

"Dickie did." I was so sure of this, I pinned Yancy with a look and waited for him to squirm. "Dickie Dunkin knew you weren't blind. He made a point of mentioning it during his act. Was he . . ." I swear, nothing people did anymore surprised me, but that didn't mean I couldn't be outraged. I'd already gritted my teeth when I remembered how much my chin hurt. The ice was melted, but the wet paper napkin soothed my skin.

"Was that Dickie's way of saying he was going to tell?" I asked. "That he was going to spread the news?"

Yancy's shoulders drooped. "Not exactly. What that was, was Dickie's way of reminding me that it was time to pay and if I didn't—"

"Blackmail!"

Yancy nodded. "Dickie Dunkin was a low-down, dirty creep."

"He knew you weren't blind."

"He suspected. I don't know how. He never said. Then a couple years ago, he set a kind of trap, a rope strung up backstage just an inch or so above the floor. It was sure to trip me if I didn't see it. I thought I was all alone. I thought I was safe. But Dickie, he was watching from a dark corner and he saw me step over the rope. That's when he jumped out and told me I'd have to start paying him or he'd tell Creosote Cal and the rest of the world."

From what I'd seen of Dickie in action, I can't say this was a surprise. He made fun of his coworkers. He made fun of total strangers. Dickie Dunkin had a mean streak a mile wide, and finding out he was also greedy, well . . .

I didn't want to miss a second of Yancy's reaction so I kept my eyes on him when I said, "You know, Yancy, that gives you a really good motive for murder."

"Yes, it does." He folded his hands on the table in front of him. "But let me tell you a couple things. Number one, I didn't do it. And number two, if I did . . . well, if I did, I would have done it a long time ago. Dickie's been getting money out of me every month for a couple years. Why would I wait until now to get rid of him? And why would I do it in such a public place? Come on, Maxie. Give me a little more credit than that."

He was right and I was grateful for his honesty, his beer, and his Fritos, and I told Yancy as much. I didn't have to tell him that his secret was safe with me because I guess he already knew that. After I called a cab and just as it pulled up to the front of his house, he put a hand on my arm.

"Thanks," Yancy said and winked.

I told him I'd see him back at Creosote Cal's and left, and on the way back to the hotel, I thought about everything I'd learned that day. I liked Yancy and I would have even if he hadn't given me beer and Fritos. I had to admit that I admired his ingenuity, his flair for promotion, and the sheer audacity it took to pull off a hoax like the one he lived in public every day.

But I also had to admit something else, and it made me so uncomfortable, I squirmed against the taxi's sticky faux leather seat.

If a guy would pull off a hoax like pretending he was blind, I wondered what else he had the nerve to do.

CHAPTER 8

Never let it be said that I shirk my job. Well, not totally and completely anyway.

The next morning, I worked like a dog at the Palace. In fact, I was so busy, I never had a chance to pick up the Chick costume from the folks who were ridding it of the itching powder. Instead, I handed out samples of the (pretty ordinary if you ask me) chili Sylvia had made the night before, helped customers choose their spices and peppers, packed bags, rang the register, and dodged Sylvia's unending questions about my chin and how it got scraped and what I'd been doing and who I'd been with and why I hadn't come right to her for help when I returned to the RV because I knew that she cared about me.

Finally just before noon there was a lull in both the crowd and Sylvia's nauseating attempts to pretend that, like a real sister, she actually cared. Seeing my opportunity, I volunteered to go to the food truck we usually worked from for some extra Texas Jack T-shirts. Once inside—and out of sight of Sylvia's prying eyes—I took a deep breath and glanced around.

If I was a no-good, sneaky, underhanded half sister, where would I hide my father's prized chili recipe?

See, Jack's recipe was what I'd spent the last week searching for.

Oh yes, she denied it, all the while batting those golden eyelashes of hers. But I knew Sylvia had discovered the basic recipe for Jack's world-famous chili in one of his old notebooks, because back in Taos (the last stop on the Showdown tour), I'd found both the notebook and the little bits of paper left near the spiral binding that showed that a page had been torn out. I also suspected what she planned to do with the recipe. Sylvia used to write for a foodie magazine back in Seattle. And before that, she had dreamed of becoming a chef.

She was out to make a name for herself in the world of food, damn her! And there was no better way to do that than to amaze and astound the culinary universe with Jack's secret recipe.

Which Sylvia, no doubt, would take full credit for.

Which, have no fear, I wasn't about to let happen.

When Sylvia wasn't around, I'd already looked through the RV and I'd gone through her clothes and her shoes and her purses. Like the sparkly evening bag she'd carried with her the night before the Showdown opened.

No luck then, no luck now.

I finished with the last of the cupboards where we stored paper plates and cups and came up empty and I grumbled a curse. Sylvia of the perfect hair and the perfect teeth and the perfect skin might be more . . . well, more perfect than me, but no way was she as smart. Or as cagey. The answer to the mystery must have been staring me right in the face.

If only I could think what it was!

I surrendered with a sigh and dug Texas Jack T-shirts in various sizes and colors out of the shipping box we stored them in, and I already had them stacked in my arms and up to my nose when someone knocked on the door of the Palace.

"There you are! Just like Sylvia said you'd be." Ruth Ann popped her head inside. The rest of her followed. "Always working. You girls are such treasures. Your dad would be so proud!"

In truth, I think Jack would be more astounded than anything else. In the exactly seven weeks, two days, and four hours since Sylvia and I had officially been in charge of Texas Jack Pierce's Hot-Cha Chili Seasoning Palace, we had not killed each other.

At least not yet.

But if I didn't find that recipe soon . . .

I would have dropped the T-shirts right then and

there and given the Palace another good reconnoiter, but Ruth Ann didn't give me a chance. She pressed a piece of paper into my hand.

Since I was holding all those T-shirts, it was a little tough to see what it was.

"Address." Like it was some big secret, Ruth Ann whispered, "It's the house where The Great Osborn is working a private party today."

I would have scratched my head if I'd had a free hand. "Is there a reason I care?"

Ruth Ann's smile was as bright as the Nevada sun. "Well, of course you care," she assured me. "Because you're going to solve the mystery. You know . . ." We were the only ones inside the Palace and there was nothing outside but a couple acres of blacktop parking lot, but still, Ruth Ann leaned in. "You're going to find out who killed Dickie Dunkin."

"And I'm going to talk to Osborn—"

"Because he was there, of course. Because he's a suspect! Just like everyone in that auditorium is. Well, everyone but me and Tumbleweed and you and Nick. We know none of us did it. In fact . . ." She scooped the T-shirts out of my arms and headed out the door. "I'll take these into Deadeye and I'll tell Sylvia I ran into you and I begged you to come over to the blacksmith shop and help me out with a project." Over her shoulder, she gave me a broad wink. "Pretty clever, huh? Sylvia won't have the nerve to question it, and that will give you a few hours to investigate. You can get over to that party and talk to Osborn. What do you say?"

I say I'm never one to look a gift horse in the mouth, and time away from work equaled time away from Sylvia, and time away from Sylvia equaled time to further look into Dickie's murder, and maybe when I got back from time away from work and time away from Sylvia and time looking into Dickie's murder, that might equal more time to search for Jack's recipe.

With all that in mind (believe me, it wasn't easy to keep it all straight), I hurried around to the front of the hotel to hail a cab. Less than a half hour later, I found myself in a neighborhood called Silverado Ranch and in front of a house where cars packed the driveway and more of them were parked out front. Since the action appeared to be going on in the backyard, I followed a path around some thirsty-looking shrubs to the back of the two-story stone and stucco house.

I was just about to step around the corner of the house when the air around me filled with flashes of neon green. Green tentacles slapped my arms and something soft and slightly sticky settled on my shoulders.

Startled, I shrieked, ducked, put my arms around my head to protect myself, and screeched some more.

That is, until I heard a high-pitched voice call out, "Gotcha!"

I plucked away the green goo that crisscrossed my face and found a redheaded boy of ten or so who jumped up and down a couple feet in front of me. He had a can of Silly String in one hand, and with the other, he pointed at the neon mess that covered me head to toe. "You're old. You weren't fast enough. Gotcha! Gotcha! Gotcha!"

Don't get me wrong. I love goofing around with Silly String just as much as the next person. What I don't take kindly to is annoying children. While the kid was still laughing his fool head off, I yanked the can out of his hands, emptied it out on the top of his head, and marched off, plucking Silly String from my clothes.

I shouldn't have bothered because, as it turned out, I'm pretty sure no one would have noticed.

Pink Silly String hung from the chairs placed in a semicircle near the aboveground pool. Yellow Silly String clothed the jungle gym and swayed softly in the hot breeze that blew through the backyard. Silly String zinged through the air above my head in multicolored, gooey rainbows propelled by the children who ran through the yard in packs. They shot one another. They shot the family dog. They shot their parents who were gathered around the barbeque grill, sipping their cocktails and—don't ask me how—talking to one another above the noise of prepubescent squeals.

"A kid's party," I mumbled to myself. "Osborn's working a kid's party."

He was, indeed, though I have to say, it took me a couple minutes of staring at the clown making balloon animals over on the back patio before I recognized his belly paunch. Then again, baggy yellow-and-blue-plaid pants hide a multitude of sins, as does a coat with one green sleeve, one yellow sleeve, a blue front, and a red back.

I got over there just as Osborn added a twist to a long blue balloon and it popped in his face.

"Do it again! Do it again!" The urchin in front of him

figured the exploding balloon was part of the act. She clapped her hands and shrieked.

Yes, there was a whole lot of shrieking going on.

Osborn blew up another balloon, twisted it a few times, and handed it off to the kid. When he was done, he stepped back and, with one hand pressed to his chest, gasped for air. That's when he noticed me. "You're not one of the guests," he said.

"No, but I need to talk to you."

A boy of five pushed me out of the way. "I want a butterfly!" he yelled.

His plastic red nose twitching, Osborn made the kid a butterfly, twisting the balloon this way and that while his gaze traveled over the army of kids who raced through the yard and skimmed the thirty or so adults who weren't even pretending they could control them. "They won't be happy if they figure out you're a party crasher," he said.

"The party givers, you mean."

Osborn's blue Afro twitched when he nodded.

"I get it. I don't want to ruin the gig for you. You could make a balloon animal for me," I suggested. "Then they might think I actually belong here."

He blew up a pink balloon and twisted it.

It popped.

Osborn mumbled a word he shouldn't have said at a kids' party. "I hate balloon animals," he added with a look toward the adults, who by this time were oblivious to the sounds of bursting balloons. "Why can't I just do card tricks? I'm really good at card tricks."

I had seen his card tricks onstage at Creosote Cal's and I wasn't sure *really good* applied, but I didn't point that out. Just so he couldn't tell me to shut up and mind my own business, I waited until he was in the midst of blowing up another balloon before I started in again. "You and Dickie had a fight yesterday. You argued about ticket sales to your shows this weekend."

Osborn gave the pink balloon a couple twists. "So?"

"So now Dickie's dead."

He glanced at me. "What happened to your chin?"

Once I'd got back to the RV the night before, I'd realized the wound I'd sustained thanks to my run-in with Yancy's fence wasn't nearly as serious as I'd feared when it happened. I'd taken care of it. Plenty of soap and water. A slathering of Neosporin. It might have been a little less conspicuous if I could have found some regular old bandages and hadn't had to go next door and ask Johnny Purdue, who ran a stand that sold cold drinks, if he had any he could spare. Not only did Johnny have bandages, but he had little kids. My injury might have been a little less noticeable if not for the Angry Birds bandage.

"It doesn't matter what happened to my chin. What happened to Dickie, that's what's important."

"You think?"

I shouldn't have had to remind him. "I think Dickie was poisoned."

"And you think I did it?"

He grabbed a green balloon, but before he had a

chance to blow it up, a small kid tugged at his sleeve. "Doggie," the kid said. "I wanna doggie."

Osborn put down the green balloon and grabbed a blue one, blew it up, and twisted it into what looked more like a misshapen soccer ball than a doggie. "There you go, kid," he said.

The little boy's bottom lip bulged. "Not a doggie."

The smile on Osborn's face never wavered. Then again, it was painted on. "It's a doggie. Take it and get lost."

The kid did.

"I didn't say you killed Dickie," I commented once the kid had walked away.

"Good thing, because I didn't."

"But you did have a fight."

One of the adults had gone over to a table at the center of which was a two-foot-high cake decorated to look like a pirate ship, and Osborn saw his chance. He motioned me to follow him to the side of the house, where, out of sight of the party goers, he lit a cigarette and took a drag.

Once again I had to face the demons of my former addiction. Lucky for me, there was green Silly String on my shorts so I concentrated on picking that off instead of on the aroma of tobacco.

"That fight . . ." Osborn scratched a hand under his bulbous rubber nose. "It was a setup, you know?"

"You and Dickie planned it?"

"His timing was bad. And doesn't it figure? Dickie was a—" He didn't finish the thought. Then again, the way his mouth twisted, he didn't have to. "Comedians, they're supposed to be all about timing. Still, Dickie screwed it up. We had it planned so we'd wait until the audience was seated."

"You wanted to fight in public?"

"We wanted to get some attention. You know, so people left there talking about us."

"And bought tickets to both your shows this weekend."

It was unnerving when the blue Afro bobbed in my direction.

I backed up a step. "Okay, I get it. The fight was all about promotion, all about publicity. You and Dickie planned it. But I bet you didn't plan that Dickie would steal Hermosa away from you."

The painted smile squeezed. "Who told you that?"

"Is it true?"

"That Dickie stole Hermosa away? That's not exactly what I'd call it."

"Then what would you call it?"

He finished his cigarette and stubbed it out beneath the sole of one red boot. "I didn't kill him."

"Like I said, I didn't say—"

"Then why come around asking questions?"

I answered as best I could. Which meant I shrugged. "Ruth Ann's upset. And the whole thing . . ." I thought back to the scene in Creosote Cal's auditorium the day before. It felt like a lifetime ago. "None of it makes sense. Bernadette's chili couldn't have been poisoned. If it was, you all would be where Dickie is now."

Even though it was coated with white greasepaint, I could tell Osborn's face got a little green. "Don't think I haven't thought of that."

"So I guess I just want some answers," I admitted. "I thought you might be able to help."

A rousing—and very off-key—chorus of "Happy Birthday" ended in the backyard, and Osborn peeked around the corner. Apparently he was still in the clear.

"I didn't see anything," he said.

"You left the judging table at one point."

"So I tasted the chili and went backstage so everybody in the audience didn't see me gag and throw up. What of it? Again you're insinuating—"

"Nothing. Honest. I'm just trying to sift through the facts. You took a taste of one of the chilies. And you coughed and pounded your chest and—"

"And got up and went backstage so I could choke in private. Man, that stuff was hot!"

"And when you walked past where Dickie was sitting—"

"Did I put poison in his bowl?" Osborn laughed. Not a pleasant sound. "What do you think?"

"I think the cops are going to be looking at everyone's motives. You and Dickie and Hermosa . . . that's definitely a motive."

"Yeah, well, if they're looking for motives, tell them to be sure to talk to the lovely and talented Hermosa."

Call me a romantic at heart (go ahead, say it—it isn't true, and after what happened back in Chicago with Edik, it never will be), I couldn't help but flinch. "You're pointing the finger at Hermosa? I thought you loved her!"

Osborn peeked around the corner one more time before he lit another cigarette. "Yeah, well, I thought I loved her, too. What a sucker I was, huh? Then one day, she marches into the theater and announces that Dickie is moving in with her."

"So Dickie and Hermosa were an item. Then why do you think she would want to kill him?"

Osborn dismissed my logic with the wave of a hand. "You met Dickie. Everyone who knew him wanted to kill him."

"I doubt that applies to the woman he was living with."

When a clown with white greasepaint smeared over his face and a huge red smile rolls his eyes, there's something particularly sinister about it. "You've never been in love, have you, kid?" he asked me, and it was a good thing he didn't give me a chance to answer. There wasn't time to get into all the ugly details of the Edik story. "Why do you suppose the cops always look at a murder victim's spouse first? Nobody knows another person as well as the person they're sleeping with. And more often than not, getting to know you turns into getting to hate you."

Even I wasn't that cynical. Or was I?

Osborn interrupted my conscience searching. "You were at the show the other night when Dickie got up onstage. He insulted plenty of people, including Hermosa."

"He did, didn't he?" I cocked my head and thought

122

this through. "Yancy said Hermosa went along with it for the publicity. Do you think that's true? It sounds crazy to me that any woman would let a guy talk about her like that. They were supposed to be—"

"In love? Yeah. Whatever!" Osborn finished his cigarette. "Hermosa didn't love Dickie as much as she loved his money. And his promises. See, Dickie claimed he had contacts at one of the big hotels on the Strip. Good contacts. He told Hermosa he was going to get a permanent gig there. And that he was taking her along with him."

"It wasn't true?"

"What do you think?"

"Did she leave you before or after Dickie promised her the moon?"

Osborn grunted. "The minute he spoke the words."

"So Dickie promises her a bigger spotlight—"

"And she walks out on me." He threw his hands in the air.

"And that's when you decided you hated Hermosa."

"You got that right, kid."

"And that's when you decided you hated Dickie, too."

He thought about it, but only for a moment. Then he shook his head and that blue Afro wiggled like a bowl of Jell-O. "Nah! Only realized how much I hated Hermosa a little while ago. Dickie—"

"Where's Osborn the Clown?" we heard someone call from the backyard.

Osborn sighed, straightened his wig, and made sure his nose was in place. "Dickie," he said, "I knew I hated a long, long time ago. And he reminded me of the fact. The fifteenth of every month."

Believe me, I would have asked him to explain if a couple little kids hadn't barreled around the corner, grabbed on to Osborn, and dragged him back to the party.

Me? I walked up front and called a cab, and it should come as no surprise that even when I got back to Creosote Cal's, I didn't head straight to Deadeye.

See, Osborn got me thinking, and thinking, I thought about Yancy and everything he'd told me the evening before about how Dickie Dunkin had been blackmailing him.

That's when I casually strolled back over to Creosote Cal's Human Resources Department, and once there, I found the answer to the question that had been nagging me since leaving the party.

No wonder Osborn hated Dickie Dunkin so much! I'd bet a case of Thermal Conversion that, just like he had Yancy, Dickie had been blackmailing Osborn. Every single fifteenth of every single month—payday.

CHAPTER 9

"It's about time."

The fact that Sylvia had customers when I got back to the Palace didn't keep her from editorializing. She packed a woman's shopping bag and glared at me from behind the cash register, all at the same time. Sylvia is just that kind of talented. "I can't believe Ruth Ann needed your help this long."

"You know Ruth Ann!" How's that for noncommittal? I grabbed a handful of the corn chips Sylvia had put out next to the tiny bowls of chili samples for customers. It had been a long day, and I hadn't even gotten a piece of cake at the birthday party. I chomped down the corn chips and gave my half sister a half smile. "I'm back now."

"And you better get to work!" Sylvia handed the woman her shopping bag and thanked her for stopping in before she glanced toward the back of the bordello. I looked where she was looking and saw a familiar flash of red.

"The Chick is back in town!" I fist-pumped and closed in on my cleaned (and itch-free, I hoped) costume and headed into the back storage room to change.

The moment I stepped back into the bordello, Sylvia pushed a pile of papers into my right hand. "Coupons for a free sample-size jar of Chili Cha-Cha with every ten-dollar purchase. And flyers advertising our latest specials, and—"

My left hand out and my stilettos dangling from it, I stopped her. "At least let me get my shoes on."

"Well, do it fast." Sylvia gave me a shove toward the front door. "The Chick is supposed to be our big drawing card and you've barely worn the costume since we got to Vegas. Look, there's a boatload of people coming into Deadeye. It must be one of those senior citizen bus tours. Get out there, Maxie. Get out there and dance!"

In fishnet-stockinged feet, I stumbled out to the wooden walkway in front of the bordello, set down the coupons, and leaned against the building to slip on my shoes. All set, I grabbed the coupons again, and since a few of the old folks who'd just walked in had spied the Chick and walked over to check out what the giant chili was all about, I dance-stepped my way over to the dusty main street of Deadeye.

"Texas Jack Pierce's Hot-Cha Chili Seasoning Palace!" I waved and tapped and—

"Whoa!" My feet slid out from under me, and I threw out a hand and caught the arm of an old guy in a white jacket who thought it was part of the act and looped an arm around the Chick, chuckling all the while.

I thanked him with a smile he couldn't see, caught my breath, steadied myself, and pulled away.

Only to have my feet go out from under me again.

This time, I wasn't fast enough. I thrashed my arms, and coupons and flyers geysered into the air, then floated down on the crowd, like overgrown confetti. I fought to regain control, but the more I shuffled my feet, the more I spun out of control. The blue sky and white puffy clouds painted on the ceiling above my head tipped. The shops of Deadeye swirled when I whirled. They disappeared from my line of sight completely when I ended up in the dust and drifts of coupons on my chili butt.

"Oh, that was just terrific!" A tiny old lady let go of her walker long enough to applaud. "Wasn't it, Harry? Wasn't it terrific?" she asked the man at her side. "Oh, wouldn't it be lovely to be able to dance like that again."

I wasn't so sure about that.

Here's the thing about the Chili Chick. She's made of heavy canvas reinforced with wire and mesh and all sorts of whatevers that keep the chili shape. The costume cushioned my fall and that was a good thing, but trying to pull myself up off the floor while encased in a giant chili wasn't so much an aerobic exercise as it was a matter of rolling, turning, and grunting.

I rolled, turned, and grunted, and finally, I was able to raise myself on my elbows and sit up. Getting to my feet, that was a whole different challenge. I looked up at the circle of senior citizen faces that looked down at me and knew I would find no help there. All I needed was to grab a hand and yank some old guy down on the floor and have him break a hip! On my own, I braced a hand against the floor and shoved. It actually might have worked if my feet didn't slip.

I ended up back where I started.

"Looks like you could use some help."

This time when I looked up, I found Gert Wilson had joined the crowd of onlookers. Gert owned the stand that sold things like cute kitchen towels and potholders, chili-themed jewelry and crockery, and she was currently working out of the general store next door to the bordello.

Gert is no fragile senior citizen so when she offered me a hand, I grabbed it. She tugged, I got to my feet. But no sooner had the soles of my shoes settled on the floor than my left foot shot back and my right foot kicked forward.

This time when I went down, I landed on my knees and I didn't care how many senior citizens were within earshot, as soon as I felt my fishnet stockings rip along with my flesh, I snarled out a curse.

"Again." Gert held on to my hand tighter this time and looped an arm around the chili. "Careful," she warned when I got to my feet and they slid to either side like I was on ice skates. "Don't try to move too fast. In fact, maybe you shouldn't try to move at all."

She didn't need to tell me twice. I stood as still as if

I'd been turned to stone and braced myself, waiting for the room to pitch, and when it didn't, I let go a long breath and kicked off my shoes.

"Thanks," I told Gert, steady on my feet now that I was stockings to floor. "I must have stepped in something."

She'd already bent to retrieve my stilettos, and she turned them over and tipped the shoes so that I could see that both of them had something shiny on the soles. She touched a finger to the substance. "It looks like Vaseline, and it's smeared over the soles and heels of both shoes. There's no way this was an accident. Somebody wanted you to fall."

"Somebody?" I shot a laser look at the Palace and at Sylvia, who, in spite of the fact that her sister was down on the ground—hard to miss a prostrate chili—and surrounded by old people who smelled like mints and arthritis cream, was engrossed in rearranging jars of spices. "Like the same somebody who claimed she didn't know anything about the itching powder in my costume?"

I pulled away from Gert and I would have stomped right into the Palace and had it out with Sylvia, but dang, it turns out senior citizens can move pretty fast when they see a chili with its chili fists curled and steam coming out of its ears; they beat me to the door. I reminded myself that customers meant sales and sales meant income and income meant paid bills, and put the knock-down-drag-out I planned to have with my half sister on my to-do list.

"Come on." Gert cupped my elbow and piloted me

toward the general store. "Your knees are scraped. Let's get them cleaned up and I'll make you a cup of tea."

Once we were inside, I ducked into a back storage room and peeled out of the costume and my ruined stockings. I dropped into one of the two director's chairs Gert had set up at the back of the shop, took the wet cloth she offered me, and touched it to my knees.

When I was done, Gert handed me a mug of tea. She was famous for the herbal concoctions that she claimed were beneficial for everything from skin tone to mood to whole body cleansing. Translation: They tasted like boiled weeds, and smelled bad, too. But this tea . . .

I pulled in a breath of the steam that rose off the mug with a bright red chili pepper on the side of it.

Blackberries, and I took a tiny sip and nodded my approval when Gert dropped down in the chair across from mine and gave me a long, hard look.

"Scratched knees to go with your scraped chin. What have you been up to?"

"Oh, this?" I touched a hand to the Angry Birds bandage. "It's nothing."

Gert looked at me over the rim of her mug. "Looks like investigating to me."

"More like being a klutz." Just to prove that it really didn't matter, I ripped the bandage off my chin. Nearly twenty-four hours after taking a tumble from Yancy's fence and the wound was dry. And itchy. I whisked a finger over my chin, then got back to taking care of my knees. Fortunately, there was little blood and the bandage Gert handed me was free of cartoon characters.

I slapped it on my left knee, then reached for the second bandage she held out and applied that one to my right.

"She's doing it because of Jack's recipe," I said.

I guess the way I ground out that *she* spoke volumes because Gert knew exactly who I was talking about. She nodded, and her auburn hair caught the light of the chandelier above her head. "You really think your sister would try to hurt you because of a recipe?"

"Jack's recipe." This was, obviously, a whole different thing from just any recipe, and Gert should have known it. Though she never came right out and admitted it, I was pretty sure Gert had a thing for Jack. Or at least she had before Jack disappeared.

This, of course, wasn't a new thought. I wondered about my dad's whereabouts pretty much morning, noon, and night. No, that wasn't what made my chin come up and my eyes narrow. It was—

"Bernadette!" I grumbled the name from between clenched teeth. "Sylvia claims she doesn't know anything about the itching powder, and I'd bet a dime to a donut she's going to say the same thing about the greasy stuff on the bottom of my shoes. If it wasn't her, it had to be Bernadette."

"And she is . . .?"

I'd been so busy, what with Dickie getting murdered and Ruth Ann begging for my help, I hadn't talked to Gert since the start of the Showdown. I filled her in about Bernadette and how she was one of the Devil's Breath contestants and how she used to work at the

Palace and how she obviously had a thing—a very sick thing—going for Jack.

"And you think this Bernadette—"

I didn't let her finish. "Don't you see?" I leaned forward in my chair. "She's obsessed. With Jack."

"And you think that means she wants to hurt you?"

I sat back. "You think I'm talking crazy."

"I think it seems . . ." Since Gert still had her mug in one hand, she gestured with the other. "Implausible."

She was being kind. But then, Gert's that type of person.

She's also loyal, and she can keep a secret.

Don't think I'd forgotten. Back in Taos, Gert had hinted that she might know something about Jack's disappearance. She'd also refused to share. No matter how much I begged, she swore she knew nothing. Nothing she could divulge anyway.

I took another drink of my tea before I set my cup on the table where Gert wrapped her customers' purchases. "Bernadette's crazy. She's fixated," I said.

"On Jack."

"The whole thing with the altar . . ." The thought made me shiver. "You have to admit, it's as creepy as hell."

"It is a little odd," she said. "But what does that have to do with—"

"Trying to make me suffer?" I stood and tossed my hands in the air for dramatic effect. "She doesn't need a reason. She's a crazy person," I wailed. "And don't you get it . . ." Desperate to have her see the error of her keeping-her-lips-shut ways, I closed in on Gert. "If there's a crazy person out to get Jack and you know anything about where he might be—"

"I don't. I told you that, Maxie." When Gert bounded out of her chair, I had no choice but to step back. Gert wasn't a tall woman, but she was substantial in an earth mother sort of way, and I didn't want to take the chance of getting flattened by her sensible sandals or lost in the folds of her ankle-length denim skirt. "Even if I did, I can't think that just because some woman remembers your father fondly—"

"Flickering candles and pictures printed from online? I'm thinking that's more weird than fond."

I expected Gert to register the same sort of panic that tapped away at my insides when I thought about Bernadette's sick obsession. That might explain why I was stunned by the tiny smile that played over her lips.

"Jack has that sort of effect on women," she said.

That might be true, but it didn't excuse attempted chili mayhem. Knowing I'd get nothing further out of Gert, I tucked the costume under my arm and stalked out of the general store.

Did I need more proof that Bernadette was behind the mischief? It came as soon as I stepped out onto the dusty main street of Deadeye and saw her lounging in front of the saloon across the street where Bob Lennox had set up his stand to sell cold drinks, hot coffee, and pastries.

She looked from my face to the costume I carried. She studied my scraped knees.

And she grinned.

When I walked back into the Palace, I made sure I was limping like a peg-leg pirate. This did not, it should be noted, get me any sympathy from Sylvia, and it was her indifference that helped me make up my mind.

I stashed the Chili Chick in the back room and, limping no more, headed out the front door. I couldn't dance, but I sure as heck could investigate, and with that in mind, I headed over to the theater, where that night, Hermosa would appear in all her glory.

Just as I hoped, the diva was mid-rehearsal.

If it was possible to call screaming at the orchestra conductor rehearsing.

"Are you a complete moron?" Hermosa didn't give the conductor a chance to answer. She stomped one gold sequin-clad stiletto and shook the voluminous skirt of her purple caftan like a raging tropical bird puffing out its feathers to make a hungry snake think it was bigger and less tasty. "I said to play the intro twice." She held up two fingers. "One. Two. Twice. And you play it once and expect me to start singing? There are millions of musicians in Vegas, Hal. Don't get the idea that you're indispensable."

Hal, to his eternal credit, kept his mouth shut. But then, maybe there are millions of musicians in Vegas.

"Try again!" Hermosa commanded with a wave of her hands. "And this time, get it right."

The music started up. The intro was played twice. And then one of the trumpet players got a little too enthusiastic when he leaned forward to hit a high note and knocked over his music stand.

"Idiots!" Hermosa screamed, and I wondered why she wasn't worried about straining her voice, then decided it didn't much matter. Maybe even Hermosa realized Hermosa wasn't much of a singer.

"I need a break," she said, and the singsong tone of her voice fooled no one. The woman was obviously about to bust a gasket.

Hermosa turned on her shiny heels and headed backstage.

I found her in her dressing room slugging back a clear liquid I bet wasn't water.

"You." Hermosa was so full of Hermosa, I couldn't believe she even remembered me from the Devil's Breath judging. That didn't stop her from giving me a look that would have frozen a lesser person at twenty paces. I, remember, have been eating hot-as-hell chili all my life. It would take a lot more than Hermosa's icy glances to turn me into a snow cone. "What do you want?"

"An autograph, of course." Never let it be said that I can't shmooze with the best of 'em. I dragged over a scrap of paper on Hermosa's dressing table, handed it to her, and waited while she scrawled her name in hot pink Sharpie. I tucked the paper in my pocket and gave her what I hoped was a fangirl smile. "And to talk about Dickie, of course," I added.

Hermosa put the back of one hand to her forehead. I swear, she really did this!

"Dickie!" Her moaning sounded a whole lot like her singing. "My heart is broken."

"Which is exactly why we need to figure out what happened," I said, and when she shot me a look, I was quick to add, "So you can get on with your life."

"Yes," she nodded and a slow smile spread over her lips. "Hermosa's Gift cannot be overshadowed by grief."

"Exactly." She didn't invite me, but I made myself comfortable in the chair across from the one she sank down in. "Do you think Dickie's murder had anything to do with the contest?" I asked, then just so she didn't get the wrong idea, I was sure to add, "Not the chili contest. The contest to sell the most tickets to this weekend's shows."

Her chin came up. "Let us be perfectly clear. I always sold more tickets than Dickie."

Ah, true love! "Of course you did," I said instead of telling her I understood because I didn't believe in true love, either. "But the others . . ."

Hermosa's eyebrows were plucked to angel-hair pasta width, and thinking, she lowered them. "The others never had a chance to sell more tickets than I do."

Not what I meant, and when I told her that, Hermosa's eyes went wide. "You think Yancy or Osborn might have . . ." She chewed over this thought while she lit a cigarette.

Did everyone in Vegas have to remind me of my late, great habit?

Hermosa blew out a stream of smoke. "Norman," she said. "It had to be Norman Osborn."

See, just what I was saying. Love is overrated. Instead of pointing this out, I said, "You used to live with him."

"Before I came to my senses."

"But if you think there's a possibility that he could be a murderer . . ."

When she smiled, Hermosa's teeth sparkled. "Oh honey, there's a possibility that we could all be murderers. Given the right circumstances."

"And you think the circumstances were right for Osborn."

"I think . . ." She tapped the ash from the end of her cigarette into a Styrofoam cup. "I just gave Norman the news about how Dickie was moving in with me. Of course the circumstances were right. Norman was insanely jealous. He was head over heels in love with me."

There was the L-word again.

"Funny," I said, even though it wasn't. "Norman isn't still so much in love with you that he worried about protecting your reputation. In fact, he thinks you might have killed Dickie."

"Son of a—" Hermosa stubbed out her cigarette on the edge of her dressing table. "He would say that. Idiot. And I suppose he gave you some half-baked reason."

"He said it was because Dickie promised you a job at some hoity-toity hotel on the Strip."

Just as she was about to throw her cigarette butt in the trash, Hermosa's hands froze. "Norman knew about that?" she asked, then realized she probably shouldn't have. She shook her shoulders and her purple caftan quivered. "Norman got the story wrong."

"Dickie didn't promise you a job on the Strip."

"He did, but—"

"But you found out Dickie was lying about the job."

"I found out—" Hermosa stood. I hadn't realized how tall she was, but then, I was sitting and I had to look up to see her face. It was a perfect mask of thick makeup and stonewalling. "If you think I was angry enough at Dickie to kill him, think again. If that was true, why would I be letting him move in with me? In case you don't believe it . . ." In a swish of purple fabric, she turned and marched out of the dressing room, and curious, I scrambled to catch up.

"The dressing rooms in this hellhole are too small," she grumbled, leading the way through a narrow hallway, and what that had to do with her adding, "Dickie's lease was up on his apartment last week," I didn't know until she stopped in front of a storage room, threw open the door, and turned on the lights.

There were metal shelves against all four of the room's walls, and they were filled with props like the bottles of fake liquor back at the bordello. Hermosa ignored that stuff and waved her hand toward what was piled on the floor.

"This is where they store the extra stuff for the casino, and nobody hardly ever comes in here," she said. "So this is where we had the stuff from Dickie's apartment delivered. We planned on having it moved to my place next week, after we figured out how to make some extra room. Damn!" Fists on hips and top lip curled, she looked over the mismatched suitcases, about a dozen cardboard boxes, and a trunk with a domed lid and rusted latches that looked as if it had come out of some granny's attic. "I guess I'm going to have to figure out what to do with it before Cal catches wind of it being here and hits the roof."

She backed out of the room and shut the door.

"Now do you believe me?" she asked. "No way I killed Dickie. Heaven help me, I loved the man, and I know he adored me. What man wouldn't?"

CHAPTER 10

"I've got to leave."

No *hello, nice to see you, glad you're back.*

But then, that's not Sylvia's style.

The moment I walked back into the bordello, she slid out from behind the cash register and left a long line of customers with purchases in their hands, who automatically looked my way.

At the door, she called over her shoulder, "See you later." And that was that.

The next hour was a blur of chili spices, peppers, and questions, and believe me, I am not complaining. When it comes to the Palace, slammed is a good thing.

But by the time I took care of all those customers and restocked the shelves, I was whooped. I'd brought a box of Hostess Twinkies from the RV and tucked it in the back room for just such an emergency, and convinced I needed a surge of sugar, I headed that way and—

Stopped cold.

The Chili Chick was exactly where I'd left her, draped over a chair in the storage room, but one look, and I knew something was wrong.

Yellow.

There was something bright yellow on the Chick.

I lifted the costume and my heart gave two mighty thumps. That is, before it stopped completely.

Someone had spray-painted a message on the Chili Chick in Day-Glo yellow.

Bitch.

As if the word were as flaming as the color of the paint it was written with, I dropped the costume and backed out of the room, Twinkies forgotten. I would have kept right on backstepping if I hadn't bumped into something that felt more like a brick wall than solid flesh.

Nick.

His hands clutched my shoulders. "What's wrong?"

The itching powder, the gunk on my shoes, that sleek knowing smile on Bernadette's face when I saw her out on the main street of Deadeye a little earlier . . . I could deal with all that, and I had, in my usual way. I was pissed, and ready to rumble.

But this . . .

There was something about seeing the Chick herself vandalized, something that deep down inside felt like a sacrilege so personal and so devastating, it took my breath—and my voice—away.

Like it had rusted shut, I worked my jaw up and down a couple times before I could get any words out. "Wrong? Somebody . . ." I made a sharp motion toward the back room and the vandalized costume, and fortunately, Nick got the message. He stepped in there, and when he came out again, his lips were pressed into a thin line.

"What did you see?"

I shook my head. "I've been busy. We had plenty of customers. And before that I was . . ."

I was what, investigating? Something told me mentioning that wasn't the best way to get Nick's sympathy. "I had the costume on earlier today and it was fine," I told him instead. "Well, except for my shoes being slippery."

"Which explains your knees."

There was something about knowing that Nick was giving my legs a careful look that shook me out of my daze. "First the itching powder! Then my shoes were messed with! Now this!" I threw my hands in the air. "Don't you get it, Nick? Somebody's out to get me. And I know exactly who it is!"

"Could it be because you're poking your nose where it doesn't belong?"

If this was a legitimate question, I would have answered it honestly. The way it was, the tone of Nick's voice told me he wasn't as interested in finding out what I'd learned in regards to the investigation as he was in reminding me that I didn't have the experience—or the smarts—to be investigating in the first place.

I crossed my arms over my chest. "Somebody doesn't like me," I grumbled.

To which, let's face it, Nick had no right to smile. "You're really hard to like."

He didn't give me a chance to level him. "Go." This time when he put his hands on my shoulders, he spun me toward the door. "Go find Sylvia so I can ask her what she might have seen. And don't worry about sales," he added because he knew that was exactly what I was worried about. "If customers come in, I'll tell them to come back a little later."

With no choice, I headed out, and though Creosote Cal's isn't nearly as big as some of those mega-hotels over on the Strip, it wasn't exactly easy finding Sylvia in a place filled with one-armed bandits, an all-you-can-eat buffet restaurant, and a pool shaped like the skull of a steer, complete with gigantic horns on the shallow end. I finally located her in the coffee shop. Notice I said *located*. No mention of talking to her.

That was because the moment I saw who she was with, I stepped out of her range of vision so I could watch.

Sylvia and Tyler York, Mr. Shiny Devil's Breath Contestant, sat across from each other at one of the two-seater tables along the far wall. Sylvia's hands were clutched ever so daintily around her coffee cup. Tyler's eyes were on her. But then maybe, like me, he was trying to figure out which of them sparkled most brilliantly in the glow of the overhead lights.

Tyler spoke.

Sylvia laughed. Even from where I stood peeking out from behind a phony wood pillar, I could hear the silvery sound. Tyler slid his hand across the table and squeezed hers.

Sylvia and Tyler York?

It took a few moments for me to process the thought and only a few after that to decide it was a terrible, awful, horrible situation. If Sylvia and Tyler ever got together—I mean really got together—they'd produce children who would be so shiny, they'd glow in the dark.

Thank goodness, before the idea had a chance to fully form, Sylvia pushed back from the table. I knew she'd see me right away when she walked out of the coffee shop, so I ducked around a corner and into the gift shop, where I stationed myself behind a rack of Creosote Cal hoodies. A funny sort of lump in my throat, I watched Sylvia walk across the lobby and back toward Deadeye with an uncharacteristic spring in her step.

I swallowed around the painful knot at the same time I asked myself what it was all about. It wasn't possible that I was actually feeling affection for Sylvia, was it? That I was touched to see her happy?

Or maybe it was the other side of the coin that had me suddenly feeling as if I'd swallowed a cotton ball.

Maybe seeing Sylvia happy and smiling with a guy as wholesome as Tyler only served to underscore what was wrong with me: I'd spent my love life brushing aside the shiny guys, the ones who were too good to be true, the guys who were steady and reliable. Instead, I'd made a play for the bad boys—every single time—and those bad boys had lived up to their reputations and my expectations. They'd left me alone and brokenhearted. Every single time.

Maybe the pang I felt when I saw Sylvia and Tyler together was nothing more than good old-fashioned jealousy.

The thought slammed into me right between my heart and my stomach, and still considering it, I watched Tyler, chin up and arms swinging, leave the coffee shop. The gift shop was directly across from the hotel registration desk, and there was a young woman with long auburn hair standing over there. The moment she caught sight of Tyler, her expression brightened. She met him halfway, and he slipped his arms around her and gave her a long and very sloppy kiss.

What had been confusion about my feelings of jealousy and longing vanished in an instant, replaced by an anger so overpowering, I didn't even realize I had stomped out of the gift shop until I was in the lobby. "Two-time my sister, will you?" I growled, only by the time I did, I realized that Tyler and the redhead, their arms linked around each other's waists, were already on their way out the front door of the hotel.

A woman possessed—though what possessed me, curiosity, jealousy, or some kind of crazy devotion to Sylvia, I couldn't say—I followed them outside, and when they hopped into a cab and it sped away, I flagged down another waiting taxi, jumped in, and delivered the classic line, "Follow that car."

We were in Vegas; the driver never questioned my motives or my sanity.

A short time later, Tyler's cab slowed in front of a gleaming (was I surprised?) white building with a steeple on one end and what looked like Rapunzel's tower on the other. There was a new sign just being installed over the front door, a gigantic red neon heart, and it swayed on the ropes and pulleys that held it.

"Love Chapel." I burbled out the words on the end of a *harrumph* of disgust. "What's that lousy, weasely two-timer doing at Reverend Love's wedding chapel?"

"Biggest chapel in town," my cab driver informed me. "They do a bunch of weddings, every single day."

"Well, they better not be doing one with those two!" I slammed out of the cab and marched inside. The main hallway was a gleaming (there's that word again) maze of mirrored walls, giant fake flower arrangements, and blush carpeting. My footsteps muffled by the plush, I followed the sounds of voices, turned a corner, and found Tyler and the redhead, lip-locked.

"What kind of lowlife are you?" I pointed one shaking finger in Tyler's direction. "How can you do this to my sister?"

The couple broke apart and Tyler looked from the redhead to me. "Meghan is your sister?"

"Not her!" There was no way to deal with the anger that pounded through me other than to tug at my spiky hair. I tugged away. "Sylvia. How can you do this to Sylvia?"

Some of the shine went out of Tyler's expression. "Sylvia from the chili cook-off?"

"Oh, that's just great! That's very sweet! One minute you're making eyes at Sylvia—"

Meghan slipped her hand from Tyler's grasp. "You were making eyes at some other woman?"

"I was not!" Tyler's denial echoed along the hall of mirrors. He scraped his left hand through his hair and curled his right hand into a fist. "This woman doesn't know what she's talking about, Meghan, darling. You're the one I'm here to marry."

"You're getting married? Now?" The news was like a slap in the face and I flinched. "But what about Sylvia?"

"Sylvia . . ." Tyler pressed his fingers to the bridge of his nose. "What on earth makes you think that Sylvia and I—"

"You were talking to her." I threw an arm out in the general direction of Creosote Cal's. Maybe. I actually wasn't sure where we were in relation to Creosote Cal's, but if nothing else, I figured the gesture underscored our little melodrama. "You were sitting in the coffee shop, and the two of you, you were chatting and—"

Tyler's laugh cut me short. "And do you always make wild assumptions about people just because you happen to see them together? Sylvia and I . . ." He turned to Meghan and took both her hands in his. "Sylvia's the one I told you about," he said. "The cooking chick. You know, the one I'm doing the job for."

Good thing this made sense to one of us. When Meghan smiled, Tyler gave her a peck on the cheek. "You'd better go finish getting ready," he crooned. "Soon-to-be Mrs. York."

Giggling, she scampered down the hallway and disappeared into a door marked *Brides Only.* It was going to take a little more than that to get rid of me.

I stepped back, my weight against one foot. "Explain," I demanded.

Tyler did. "Sylvia, she's your sister, right?"

"Half sister," I corrected him.

"Well, I can't believe she didn't tell you. The whole thing about me being a chili contestant—"

Before he could say another word, the truth dawned as bright as Tyler's smile. "You're a phony!"

"I'm an actor."

"And Sylvia hired you—"

"To pretend I'm a chili chef." Tyler nodded. "Only the recipes I've won the regional competitions with—"

"They're Sylvia's recipes." My jaw flapped. "She . . . you . . ." I shook my head, hoping to order my thoughts. "You and Sylvia aren't—"

"Involved?" Tyler threw back his head and laughed. "Not hardly! Sylvia is the most straitlaced, uptight, inflexible, hidebound—"

It was all true, but that didn't keep me from growling, "That's my sister you're talking about!"

"Well, your sister and I are not romantically involved," he told me in no uncertain terms. "We never have been. We never will be. Meghan and I are getting married today."

"Then why were you holding Sylvia's hand?" I asked. "Back at the coffee shop."

Tyler reached into his pocket and pulled out a check. The signature was Sylvia's. "I wasn't holding Sylvia's hand, I was getting the last of what she owed me, and we were trying not to be too obvious about the payoff. You know, in case any of the Showdown people were around. I'll say this much for your sister—she agreed to pay me in full for this last gig, even though the contest was canceled. So . . ." He tucked the check back where it came from, turned, and walked away. "If you'll excuse me, I'm going to get married now."

My head spinning, I stood in the center of the hallway and stared at my own dazed reflection in the mirrors that surrounded me. As far as I knew, there was actually no written rule about how a Showdown vendor couldn't enter one of the competitions, but I'd bet any money that Sylvia realized if she entered, she'd never win. Not in a million years. Sylvia, see, has a reputation. What was it Tyler said? Straitlaced, uptight, inflexible, hidebound? Sylvia was all those things, and everyone who ever got close to the Showdown knew it. It was no surprise to me that she was also a little sneak. If Tyler won a few cook-offs using Sylvia's recipes, she could take advantage of the publicity and talk up how she'd taught him everything he knew, and once he made a name for himself on the chili circuit, she could piggyback off his fame and publish that cookbook she'd always wanted to write. A cookbook that would, no doubt, feature Jack's famous—and currently missing—recipe as its centerpiece.

It was so devious a plan, it made me see red, and I turned on my heels to leave the chapel so I could go back to Cal's and have it out with Sylvia. That's when I caught sight of a door with a tasteful brass plaque on it: *Reverend Linda Love.*

Chili judge, I reminded myself, and there when Dickie (literally) bit the big one.

The thought knocked up against my anger and nudged it out of the way. Maybe it wasn't too late to salvage something useful out of the fiasco that was my visit to the Love Chapel.

I knocked and was ushered into an outer office by a middle-aged woman in a neat, and a little over-the-top, pink suit.

"The reverend is officiating at a wedding," she told me. "If you like, you can wait in her office."

Linda Love's office was bigger than my apartment back in Chicago. It featured a tasteful mahogany desk that was about a mile wide, with a matching ceiling-high bookshelf behind. There was an Oriental rug in shades of red and deep green on the floor, and framed photos on the walls. I strolled over to take a gander.

Reverend Love with her hands out in blessing over a newly married couple, an Elvis impersonator at her side.

Reverend Love standing between a bride and a groom both dressed in purple, a black-caped vampire looming behind them, his arms out and his fangs bared.

Reverend Love with marrying couples decked out like aliens, and some in Renaissance costumes, and others in gangster gear complete with toy tommy guns.

From the photos, I moved to look over the bookcase, but there wasn't anything there nearly as interesting as aliens or vampires. She'd been awarded a crystal bowl from the local Chamber of Commerce for congeniality. She'd matted and framed her minister's license and had it set up on an easel next to a tasteful bouquet of red and white fabric flowers.

It was all pretty ordinary and just what couples would expect to see when they came to sign up for what a framed poster on the opposite wall said could be a Standard, a Special, or a Theme Wedding Package.

In fact, the only thing that struck me as interesting was the one thing on the bookshelf that seemed out of place.

It probably goes without saying that I am not the doll type. I never was, even as a kid. Skateboards were more my thing. And bikes, and softball. Fistfights and football. Even so, I will admit that the doll propped against a fat book was way cute.

She was a foot tall, and not scary like so many of those dolls that are meant to look realistic. This one was completely made of fabric, from her skinny little stuffed legs and arms to her big round head. Her dress was pink satin and she wore a black felt scarf and beret. Her brown hair was made out of felt, too, strips of it sewn close to her head to look like a bob, and she had rosy pink cheeks (also round dots of felt) and a sweet little bowed mouth.

I couldn't resist; I had to play with her. She wore a white cotton petticoat under her dress, and I fluffed it and noticed that there was a name embroidered in powder blue on the inside. Curious, I turned to the light to read the lettering and saw that there were, in fact, two names.

"Noreen Pennybaker." I read the name that flowed along the hem of the petticoat in slanting stitches that made it look like a signature. Above that in blocky, more childlike letters were the words *Tout Sweet*.

Finished looking the doll over, I set her back where I'd found her, but before I could turn around, I heard a voice behind me, "Cute, isn't she?"

Reverend Love crossed the office, her footsteps silenced by the thick Oriental rug.

"I'm glad you knew better than to touch her," she said. "This doll is very special to me. She was handmade for me by my Aunt Louise, and I'm afraid I'm a little overprotective. I'd hate to see anything happen to Tout Sweet."

The reverend slipped behind her desk. "You look familiar so I know we've met. You're . . . Maxie!" Her eyes lit when she got the name right. "You were at the Showdown. Are you looking to schedule a wedding?"

"Wedding?" The word barely made it past the sudden clog in my throat. "Oh, no!" For the second time in as many minutes, I backed away, this time from the very thought. "I just happened to be here. On account of Tyler and Meghan."

The reverend smiled. "Cute couple. I'm sure you're very happy for them."

"You betcha!" She hadn't invited me, but I took the

chair across from her desk. "I figured as long as I was here, I'd ask you about the other day. You know, about Dickie."

Her smile dissolved and she puckered her lips.

"Did you know him?" I asked.

The reverend's shrug was as elegant as the steel gray suit she wore with tasteful pearls and a white cami. "Everyone in Vegas knows . . . er . . . knew Dickie," she said when she sat down. "He was quite a character."

"And now he's dead and someone murdered him."

The reverend opened a desk drawer and brought out an eight-by-ten glossy. "He just did a wedding here," she said, sliding the photo across the desk to me. "I haven't even had a chance to have the picture framed yet."

I studied the photo that showed a grinning Dickie in a pink-and-black-plaid sport coat standing with a middle-aged couple. "Dickie was a minister like you?"

Reverend Love laughed. "Oh, my goodness, no! But like so many people, this particular couple wanted to make their wedding ceremony different and distinctive. They were both fans of Dickie's so—"

"Dickie had fans?"

Her smile was mischievous. "That's the rumor. My own personal opinions aside, we are a full-service chapel. So when this couple asked for Dickie, I got them Dickie. He wasn't everyone's cup of tea, but hey, who am I to judge?"

"He sure got on people's nerves. But Dickie liked you." I cocked my head, thinking. "At the show the night before the cook-off started, and that morning when Dickie died . . . he was nasty to everyone else, but he said you were a doll. A doll!" I glanced over the reverend's shoulder. "Like Tout Sweet!"

I don't know if the reverend got the joke. She folded her hands on the desk. "Believe it or not, Dickie Dunkin was a smart businessman. He knew which side his bread was buttered on. Of course he went out of his way to be nice to me. This is the biggest and most successful chapel in Vegas. He knew if I was going to hire him to appear at comedy wedding services—"

"Then he had to stay on your good side and then he'd get the jobs, and a little publicity while he was at it."

"Exactly."

"Whoever sells the most tickets this week and appears with you at the big wedding ceremony on Sunday, that person will get publicity, too."

"And let me guess, Dickie claimed he was going to win."

"Hermosa and Osborn and Yancy . . . they all claim they're going to win," I told her.

The reverend's eyes went wide. "You don't think that the silly contest had anything to do with—"

"I can't say. I do know there are plenty of people who didn't like ol' Dickie."

"Oh, come on! I know there were people who didn't appreciate Dickie's sense of humor, and I can certainly understand why. He could be pretty scathing. Not to mention insensitive and insulting. But I can't imagine there are people who would take that shlock act of his so seriously that they'd want to kill him. Maybe wring his neck!" She grinned, but only for a moment. Then her mouth settled into a hard line. "But murder? No, not murder."

I weighed the advantages of letting her in on Dickie's dirty little secret against keeping it to myself and decided that I might find out more—and possibly cultivate a useful ally—if I was aboveboard. "There was obviously somebody who really wanted Dickie dead because we both saw him do a header into the Devil's Breath. I can't say for sure at this point, but I think it might have been one of the people he was blackmailing."

The reverend opened her mouth in astonishment, but before she had a chance to say a word, her phone buzzed. She flinched and picked up the receiver. "Is it time already?" she said, then nodded.

"I've got Tyler and Meghan's wedding to take care of," she said, and when she stood, her message was clear.

I got up and moved to the door.

"You'll be at the wedding on Sunday?" the reverend called after me.

I was already at the door so I pretended I didn't hear her. Me, watch dewy-eyed suckers get hitched? I'd sooner eat an entire pot of Sylvia's flavorless chili.

I was still mulling over the unsavory thoughts of both weddings and Sylvia's cooking when I walked outside and got out my phone to call a cab.

I can't say if it ever arrived.

Because then, as I stood there waiting under that

gigantic neon red heart, I heard a snap. And a screech. And a whoosh.

Automatically, I looked up, and what I saw made my stomach leap into my throat.

That gigantic red heart was headed for the sidewalk at lightning speed.

Right at me.

CHAPTER 11

Here's the thing about having a crisis:

When it happens (and the way things were going, it seemed to be happening pretty regularly), most people can't wait for someone to show up and fuss over them and hold their hands.

But when it happens to me, I'd rather just be left alone. I can handle things. On my own. I don't need someone else butting in.

Especially when it turns out that someone is Nick.

The moment the curtains draped around my little cubicle in the ER swept aside and he swept in, I groaned.

"What the hell!" Nick marched over to the bed and sized up the situation with one pinpoint look at me propped up in bed and the blood-soaked bandage on my left arm. "What have you been up to?"

Like I said, I didn't want coddling. But a little understanding would have been nice.

Maybe that was why even my gritted teeth didn't stop me from adding a note of sickening saccharin to my voice. "Maxie, you poor thing! I came as soon as I heard the news. You must be in terrible pain. Let me get you a sip of water."

Dumbfounded, he stared at me for a couple seconds before he got the message. "Oh." There was a glass of ice water with the straw in it on the table next to my bed and Nick grabbed it. "You want a drink?"

I did. Desperately. I'd been alone in the little curtained cubicle ever since the paramedics scooped me up off the sidewalk in front of the Love Chapel and dumped me here, and that was . . .

I glanced around but there weren't any clocks, and I wondered how long I'd been waiting for the doc who was supposed to stitch up the wound caused by the shattered glass from the fallen heart sign. My sense of time was warped, but then from the looks of things, I'd lost quite a bit of blood. I was woozy. Shaky. Thirsty. And more than a little scared.

I wasn't about to admit to any of it. Especially not to Nick.

"What are you doing here?" I asked him.

He dropped into the chair next to the bed, and even though I didn't ask for it, he put the glass of water up to my mouth and stuck the straw between my lips. "Drink."

When the cool water hit the back of my parched throat, I closed my eyes and sighed.

"You're not going to pass out, are you?"

I opened my eyes to find Nick's face only inches from mine. "You okay?" he asked. "Do you have a concussion?"

I would have pushed him away if I'd had the energy. Instead, I shook my head. "How long have I been here?"

"I don't know. I got the call . . ." Nick sat back and plucked his phone out of his pocket to check the time. "About twenty minutes ago."

I wasn't sure exactly where the hospital was in the scheme of Vegas geography, but believe me, when we arrived for the Showdown and I drove the RV with the Palace towed behind it through town, I got a sense of Vegas traffic. Twenty minutes? No matter where he'd come from, Nick must have moved like a bat out of hell.

I was still in shock from the whole incident. That would explain why my throat clogged and my eyes watered.

"All I did was walk out of the wedding chapel," I said.

"I know. I heard." Nick was on my right, and he rested his elbows on the bed and leaned forward. "Reverend Love told me."

I didn't have to ask. He filled me in on the details.

"She told me you came to see her at the chapel. To ask about Dickie. Believe me . . ." For just a moment, his eyes darkened to the color of a stormy sea. "We'll talk about that later. For now, what's important is that

Reverend Love remembered you from the Showdown. Then again, she was pretty shaken up. I mean, by that sign coming down."

"She wasn't the only one."

A smile touched Nick's lips. He had the good sense to control it. "Since she didn't know who else to call, she got ahold of me."

Was I supposed to say *thank you*? Something told me it was how most people would have handled the situation. People like Sylvia. Rather than be accused of acting anything like her, I decided a middle-of-the-road reaction was called for. "That was nice of Reverend Love."

A smile darted over Nick's lips. "She's a caring woman and she was plenty worried. She said she was about to start a wedding ceremony when she heard the crash and she ran out and saw the sign and you, sprawled out on the sidewalk. She's the one who called 911, and she waited there with you until the paramedics arrived. I told her I'd call her after I found out how you were."

I glanced at his phone where it lay next to my right hip. "Yeah. Sure. Go ahead and call."

Nick nudged the phone aside. "There's plenty of time for that. For now—"

The curtains Nick had just pulled shut were whisked aside and a heavyset African-American nurse scurried in and introduced herself as Yolanda. "Dr. Wu is on her way to stitch up the wound," she assured me. "How you feeling?"

I told her I was fine.

Fists on hips and her lips pursed, she looked me over before her gaze traveled to Nick.

"You care if this guy's here?" she asked, and before I could answer, she added, "Because I'll tell you what, one look at him and my heart is already pumping hard. I'm afraid if that's what's going on with you, you're going to lose more blood."

"It's not like that between us," I assured her and reminded myself. "We're not—"

"Uh-huh." She rummaged around in a drawer for saline and cotton balls and such. "You want him to stay?" she asked.

I was about to tell her I didn't when Nick laid his right hand over mine.

The nurse glanced over before she got to work. "Smart man. 'Cause this might hurt a little, and you're going to want someone to hang on to."

"I won't," I vowed at the same time some crazy reflex action took hold, and I turned my hand over in Nick's.

Reflex action again. It had to be. He wound his fingers through mine.

When the nurse took off the bandage the paramedics had applied back at the chapel, I tensed and sucked in a breath. It's not like blood bothers me all that much. At least it doesn't when it's not mine.

The wound was surrounded by dried blood the color of rust, and even as I watched, fresh blood welled up from inside the cut, which was maybe three inches long and as neat and thin as if I'd been sliced by an experienced sous chef. This blood was a brighter shade of red, and it smelled sweet and hideous. My stomach flipped and my vision blurred. Still, it was impossible for me to look away.

"Tell me what happened," Nick said, and when I kept right on staring at the cut and the blood and the way Yolanda's hands were poised over it all, ready to get to work, he said it again. "Maxie . . ." He crooked a finger under my chin and turned my head. "Tell me what happened."

My voice was breathless. "The sign came down."

"Just as you stepped outside."

When Yolanda wiped down my arm with liquid, I flinched. When she poked around inside the wound looking for bits of glass, I squeezed my eyes shut. She wiped again, and it wasn't until she was done that I realized I was holding on to Nick so tight, I'd probably cut off circulation in his fingers.

I loosened my hold. "Sorry," I said.

He closed his hand over mine. "You were telling me . . . about walking outside . . ."

"Lucky thing I have good reflexes. Because I looked up and all I could see was that big red heart coming closer and closer. The next thing I knew . . . kerblam!" I was a little too enthusiastic about my description, and I jerked my left arm and got a stern look from Yolanda.

"Sorry," I told her, too, before I turned back to Nick. "You know where this is going, don't you? A sign falling right at the moment I was under it? No way that was an accident. It had to be Bernadette."

"The woman with the altar."

"The crazy woman with the altar. With flowers and candles and pictures of my missing father on it," I added with emphasis for Yolanda's sake. Her gaze never left her work, but her eyebrows did a slow slide up her forehead. "Bernadette hates me, Nick. This proves it. She tried to hurt me with the slippery stuff on my shoes, and then she painted the graffiti on the Chick. Then she followed me over to the Love Chapel, and she must have cut the cables that kept that sign above the door. She tried to kill me. You believe me, don't you?"

"I believe you believe it."

It was one of those comments that would have gotten him skewered if I wasn't a little busy biting my bottom lip when Yolanda wiped down my arm again, this time with some sickening yellow stuff that burned.

"Anesthetic," she told me and gave me a pat on the shoulder. "When the doctor does the stitching, you won't feel a thing."

I was grateful. Especially when the doc arrived and started her work.

"Maxie." I was staring again, at the doc's neat, economic movements and the glint of the needle and the long thread she worked up and down into my skin. Nick's voice made me turn to him. "It's not like I don't believe you, but—"

"But you don't believe me."

"I just don't see why some woman you knew fifteen years ago—"

I guess the way I sighed told him I was ready to fess up.

"If I was Bernadette . . ." I'd never spoken the words. Not out loud. Not to anyone. Not even to Jack, and he was the one who needed to hear them the most. I forced myself to look Nick in the eye. "If I was Bernadette, I'd hate me, too."

He sat back but he didn't let go of my hand, and I pictured him as he must have been back in his cop days. Oh yeah, that gleam in his eye told me he knew he was about to hear something both interesting and relevant. If he was still a cop, no doubt he would have pulled out a notebook and started writing down every last word I said so he could use it as evidence against me. "Tell me about it."

"Like you said, it was fifteen years ago. And that's a long time."

"Tell me anyway."

This time when my stomach clutched, it had nothing to do with Dr. Wu and her shipshape stitches. I thought back and filtered through what I knew was the truth and the excuses I'd piled on top of it to smother it in the years since.

"Every year after school let out," I told Nick, "Jack would show up in Chicago to get me so I could spend the summer with him at the Showdown. That summer . . ." I did some quick mental math. "I was fourteen, and just like every year, I couldn't wait to get on the road with him. The first Showdown that summer was in Saint Louis, and I remember he borrowed a car to pick me up at home. He said it was because a car got better gas mileage than the RV, but when we got to the fairgrounds in Saint Louis—"

"Sylvia was there."

I shook my head. "Sylvia had her wisdom teeth out that summer. We didn't go to Seattle to get her until after the Fourth of July. No, it was just going to be me and Jack for a whole month, and I can't tell you how thrilled I was." Thinking back, I grinned. "He's really something, Nick. You're going to love him. I mean, when you meet him. When he comes back. Everybody loves Jack."

"Did Bernadette?"

My smile disappeared in a wave of memory. "We got to the Showdown, me and Jack, and that's when I met her. She'd been working as the Chili Chick for a few months, and she and Jack . . . well, it's not like he's some kind of crazy womanizer, but—"

"I've heard the stories." Nick didn't judge, he just reported the facts, and I was grateful.

"She was there, Nick. She was in the RV when I got there." Maybe he didn't see the importance of this little fact. Maybe that's why I had to raise my voice to make sure he heard me loud and clear. "I thought I was going to have part of the summer all alone with my dad and—"

"And you had to share him with Bernadette."

Dr. Wu finished her work, gave me a short lecture on wound management, and left the cubicle. Yolanda patted my arm. "You wait until I get you some written information to take home with you," she said, and her gaze traveled to Nick. "You two just sit and talk for a while."

When she left, she closed the curtains behind her.

"How did you feel about that, Maxie?" Nick asked.

I knew he wouldn't think it was funny, but I tried anyway. "About getting stitches?"

Nick's lips thinned.

I got the message.

"About sharing Jack. Okay. All right. I know that's what we're talking about." I made a face at him, the better to hide the fact that, even all these years later, I felt like there was a fist in my stomach. "I was hurt," I admitted. "I felt betrayed. That very first day I decided right then and there that I hated Bernadette with the passion of a thousand burning suns. I hated her as only a fourteen-year-old can hate. More than I'd ever hated anyone or anything in the whole world."

"And she hated you right back."

I glanced away. "That's the crazy thing. I don't think she did. Not at first anyway. She tried to be nice."

"And you—"

"Oh, I took my mission very seriously, and the way I saw it, that was to make her life a living hell!" It wasn't funny, but I laughed anyway. "I talked back and I broke curfew and I got into fights and I created all the trouble I could that summer. I guess I was trying my best to make sure Jack didn't forget that I was around."

"And you needed to make sure he'd turn his back on Bernadette and come running to you when you needed him."

I'd never thought about it like that, but Nick was right. Rather than admit it, I continued on with my story. "When it was time for Jack and Bernadette to disappear into their bedroom at night, I'd pretend to be sick so

Jack would have to sit up with me. It might come as something of a surprise, but I can be a pretty good little actress when I put my mind to it."

Apparently, this did not come as something of a surprise. Nick simply nodded.

I kept talking. "When Bernadette brought home little presents for Jack—a special kind of chili spice she'd bought from one of the other vendors or his favorite candy or a book or something—I got to them first and threw them away. When she brought me a cute little top she'd picked up at one of the local stores, I pretended it didn't fit. When she gave me a magazine, I said I'd already read it. Once I stole her shoes so she couldn't dance as the Chick, and once—"

My mouth fell open: I'd forgotten all about it!

"I wrote on the Chick costume. In yellow marker. *Bitch*."

"Well, that explains that." I could practically see Nick ticking off the solution to the mystery of the vandalized costume on his mental clipboard before he asked, "And Jack?"

I raised my chin. "He loved me more than he loved Bernadette."

"Which means he stuck up for you. Like most fathers would. Except I have a feeling most fathers wouldn't have put up with your shenanigans as long as he did. Am I right?"

Who uses a word like *shenanigans* in actual conversation?

I considered this while I looked down at the white

cotton blanket that covered me, counting the crossed threads at the same time I examined my conscience. "I didn't deserve Jack's loyalty," I finally admitted. "Not with the way I was acting."

"But like you said, he was a good dad, and he loved you. I don't doubt that he knew exactly what was going on."

I wiped a hand over my suddenly wet cheeks. "Something in my eye," I told Nick, who didn't believe it any more than I did and proved it by changing the subject just enough to allow me time to recover my cool.

"After Fourth of July," he said, "when Sylvia got there, what did she think of Bernadette? How did they treat each other?"

I swallowed hard. "By the time Sylvia got there, Bernadette was already gone. She couldn't take it anymore, and I . . . I was so happy." For just a moment, the old feelings flooded me, and I pictured myself as I had been the day I'd won the war for Jack's heart and driven Bernadette away. I spent the day grinning like a fool and completely oblivious to what I'd only come to realize later was the look of complete and utter desolation on Jack's face.

The thought sobered me. "That day she left, I put on the Chick costume and danced around the Showdown all day long." I shrugged. "At the time, I thought it was the happiest day of my life. I guess deep down inside all I knew was that she was gone, and that was all that mattered to me. It took me years to admit to myself that I drove Jack and Bernadette apart."

Nick squeezed my hand. "Hey, you were a kid. You didn't know any better."

"I should have."

"Maybe, but it doesn't matter anymore."

"But don't you get it?" I turned in bed, the better to give Nick a careful look, and winced when I moved my arm. "It matters plenty to Bernadette. She still loves Jack. That weird altar of hers proves it. And Jack . . . well, he's had plenty of girlfriends since Bernadette, but never one he moved into the RV, at least not during the summer when Sylvia and I were around. What if . . ." I coughed away the sudden tightness in my throat. "What if Bernadette was the one woman who could have made Jack happy? Who would have settled him down? What if things turned out different and she was the one who could have kept him from disappearing?"

"You don't know that."

"But, Nick. What if—"

"No." He refused to listen and it didn't matter anyway, since Yolanda picked that moment to walk back in. She gave me a prescription for painkillers that I knew I wouldn't fill and written instructions about how to take care of the wound, and when she was all done, she said I could go.

Since he wasn't listening to me anyway, we were all the way back to the RV parked near Creosote Cal's before Nick and I spoke again.

He tossed his car keys down on the table. "No wonder Bernadette hates you."

I dropped my denim hobo back on one of the

vinyl-covered benches next to the built-in table and rummaged around in the cupboard—one-handed since my left arm throbbed—for the box of chocolate cupcakes I knew I'd stashed there, and when I found it, I ripped into it and sat back down.

"Better than pain pills," I told Nick.

He glanced over the ingredients listed on the side of the package. "I'm not so sure about that."

"Well, at least I can't get addicted." I finished one cupcake and reached for another.

"I'm not so sure about that, either." With one finger, Nick pointed my way. "You have . . ."

White gooey frosting. I could feel it on my chin. I swiped a hand over my face.

Nick shook his head.

I swiped again.

"You're missing it by a mile." He leaned across the table and brushed his hand over my chin. "Better," he assured me.

I wasn't so sure. Because suddenly, the spot where his fingers rested felt as if it were on fire.

I am usually cool, calm, and collected when it comes to guys, but all of a sudden, I was at a loss for words. "Cupcake?" I squeaked.

Nick cupped my chin. "Let's skip the cupcakes and the preliminaries."

Was he talking about . . .

I gulped at the same time I glanced over Nick's shoulder toward my bedroom.

Was he talking about what I thought he was talking about?

A slow smile inched up Nick's lips. "Let's get right down to business and talk about what you were doing at the Love Chapel in the first place."

His touch might have been hot, but it was incinerated beneath the fire of the anger that flared up inside me. "You're going to tell me to mind my own business."

"Well, look what happened!"

"What happened had nothing to do with me talking to Reverend Love. It was a what-do-you-call-it. A crime of opportunity. Bernadette followed me when I left the hotel. She saw her moment and she took it. I bet if you check with Reverend Love, you'll find out that there was some kind of problem with that sign. They were just installing it, you know. I bet it was loose. Or it needed to be fastened better or something. What happened to me has nothing to do with me asking Reverend Love about Dickie."

"What Reverend Love knows about Dickie isn't any of your business." The RV isn't exactly spacious, and Nick's voice ricocheted around it like rifle fire. He poked a finger in my direction. "I just found out this evening, Maxie, the detective in charge of Dickie's case just told me . . . they figured out what killed Dickie. It was a poison called datura. It's a native plant, grows pretty much everywhere. It would be simple for someone to pick some, dry it, then use it on a victim. We're dealing with someone evil, someone who doesn't care who gets in the way. For your own safety, you need to keep out of things that don't concern you."

"You"—I poked right back—"need to get your priorities straight. You're supposed to be head of security for the Showdown so you should be concerned with Showdown business so why don't you go . . ." I made a shooing motion toward the door. "Go slap the cuffs on Bernadette. Or grill her under a bright light. Or do whatever it is you cop types do when you know you have a perp and you have to get her to confess."

"Perp!" Nick hopped to his feet. "For all we know, the sign was faulty and the wires just snapped at the perfect moment."

"Perfect?" I jumped to my feet, too, and fists on hips, stared him down. "So now you're saying that the sign falling was a good thing? Because I was the one under it? Now you're saying—"

"So there I am working my butt off and you two are sitting here eating cupcakes?" Sylvia stomped through the door and proved what I'd always suspected of her. She's delusional. We weren't sitting. And we weren't eating cupcakes. In fact, Nick and I were toe to toe, shooting death rays at each other.

Sylvia was oblivious. "Thanks for coming back to the Palace and relieving me, Maxie." She yanked open the refrigerator and took out a head of lettuce and a couple tomatoes. "I didn't even have a chance to get dinner."

"Uh, bandage!" I held up my left arm. "Stitches. Attempted murder!"

Sylvia rolled her blue eyes. "Yeah, right. Whatever."

By this time, Nick was already out the door. He didn't bother to say good-bye.

Sylvia grabbed a bowl from a nearby cupboard and threw a sidelong look in my direction. "What happened to your arm?" she asked.

I am not often at a loss for words, but in that moment, I was struck dumb. Rather than deal—with Sylvia's insensitivity or Nick's hardheaded attitude—I stomped out of the RV and slammed the door behind me.

A couple minutes later (I hung back to make sure Nick was nowhere around), I was back in Creosote Cal's. I avoided Deadeye, closed at this late hour, and instead, headed into the casino. Sure, I remembered what Yolanda had told me about not mixing painkillers and alcohol, but like I said, I had no intention of taking any painkillers. For now, I knew a beer would do the trick, and it might help calm the irritation that bubbled in me like hot lava.

I'd just slid up on a bar stool and was waiting semi-patiently for the bartender to finish up with the already drunk young guys at the other end of the bar when my attention was caught by a man out in the lobby who looked vaguely familiar. Fifty or so. Washed-out hair that had once been sandy. Wide nose. Weak chin. It wasn't until I also noticed his silver belt buckle studded with turquoise chips that the pieces fell into place and I remembered George Jarret, the man I'd found snooping around outside Dickie's dressing room the day of the murder.

Bad timing, because I never did have a chance to order that beer.

Instead, I crossed the bar and went out to the lobby, and making sure to stay far enough back so he wouldn't notice me, I followed George Jarret.

All the way to Dickie Dunkin's dressing room.

The crime scene tape was gone from the doorway and the door was closed, but it was clear from the start that George wasn't going to let that stop him.

He tried the knob.

Locked.

George took something out of his pocket, slipped it into the lock, and jimmied it. The next time he tried the door, it popped right open. He looked left and right, and I ducked behind a wall just in time to avoid being seen. Sure that the coast was clear, George went into Dickie's dressing room and closed the door behind him.

CHAPTER 12

Ten minutes later, George Jarret emerged from Dickie Dunkin's dressing room with a stack of photos of Dickie tucked up under his arm.

I will admit that while this was mildly interesting, it was not the bombshell I'd been hoping for. The first time I met George, he told me all he wanted was an autographed picture of Dickie. It looked like he was actually telling the truth.

As disappointing as this was in terms of my investigation, I was not about to let it stop me. I waited until George had disappeared back the way he'd come and slipped into the now empty dressing room.

Like all of the performers I'd been in touch with

lately, Dickie had a dressing table with a mirror in front of it and a chair pulled up to it. There was a scattering of jars on the table, one of face powder, one filled with some goo guaranteed to remove age spots, one that was apparently where Dickie kept loose change. I spilled it out and counted. One dollar and seventy-nine cents.

There were three plaid sport coats hanging on a nearby rack, and I went through the pockets and found nothing but a pack of gum and a roll of antacids.

At the door, I took one last quick look around. There was nothing even mildly interesting in Dickie's dressing room, nothing that spoke of his life (other than his bad taste in clothes) and certainly nothing that explained the terrible way he died. In fact, it was all so ordinary and so boring, I couldn't help but wonder why George Jarret had spent ten minutes in there to begin with.

I was still turning the thought over in my head when I slipped back outside and started through the lobby. That was when I saw Carmella, one of the ladies from the costume shop, heading out the door. She waved, I waved back, and I thought about the Chili Chick.

I knew that Yancy was performing that night and that his show was sold out. I also knew that the costume people stuck around until the last show of the night was over, and eager to see how the repairs on the Chick were going, I skirted the auditorium and went around backstage. From there I could hear Yancy's piano, and I stopped for a moment and let the music wash over me. It was a slow, bluesy song, with a bass that crawled along my spine and wormed its way deep down inside, and when Yancy started singing, I caught my breath.

Take that, Dickie Dunkin. And Hermosa and The Great Osborn, too. Oh yeah, take that. Because blind or not, Yancy Harris was one heck of a talent, and with his sold-out show, I was sure he'd be standing at Reverend Love's side on Sunday for the big wedding ceremony.

I waited as long as the song took, then scooted down a hallway filled with hanging costumes. I stuck my head in the first open door and waved to two ladies who sat in front of sewing machines.

"Is the Chick done?" I asked.

The first woman was ninety if she was a day, a tiny thing with about a million wrinkles and a bent back, and she took off her reading glasses before she looked up. "Finished it a couple hours ago," she assured me. "I left it with Elaine. You know, over there." She jabbed one scrawny finger across the hallway.

It was Elaine's job to make sure all the performers had the costumes they needed, and she was easy enough to find. She sat behind a wide counter, her feet propped up next to a computer screen and a copy of *People* open in front of her.

"Chick?" I asked.

Elaine grinned. "They did a great job, didn't they? Glad I took before and after pictures so I can show them to Cal. He needs to know how good we are at what we do."

"I'm glad. So . . ." I glanced around. There was a

cocktail waitress's pseudo-sexy cowboy outfit nearby, a long and very pink shiny gown next to it that was just tacky enough for me to guess that it belonged to Hermosa. "Where's the Chick?" I asked Elaine.

She swung her legs off the table and stood, glancing toward an empty rack. "I guess somebody picked it up. If it wasn't you, it must have been your sister." Elaine bustled around to my side of the counter. "I know the costume was here when I left for dinner. And it was gone when I got back. It was nice of your sister to get it for you."

Nice? And *Sylvia*? Both in the same sentence?

I wondered what Sylvia was up to and twitched the thought away when Elaine waved me closer. "We've got a sign-out log. Come and look. Oh." She squinted and gave the log another careful look. "What did you say your sister's name was?"

I told her.

"Well, this is written kind of sloppy, but it sure doesn't say Sylvia. It looks like . . ." Elaine lifted the book so she could tip it to the light. "You sure you haven't been drinking, honey?" she asked me. "Because I'll tell you what—according to the log, the Chili Chick costume was picked up by one Maxie Pierce."

Sylvia was hilarious.

At least, she thought so.

In keeping with her opinion of herself, I figured she'd bust a gut when I stomped into the RV and did a quick-and-dirty search of the place. "So . . ." My breaths coming in short gasps, I got back to our combined kitchen/living area. "Where did you stash her?"

When she pretended she didn't know what I was talking about, and I gave her an abbreviated (and expletive rich) account of how I'd gone looking for the Chick and couldn't find her, Sylvia froze at the sink where she was cleaning up her dinner dishes. Now she turned to me, her jaw slack. "What do you mean, the Chick is missing?"

I am not an eye roller. I mean, not like Sylvia. But let's face it, if an occasion ever called for it, this was it. I rolled with wild abandon. "You can quit fooling around, Sylvia. If you expect me to dance as the Chick tomorrow, I need the costume."

"But I don't have it." She dried her hands and hurried over, and before I knew what she was going to do, and so could back out of her reach, she grabbed my hands. "This is terrible!" she wailed.

And I thought I was a decent actress?

I yanked my hands out of Sylvia's grasp. "All right, I get it," I admitted. "You're pissed because I didn't get back in time for you to take a dinner break. You're getting even. Point taken, lesson learned, and all that jazz. Now quit messing around and tell me what you did with the Chick."

I wasn't sure how she managed, but Sylvia even got her peaches-and-cream complexion in on the act. She looked a little green around the gills. This time when she grabbed me, she dragged me over to the table. She plunked down on one bench and urged me to sit on the one opposite.

"I swear, Maxie, I don't have the Chick. Somebody must have stolen the costume."

"But no one even knew the Chick was getting repaired. Just Nick and you and me."

"And whoever spray-painted the costume in the first place."

The *why* was as murky as ever, but suddenly, the *who* was as plain as day. I ground my teeth together. "Bernadette!"

Sylvia's perfectly bowed lips twisted. "You think?"

"She tried to kill me tonight."

To Sylvia's everlasting credit, she did not question this. Instead, she reached for her phone and hit one of the numbers on speed dial. "Nick," she said while she waited for him to answer. "We've got to tell him the Chick's been stolen."

I agreed.

That didn't keep me from wondering why Sylvia had Nick's number stored in her phone. Or why my half sister suddenly cared so very much about what happened to the Chili Chick.

Nick took all the information and assured us that he'd get in touch with both hotel security and the Vegas police to report the robbery.

I—for about the one-hundredth time—told him he didn't have to bother. We could just march over to Bibi's Bump and Grind and have it out with Bernadette.

"It makes sense, doesn't it?" I demanded, and not for

the first time. "It's one of those things you cop guys call a . . . a whatever you call it. You know, like when you profile a serial killer. The fact that the Chick is missing says something about Bernadette's mental condition, and her emotional state, too. It would make perfect sense for her to swipe the Chick. The woman is a nutcase! And . . ." Just in case Nick had forgotten, I laid a gentle hand on my left arm. "She did try to kill me."

"Maybe, maybe, and maybe." Nick actually had taken notes after he arrived at the RV and Sylvia and I explained what was going on. He flipped his notebook closed. "It's not like I have any jurisdiction," he explained. This, he had already said, but I guess he thought the way I was jumping around meant I needed the reminder. "We'll take care of it."

"And by then, who knows what Bernadette might do to the poor Chick!" The scenes flashed before my eyes, each more terrifying than the last.

The Chick hanging off the front car of one of those crazy Vegas roller coasters.

The Chick, roasting over an open fire.

The Chick, locked in that closet with all those flickering candles and the pictures of Jack.

I shook away the thought before it could derail what little self-composure I had left. "You know she's got it, Nick."

"I can go talk to her."

"And I can come with you."

Really, he didn't have to look at me that way.

Nick reached into his pocket and pulled out one of

those gaming cards that activate the machines in the casinos. "Go play some slots or something," he said, pressing the card into my hand. "Relax."

"You mean, stay out of your way."

"I mean, relax." He folded my fingers over the card and left the RV.

"Well, he's got a lot of nerve," I grumbled.

"That's not all he's got." When I turned to her, I saw that Sylvia was staring at the door, a smile on her face.

And I mean, really, I should have to put up with that? After the hogwash I'd just put up with from Nick?

Rather than think about it, I grabbed my purse and headed out of the RV and back into the casino. In Vegas time, the night was still young, and don't think I forgot that I owed myself a beer.

A couple minutes later I was settled in at the bar, a chilly one in front of me, watching The Great Osborn do a card trick on the other side of the room. No doubt he'd decided to pick up a few extra bucks, and maybe sell some tickets to his show the next night while he was at it, by shmoozing with the bar crowd. He was decked out in his tux and that silly blue cummerbund of his. At least there was no sign of the Afro.

Hermosa was there, too, enthroned at a table on the other side of the bar, her diaphanous green gown spread out around her so that she took up one entire side of a booth. Maybe she hadn't sold as many tickets to her show as she would have liked. Or maybe she was thinking about Dickie Dunkin and (go figure) getting all mushy. Either way, there was an empty glass in front of her and a fresh drink next to it, and the way the light above her table cast a glow on her, I swore her cheeks were wet. Even as I watched, an elderly guy in a golf shirt and khakis sat down across from Hermosa and ordered drinks for the two of them, and her expression brightened considerably.

"You look like you had a hard day."

I'd been so absorbed in my own thoughts, I hadn't noticed anyone sit down next to me. I glanced to my right and into the most glorious set of hazel eyes I'd seen in a month of Sundays.

The face that belonged to those eyes was just as delicious. Square jaw lightly dusted with honey-colored whiskers, a nose with a bump on the bridge of it that made me think its owner had been in a fight or two, and a smile . . .

A few minutes earlier, I wouldn't have thought I was capable, what with having survived a murder attempt, learning the Chick was missing, and being annoyed past all reason by Nick, but I found myself smiling back.

"That's better." The guy next to me stuck out a hand. "Noah," he said.

I could have kicked myself for the breathiness of my voice. "Maxie."

Those astounding eyes traveled to the bandage on my arm. "You've been hurt. And just recently. If I buy you a drink, will it make you feel better?"

I was pretty sure it would, but before I had a chance to tell him, Osborn oozed over. "Pick a card, any card," he said, ruffling the deck right under my nose.

Since I was pretty sure he wouldn't get the subtle message of a not-so-subtle look, I threw Osborn a smile that would have frozen any man with half a brain. "I'm a little busy here, Osborn," I said.

"But it's a new trick." He rippled the cards another time. "And I need to practice before my show tomorrow. Besides, there's a photographer here from the *Review-Journal*." Osborn looked down the bar out of the corner of his eye toward a shaggy-haired guy in jeans and a T-shirt. "If I make the trick really showy and you pretend you're really impressed, maybe he'll take a few shots and that will get me some free PR. Come on, Maxie—"

"You know this guy?" I'd seen similar scenarios played out so many times in so many bars, that the way Noah asked it, I knew what was coming. If I said Osborn was a stranger and he was bugging me, there would be a fight. Sure, Osborn was a little strange (and he might actually be a murderer), but he was old enough to be my father and he wouldn't stand a chance against fit-and-trim-looking Noah. If I said Osborn was a friend, or at least a friendly acquaintance, Noah would get all huffy the way guys do when it comes to things like this and find someone else to spend his time and his money and that great smile of his on.

I gave Noah what I hoped was a reassuring look before I turned back to Osborn. "Get lost," I said.

The Great Osborn got lost.

I spent the next fifteen minutes in pleasant conversation with Noah. He was in town for a convention, a tax accountant from Portland, and so all right, I knew from the start that things would never work out between us, what with me not even knowing what a tax accountant did, but hey, who am I to question it when sparks fly? Fly they did, and even before I finished my drink and started in on the one Noah ordered for me, I knew where things were headed. Since I also knew Sylvia was back at the RV, I hoped Noah didn't have a roomie.

"So . . ." He sat back, and even though I knew what was coming, I tensed just a little. That was fine. Anticipation was part of the game. "If you're not busy for the rest of the night, how about if we—"

"Poison!" As Hermosa had proven onstage, she could hit the high notes when she wanted to even if they weren't always on key. The way she screamed this single word nearly shattered the glass in my hand. Like everyone else in the bar including that photographer, who sat not too far away, I looked her way and found her crumpled against the faux cowhide bench, her jaw slack and her eyes shooting daggers at The Great Osborn, who stood near her table.

"You!" Hermosa pointed an accusatory and very shaky finger in Osborn's direction. "You dare to approach Hermosa . . ." Was it my imagination, or did she really make sure she got her name in there just a little louder than she said the rest of her piece? "You dare to come over here and offer to buy me a drink? You don't think I know what you are really trying to do?" She put the back of one hand to her forehead.

"Poison! Poison! Poison! You're trying to poison me

the same way you poisoned Dickie, my dearly beloved Dickie. You are trying to take advantage of a woman with a"—her voice clutched and she pressed her hands to her chest—"broken heart whose soul has been ripped in two by the terrible tragedy that has befallen her."

The Great Osborn stood with his arms hanging at his sides. "But, Hermosa, I was just—"

"You are jealous! You are seething with anger as only a man who has been rejected can be. You know that Hermosa . . ." She sat up a little straighter and, while she was at it, smoothed a hand over her hair and shot a look in the direction of the bar. Believe me, I didn't think she was looking at me. "You know that Hermosa has turned her back on your love, that she has left you for another man. You can no longer live with the terrible truth or with the heartache that haunts you day and night. This is why you poisoned my beloved!"

Her say-so said, Hermosa topped it off by tossing her drink in Osborn's face. She swept out of the bar but not—it should be noted—before she stopped long enough at the door (one hand on the jamb and the other resting over her heaving bosom) and had a photo snapped.

Damn, how I hate it when investigations get in the way of my real life!

Knowing it might be my only chance to seize the opportunity, I told Noah I'd be right back and scooted over to where The Great Osborn stared down at his wet suit coat and pants.

"Looks like you could use some help." I plucked a

pile of paper napkins off a nearby table and handed them
to the magician, who didn't bother to thank me.

The Great Osborn blotted. "She's out of her head."

"Well, you did say you and Hermosa were once an
item."

"Yeah, everybody knows that." When one pile of
napkins was soaked, he took the second pile I offered
him. "But that doesn't mean I killed Dickie. And it sure
doesn't mean I tried to poison Hermosa's drink just now.
I didn't go anywhere near her drink, did I?"

The Great Osborn looked toward the guy in the khakis who'd sat down with Hermosa only a little while
earlier. The poor guy was as pale as a corpse and
couldn't catch his breath. "You people . . ." He shoved
out of the booth and headed for the door. "You theater
people are all crazy!"

"Is that what it was?" I asked Osborn. "Just Hermosa
being crazy?"

His gaze slid toward the bar. "And making sure she
got a few inches' worth of coverage in tomorrow's paper.
That had to be it, because I'll tell you what, I didn't try
and slip poison in her drink. How could I?"

How could he, indeed, but don't think that I forgot
that The Great Osborn, for all his stumbling and bum-
bling, was a magician.

And magicians are all about sleight of hand.

I pushed the thought away and decided to concentrate
on better things. More interesting things. More exciting
things.

Like Noah.

"Noah." The name fell from my lips with a proverbial thwack when I got back to the bar and realized that some guys don't like to play second fiddle, especially when first fiddle is a woman's investigation.

Noah was already long gone.

CHAPTER 13

Without the Chick, I was condemned to working behind the counter at the Palace. First thing Saturday morning, I rang up a bunch of sales for a ladies' group before they got on a bus and headed home to Albuquerque. I'd just finished up when I heard a familiar tap, tap, tap.

The ladies, just trooping out the door, stepped aside to let Yancy in, and a couple of them shook their heads as if to say *poor, blind man*. I wondered how much he saw of that, and how much it annoyed him.

Yancy waited until the ladies left, then he scooted over to the counter. He had a copy of the day's newspaper in his hands, and with a look over his shoulder to make sure there was no one around to see, he spread it open and pointed.

"Lookee here! Hermosa got herself some major publicity this morning!"

The picture showed our resident diva just as I remembered her from the bar the night before, leaning back in the doorway, one hand on the jamb and the other pressed to her broken heart.

"I was there," I told Yancy. "I saw the whole thing. She accused Osborn of trying to poison her."

"So it says here." Yancy inched his dark glasses down the bridge of his nose so he could look at me over them. "You think he really did it?"

"I think he's way too bad of a magician to pull that off right in front of Hermosa. And I think Hermosa worked a little magic of her own to get her picture in the paper."

Yancy chuckled. "You got that right. But I'm the one who sold out my show last night!"

"I know. I heard part of it." A customer came in and I gathered up the newspaper and tucked it behind the counter, then waited while the man decided what kinds of spices he wanted to take home to Buffalo. Since I've never been that far east, I can't say for sure, but something told me New Yorkers in general aren't anywhere near as adventurous as Texans, say, when it comes to chili; I recommended our mildest mixes. He made his purchases and left and I turned back to Yancy.

"You're really good," I told him. "You should be a star."

He waved a hand like it was no big deal, but I didn't fail to catch Yancy's smile. "I wouldn't have the job at all if folks around here knew I could—"

Another customer walked in and Yancy didn't say another word. By the time I was done taking care of that lady, Yancy had gone over to sit on the red velvet fainting couch against the far wall of the bordello.

"I don't know," he said when I went over there. "I mean about Osborn and how he's not skilled enough to slip something in Hermosa's drink. Maybe he's just playing at being a bad magician."

"Maybe."

"And he was plenty steamed when Dickie stole his girl."

"Plenty steamed at Dickie, maybe, but now that he's out of the picture, maybe Osborn's going to try to get Hermosa back."

Yancy nodded. "Maybe."

"So he wouldn't be trying to poison her."

"Unless she needs to be taught a lesson."

The comment brought me up short and made me think that the blues song I'd heard Yancy sing the night before wasn't full of heartbreak and longing for nothin'.

"You think the fight wasn't just for publicity? That it could have been the real thing?"

"I think anytime you get more than one performer in the room, there's bound to be drama." Yancy laughed. "Except if one of those folks is me, of course. I'm the most laid-back cat in the city!"

"I agree with you there!" I plunked down next to Yancy. "Is it like that all over the hotel?" I asked. "What I mean is, could there be other performers around here we haven't looked at yet? Somebody else who might have had it in for Dickie?"

"Everybody who ever met the man had it in for him. But I see what you're getting at. Sure. It's true. It could have been anybody. Most of the waitstaff here are performers of some kind just waiting for their big break as dancers or singers or comedians. And most of the folks behind the bar, too. Why, I remember back in the day when they didn't use Deadeye to host things like this Chili Showdown. It was sort of a carnival midway. You know, with a Western theme. And Reverend Love, one day when she was working—"

"Reverend Love used to work here at Creosote Cal's?"

"Yeah, sure." Yancy nodded and I told him to hold that thought when another group of shoppers came in. They were a demanding bunch, but I wasn't complaining. By the time they left, they had enough spices with them to ignite their little hometown back in Iowa.

As soon as they were gone, I poured a couple cups of coffee and took one over to Yancy. "Milk," he said, peeking into his mug. I went and got it, fixed it just the way Yancy liked, and when he looked it over a second time and nodded, I handed it to him.

"Tell me about Reverend Love working here," I said. "Was there a wedding chapel?"

"No, no. Nothing like that! It was quite a few years back, but the way I remember it . . ." He tipped back his head, thinking. "Linda Love was Linda Green back then. Or some name like that, a kid fresh in from somewhere or maybe from nowhere like so many of them are. That was long before she married Bill Love. He's the one who started the wedding chapel, but Linda . . . Linda was the one who made it into the glory it is these days. When Bill died, she inherited, see, but she wasn't stupid and greedy. She took all his money and sank it back into the business. It's paid off for her, too."

"But back when she worked here at Cal's . . ."

"That was long before she'd made a name for herself in this town," Yancy said. "She was one of those folks over on the midway. You know, the ones who guess at your age or your weight, then give you a prize if they're wrong."

It was hardly the way I'd ever pictured the woman with the neat hair, the trim suits, and the pricey jewelry, and I laughed. "She doesn't seem the type."

"Oh, she was a cagey one. Knew all the tricks! You know there's a formula for making the right guesses about those things. Still, it takes a slick personality to pull it off and make it look like it's some kind of magic. The reverend? Oh yes, she was good at what she did."

"Funny nobody ever mentioned it before."

Yancy pulled himself to his feet. "Didn't seem to matter. And besides, like I said, it all happened a long time ago. It's not like it can possibly have anything to do with Dickie's murder."

I knew Yancy was right about how Reverend Love's job years ago couldn't have anything to do with what happened to Dickie, but later in the day when I took my lunch break and saw Reverend Love outside the Palace, I figured it wouldn't hurt to question her about what I'd heard. Besides, I knew she was concerned about what had happened to me outside her chapel the day before, and I wanted to prove to her that I was as right as rain.

Before I could head her off at the pass (that's Deadeye-speak), though, I ran into Creosote Cal.

"Hey, what's the hurry, little lady?" Since Cal stepped directly in front of me, I had to look around him to keep an eye on Reverend Love. I saw her go into the auditorium. "You're a-movin' like your boots are on fire!"

I glanced down at my sneakers, then realized Cal was just playing his Western persona to the hilt, so I ignored the comment. "I just wanted to talk to Reverend Love," I told him. "I hear she used to work here."

"Darn tootin'!" Cal hooked his thumbs in his suspenders and rocked back on his heels. "And aren't we just proud enough to burst our buttons to say that the little lady got her start right here at Creosote Cal's Cactus Casino and Hoedown Hotel."

"Funny place for a minister to get started."

"Maybe." Cal grinned. "But you know what they say about Vegas. It's the city of miracles!"

I'd always thought that was Rome.

"Anything can happen here," Cal continued. "To anyone. Why, look at me. Came here back in '65 with nothing but a couple bucks in my pocket. And now all this . . ." When he glanced around Deadeye—from the painted sky above our heads to the phony street of shops around us and the made-from-recycled-plastic street dusted with just enough real Vegas dirt to make it feel gritty—he practically busted a gut with pride. "Same thing happened to our Linda. She started out here all right, but then she married Bill and became a minister herself and now she's really something. One of the biggest names in Vegas. And I'll tell you what, she's not ashamed of her past, either. Oh, no siree. Not like a lot of people would be. She's as proud as she can be of what she did here."

"Guessing people's weights?"

"It ain't as easy as it looks," Cal confided, and gave me a wink. "Takes a special talent. Oh yes, it does! And our Linda, she's got plenty of that."

When Cal stepped away, I headed for the auditorium. Both Hermosa and Osborn would be performing in there later in the evening, but for now, it was set up like an assembly line of sorts. Long tables filled the stage, and from where I stood near the doors, I could see that each table was lined with pieces of paper. Reverend Love went from paper to paper to paper, hitting each one lightly with an inked stamper.

"Hey, Reverend!" I called from the back of the auditorium. "Want to guess my weight?"

Her stamper poised above a paper, the reverend froze. But only for a second. She set down her stamper and waved me over.

"I see you survived your ordeal," the reverend said. "I'm glad Nick was right and you weren't seriously hurt. Has my insurance company contacted you?"

I told her they hadn't, but when they did, I would

cooperate fully. I didn't bother to mention that it wasn't her fault that Bernadette was a crazy person intent on revenge. There was no use muddying the waters.

"So . . ." By this time, I was up onstage with the reverend and I looked over the papers she'd already stamped. "What's up?"

"The wedding licenses for tomorrow," she told me. She started stamping again, lightly whacking page after page as she made her way up and down the tables. "I thought it would be easier to stamp them than to sign my name to each one, and my goodness, I'm glad I did." She glanced at the sea of papers. "You don't really get a sense of how many people will be involved until you see the licenses like this."

"That's a lot of happy couples," I said.

The reverend didn't exactly laugh. It was more of a snort. She kept stamping away. "Half of all marriages end in divorce," she said, finishing up with the papers on one side of a table and starting down the other. "My guess is that the rate is higher for marriages I perform here in Vegas."

It was a surprisingly candid—and skeptical—comment from a woman I expected to be anything but.

"Wow." I looked over the sea of papers. "That's a lot of couples who may not make it. Doesn't that make you sad?"

The reverend glanced up from her work. "Welcome to the real world."

Maybe I looked stricken by her cynicism. Maybe that was why the reverend smiled. "I didn't really mean it!"

She patted my shoulder. "You don't think I'm that much of a curmudgeon, do you? I actually do believe in happily ever after."

It was nice to know, but hey, I understood. When it comes to romance, I'm pretty cynical, too.

The note was waiting for me when I got back to the Palace.

It was a single sheet of paper, and the letters that had been glued on it were cut out of newspapers and magazines. Some of them were black and white. Some were colorful and glossy. The whole thing was such a hodgepodge that after I pulled the note out of its envelope, it took me a few moments of staring before I could focus.

By that time, Sylvia was already standing at my side, reading over my shoulder.

If u want to see the Chick again, I must talk to Jack.

"Are you kidding me?" The way my voice ricocheted from the rafters, I don't think kidding had anything to do with it. My hands shook so badly, I had to set down the note or risk tearing it to tatters. "That crazy woman is holding the Chick for ransom!"

"She doesn't know Jack is missing."

Oh, how I hate it when Sylvia says something that I hadn't thought of myself.

The idea brought me up short, and thinking, I narrowed my eyes and propped my fists on my hips. "You might be"—I had to swallow hard before I could get the word out—"right. That's what this whole thing has been all about. She thinks Jack's avoiding her. That he's here somewhere and he's dodging. She thinks that if she does enough weird stuff, he's bound to show up to talk to her about it. And when he doesn't, she ups the ante. That's why she stole the Chick. She doesn't know Jack is missing."

"But she does know where the Chick is." Was that blue fire I saw shoot from Sylvia's eyes? In all the years I'd known her (and that was all my life), I'd seen Sylvia be calculating and sly. I'd seen her annoyed at the things I'd done to her (real and imagined), and I'd seen her royally pissed. Just a few short weeks earlier, I'd seen her scared and vulnerable when she was arrested for murder.

But I'd never seen the fire of righteous indignation in her eyes.

At the same time I marveled at how amazing it was that she cared as much as I did about the Chick, I worried about the fact that Sylvia and I might actually agree about something. If I wasn't careful, I'd end up admiring her for her convictions.

The thought sat on my shoulders like a too-tight jacket, and I twitched and shrugged to get rid of it, and when that didn't work, I cleared a ball of uncomfortable emotion from my throat. "We'll get the Chick back," I promised my sister. "We have to. She's the symbol of everything Jack did in his career."

Too late, I realized just how literally Sylvia would

DEATH BY DEVIL'S BREATH

take my words. Oh yeah, the Chick was a symbol of Jack's work, all right. The way he worked to steal Sylvia's mother's heart, and the way he worked (I hear it didn't take him long) to cast her aside so he could win my mother over. The Chick was a legend on the chili cook-off circuit and I'd never thought of it before, but some of what was legendary had more to do with Jack's love life than his chili spices.

I held my breath, waiting for Sylvia to remind me of all this in her snippy Sylvia sort of way, but instead, all she did was sigh. "It would be awful if we never saw the costume again. But now that we've got the note . . ." When I put a hand out to pick it up again, she stopped me. "Fingerprints," she said. "We'll give it to Nick and he'll give it to the cops and they'll for sure find out who took the Chick."

"We don't need to find out. We know. It's crazy Bernadette."

No truer words had ever been spoken because just as I said them, I glanced out the window and pointed.

"It's crazy Bernadette!" I said when I caught sight of her outside in the street. "The woman has more nerve than a bad tooth."

"Maybe. But, Maxie, you're not—"

I didn't wait around for Sylvia to tell me what I was *not* going to do. Before she could stop me, I stomped out of the bordello and into the dusty main street of Deadeye.

By now, Bernadette was two storefronts down from the Palace.

201

"You're a no-good Chili Chick rustler," I called out, and when I did, she stopped in her tracks.

Slowly, she turned to face me. That day, Bernadette was dressed all in black in vivid contrast to me in my khakis and a shirt the flaming red color of a Satan's Kiss pepper.

She stood tall in her black boots. "You can't possibly be talking to me," Bernadette said.

I took one step forward. "You know I am. And you know why. You kidnapped the Chick."

Bernadette took a step in my direction. "Did I?"

"You can't deny it. I know you did. And you'd better give her back."

"Or what?" She laughed and something about the brittle sound attracted attention. Before I knew it, the people who'd been browsing the shops of Deadeye were lined on the wooden sidewalk, watching the scene. Sylvia stepped onto the walk in front of the bordello. Gert walked out of the general store. I didn't have to see Nick to know he was outside of the sheriff's office with his eyes on me. I could feel the waves of heat coming from that direction, like the sun at high noon.

Bernadette hooked her fingers in her belt. "Even if it was true, what could you possibly do about it, Maxie? What could you do if you thought I had the Chick?"

"I could call the cops. I have called the cops. That costume's worth a bundle. Stealing it is a felony."

"That's too bad for whoever stole it. If the cops ever find the person."

The way the anger seethed in me, it was impossible

to keep still. I took another step toward Bernadette. "Too bad for you, you mean. If you hurt the Chick—"

"Who said anything about hurting her? If all it takes is for Jack to make an appearance—"

"Aha!" I pointed my trigger finger at her. "I knew it was you. Only the person who wrote that lame ransom note would know that's what it said. You want to see Jack. You'll only give back the Chick once you talk to Jack."

I guess she thought it was a real possibility because her gaze flickered over the crowd, hungry and searching. When she didn't see Jack anywhere and looked back my way, she frowned. "Prove I took the costume," was all she said.

"The cops will search your house. They'll go over to Bibi's Bump and Grind and—"

"And you think I'm that stupid?"

This was not the time for honesty. I drew in a breath and held it deep in my lungs, then forced myself to let it out slowly. "It's not going to happen," I told Bernadette. "You're not going to see Jack."

"Avoiding me is that important to him?" She tried for a laugh but it didn't fool me; I heard the way her voice clogged with emotion. "Can he really be that mean? That's not . . . that's not the Jack I remember."

"He isn't mean." I stepped closer to her. "There's something you need to know, Bernadette. Jack . . ." I coughed away the sudden tightness in my throat. "Jack is missing."

She threw back her head and swaggered nearer. "Oh

yeah, and I should believe that from the world's biggest liar!"

"I was. I was a liar," I admitted. "But give me a break, that was a long time ago, and I was just a kid, and besides, I had my reasons."

"Like you hated me."

"Like I hated the thought of losing Jack." Unconsciously, I'd mirrored her stance, my fingers hooked in the waistband of my khakis, my shoulders back. "I finally figured it out, Bernadette. It didn't matter who it was, you or some other woman. I would have done the same thing. I couldn't take the chance of losing Jack."

"But now you say . . ." We were still twenty feet from each other, but she swallowed so hard, I saw her throat jump. "You're telling me that he's not here? That he's gone?"

"He hasn't been with the Showdown since back in Abilene. So I guess you wasted your time being in the Devil's Breath contest. That is why you did it, isn't it? That is why you used one of Jack's old recipes. You thought for sure he'd be here, that he'd see you. That he'd realize you were still in love with him. You need to understand that's not going to happen."

She looked as stricken as if she'd been shot. "Missing?" The word escaped her lips on the end of a moan. "You don't think he's—"

I refused to let her say it. "I thought maybe you could tell me. I thought maybe you knew—"

"No." Bernadette shook her head back and forth, faster and faster. "You can't believe I'd ever have anything to do with something like that! I love Jack. I always have. And I haven't . . ." She swallowed her tears. "I haven't seen him in years. And now you're telling me . . ." By this time, she was breathing hard. Her voice rose, a soft, high keening that echoed through Deadeye like the cry of a banshee. "Missing?" When she looked at me, Bernadette's eyes brimmed with tears. "Maybe if you would have let him be happy with me, he'd still be here."

It was my turn to clutch my chest. A second later, I knew there was only one way to handle both my pain and Bernadette's. I raced forward and pulled her into a hug.

Dang. I wish there weren't so many people standing around watching. I'd hate for word to get out that I actually have a heart.

CHAPTER 14

I didn't care if Sylvia liked it or not (and believe me, Sylvia did not like it), after that scene with Bernadette I needed to get out of Deadeye, and fast.

Desperate to clear my head and avoid the looks I was getting from the crowds who'd watched my close encounter of the uncomfortable kind with Bernadette, I darted outside and regretted it instantly. Hot. It gets hot in Las Vegas. And that Saturday afternoon it was sizzling enough to melt the soles of my sneakers to the pavement. Unwilling to go back into Creosote Cal's, where people were still pointing at me and whispering about how wonderful it was that I'd consoled Bernadette over her broken heart, I started off across the street. There was another hotel over there and a sign outside flashing out the news that the IADL & C was having its annual meeting there. I had no idea who or what the IADL & C was; I only knew that, with any luck, no one there would recognize me. And the AC would be cranked up, too.

When I stepped into the lobby and a wave of cool air washed over me, I breathed a sigh of relief.

That sigh stuck in my throat when I realized I was surrounded.

Dolls.

There were dolls everywhere. Armies of them were displayed in glass-fronted cases around the lobby. Posters of them hung on the walls. There was a doll bigger than me (and dressed as a bride . . . eesh!) standing near the hotel registration desk and another doll (this one a giant pseudo-Barbie in a pink bikini) near the entrance to the ballroom, where a sign welcomed conventioneers and visitors alike to the International Association of Doll Lovers & Collectors annual meeting. Personally, I would have much preferred a stop at the bar for a chilly one, but remember that cute little doll in Reverend Love's office? And now this? Never let it be said that I don't know a sign when I see it. Even if I don't always know what the heck it means.

Curious to find out, I strolled into the ballroom, where conventioneers mixed, mingled, and swarmed a few dozen vendor booths devoted to dolls, doll clothes, books about dolls, calendars that featured dolls, and even pieces and parts of dolls. I passed a booth where doll eyes stared at me from jars and plastic and porcelain doll arms and legs hung like so many sides of beef in a butcher shop. Bad enough, and even worse when I saw the display of doll wigs. Real human hair? They use real human hair to make the higher-priced doll wigs? If I wasn't already completely creeped out, believe me, that would have put me over the edge.

The good news is that—grossed out—I spun the other way, and when I did, I saw that the booth directly across from the pieces/parts store was manned by a guy who looked awfully familiar.

George Jarret, the guy I'd seen first lurking around, then sneaking into, Dickie's dressing room!

More curious than ever, I strolled over in his direction and checked out the sign suspended above his table: *Jarret Collectibles, Dolls of Distinction.*

Obviously, dolls weren't the only things in his inventory. A section of his table was draped in black, and in the center of it was a framed photograph. It was surrounded by piles of the same photograph of none other than the late, great (hey, that's what the sign that leaned against the framed picture said) Dickie Dunkin.

So I was right about Jarret's felonious ways! I saw him walk out of the dressing room with the pictures of Dickie, and now he was selling them for fifteen dollars each. Fifteen dollars for a picture of a guy in a plaid sport coat!

I guess my expression registered my disgust, because Jarret stepped right over, his eyes eager.

"Collector's item," he said, pointing to the photo. "And since the pictures are autographed, sure to gain in value year after year. A real investment. You know Dickie Dunkin was murdered just a couple days ago."

"I know you took these photos out of his dressing room."

Jarret's face paled. "You can't possibly—" Before he could say too much, he swallowed his protest and shuffled from foot to foot. "That's preposterous."

"Just joshing!" I gave him a wide smile. "How could I possibly know anything like that? And why would I possibly care?" To prove it, I inched down the table and away from the pictures of Dickie, looking over Jarret's merchandise as I went. It included new dolls still in their boxes, plastic baby dolls, and some of those eerie porcelain dolls that are meant to look realistic and instead look like something straight out of a horror movie writer's warped imagination.

Still, in the name of my investigation, I would have pretended I was interested, but I never had the chance. Something at the end of the table caught my eye, and before I even realized I was moving, I'd zoomed over there for a better look.

It was a single doll inside a tall glass display case, and I took one close look and caught my breath.

She was about a foot high and entirely made of fabric, from her skinny stuffed arms and legs to her big round head. This doll had yellow strips of felt for hair, and she was dressed in a white dress dotted with pink and blue flowers.

"She's great, isn't she?" Jarret mistook the expression

on my face for interested-in-doll instead of the interested-in-what-looked-awfully-familiar it really was. The scent of a sale hanging in the air, he rubbed his hands together and closed in on me and the doll. "You have good taste. And you're knowledgeable. You know exactly what she is, don't you? Then you also know she's one of a kind."

I thought about my visit to the Love Chapel and the doll I'd seen in Reverend Love's office. "But I've seen another. Not exactly the same, but similar."

"Really?" Jarret's dark eyes lit up. I swear, if there wasn't a display table between us, he would have pounced. "Where?"

"Maybe in a book." I must have been a pretty good liar, because his expression fell. "That must have been it. A book about doll collecting."

"Well, I can see how the picture attracted your attention," he said. He raised a hand toward the glass display case, not quite touching it, but caressing the air around it. "These dolls . . . they're the Holy Grail of doll collecting."

"These dolls? But you said this was the only one."

He realized his error and cleared his throat. "Did I say *they* were a legend?" Jarret laughed. "Just a slip of the tongue. There were more of these wonderful dolls at one time. You probably saw photos of them in that doll collecting book you said you saw. Unfortunately, they're long gone. If there were more of these dolls, this one wouldn't be worth as much as it is."

I glanced from him to the doll. "And this one's worth . . .?"

"Seven-fifty," he said.

It took a couple seconds for the number to sink into my brain. "Seven *hundred* and fifty dollars? For a rag doll?"

"Handmade," Jarret said. "One of a kind."

I remembered what Reverend Love had told me about the doll I saw in her office. "And this doll was made by a woman named Louise, right?"

Jarret got that smile on his face, the one I'd seen people sprout when they were about to lecture me about how they were right and—oh, as much as they hated to admit it, they couldn't spare me from the painful truth— how I was very, very wrong.

"This is a Noreen Pennybaker doll." He said this like it was supposed to mean something. Maybe it did in the world of doll collecting, but it didn't mean squat to me.

It did, however, spark a memory.

I bent to peek up the doll's dress, but because of the glass display case, it was impossible to get a good look. "Noreen Pennybaker?" I glanced up at Jarrett. "Should her name be inside the doll's petticoat?"

"I assure you, it's embroidered there. Along with the doll's name, of course. That's how we know Honey Bunch here is authentic. If you're a serious buyer . . ." He didn't finish the thought. He didn't have to. Obviously, if I was serious and had seven hundred and fifty dollars to burn, he'd whip out the doll and throw her skirts in the air to show me the embroidered signature. If not, then I wasn't worth the effort.

Jarrett backed away from the display case. "Take my word for it, everything is just as it should be. Just as the story says it is. You *do* know the story?"

I gave him the smile that had once been known to charm men. Yeah, the one I didn't bother with much these days because, let's face it, none of the men I knew were worth the effort. "I bet anything you can tell it like nobody else can."

It worked. Jarrett's shoulders shot back. "Legend says there are others of these dolls. But this is the only one that's ever been found anywhere," he added quickly, just so I didn't get the idea that the seven hundred and fifty dollars was the rip-off I'd already decided it was. "Each and every one of them was made by a woman named Noreen Pennybaker. Woman? I should say *artist*! Look at the sweet details." He pointed. "The darling expression on Honey Bunch's face. The cute little outfit. Those adorable spots of pink color on her cheeks. This doll has personality, and . . ." He leaned over the table toward me. "I have the little book, too. I don't like to say it too loud because I wouldn't want to start a stampede. But I do, I do have the book, the storybook Noreen Pennybaker wrote and illustrated to go along with each of the dolls she made."

"Each of the dolls that have never been found except for this one."

Jarrett nodded. "Pity. If I could only find the rest of them!"

"Wouldn't that make this one worth less?"

"Ah, you are a sly buyer!" He waggled a finger at me. "Of course, if more dolls came on the market, Honey Bunch here would lose some of her value. But none of her charm! The trick is, there have been rumors about these dolls for thirty years or more. But this is the only one that's ever come to market. If there were more, they're gone now. And if someone ever discovered them . . ." His brown eyes lit up. "My goodness, what a collector would pay for all of them would be simply astounding." Jarret seemed to remember himself and wiped the smile off his face. "Since that's not ever going to happen, that makes Honey Bunch unique."

Maybe not so much.

Rather than point this out, I stepped back and out of the way when a middle-aged woman raced to the table.

"I just heard the news!" As if she might have a heart attack, the woman pressed a hand to her ample chest. "You said you'd do it, George, and you were right. You got Honey Bunch! She's . . ." She sucked in a breath and let it out slowly. "She's exquisite. And the book? You have the book, too?"

Jarret assured her he did, and I didn't wait around to hear any more. See, I'd just learned all I'd needed to learn, not from George Jarret, but from his customer.

He hadn't had Honey Bunch.

And now he did.

Just like he hadn't had those pictures of Dickie Dunkin.

And now he did.

Of course I knew just how he got the photographs.

The only question now was where Honey Bunch came from.

When I got back to the Palace, a couple things happened that made me forget all about George Jarret and Honey Bunch.

First of all, Sylvia met me at the door. "I'm going to dinner," she said, even before I set foot inside the bordello. "And just so you know, I've learned a thing or two from you, Maxie. I'm not going to hurry back. I'll let you see what it's like to work here for hours and hours all by yourself."

Before I had a chance to make a face at her, she was gone.

Work by myself I did and—don't tell Sylvia—but it actually was kind of fun. Instead of thinking about murder, I got to think about chili and chili peppers and chili seasonings and all the wonderful ways chili can be served. I took the bland chili that Sylvia had prepared for samples and jazzed it up with spicy goodness and watched with real satisfaction when customers tasted, smiled, and said they had to buy whatever seasoning it was that was in there, it was that good.

I rearranged the shelves, not because they needed it, but because I knew it would push Sylvia's buttons, and I did a quick mental inventory of what we had left in the way of dried peppers and spices and figured out what we might need for the next day, the last day of the

Showdown. With all those weddings that were going to take place in the auditorium the next afternoon, I knew there would be plenty of extra potential customers around, and thinking about how I could turn them into buyers, I made up some signs that said things like *Spice Up Your Honeymoon* and *Every Romance Needs a Little Extra Heat* and taped them in the windows.

At the last minute, I decided to add a little more pizzazz to my display and ducked out to the RV. Even though Sylvia and I had long outgrown the crayon stage, I knew there was still a box of colored pencils and crayons and glitter on the top shelf of the closet in my bedroom that Jack used occasionally to make up signs and jazz up displays. When I returned to the Palace, I found Gert behind the cash register.

"I didn't think you'd mind if I took care of a couple sales for you," she said. "I've got Janna from the coffee place watching my stuff for a couple minutes and no customers right now so I stopped by. Wondered if you'd seen today's paper. There's an obituary for Dickie."

I told her that while I'd seen enough of the morning paper to catch the photograph of Hermosa along with the story about how she claimed that Osborn was trying to poison her, the obits were something I didn't normally pay any attention to.

"I think they're fascinating." Gert laid out the paper on the counter. "The well-written ones say so much about a person's life. Look, look at this one here."

I glanced at the picture Gert pointed to. It showed a

woman with bare shoulders, long, dangling earrings, and hair piled up on her head.

She laughed. "Where else but in Vegas would you read an obituary that says this woman was proud of the fact that she was the first to ever dance topless at a charity fund-raiser? I swear, this town is unreal!"

I looked over the rest of the obituaries. Dickie's stuck out like the sore thumb Dickie was. It was longer than the rest of the obits, and the picture that went along with his life story was the same publicity photo I'd seen George Jarret selling just a short time before.

"He was such a nasty man, wasn't he?" Gert's shoulders trembled. "I mean, that act of his certainly was. He poked fun at everyone. He said mean things. But then you read this and you get insight into the real person. Listen."

Gert read from the paper. " 'Richard (Dickie) Dunkin, Vegas mainstay and master comedian.' " She screwed up her mouth. "Obviously written by a friend. But that's not the important part. Here it says that every year, he gave a performance for the local animal rescue organization. And here it says that he was involved with the Shriners. They do lots of good things for kids. So maybe Dickie wasn't such a terrible person after all."

"Maybe," I conceded. "But somebody sure didn't like him. It doesn't say anything about who's left behind, does it?" I asked her. "Like maybe he was some kind of secret millionaire and somebody was going to inherit a whole bunch of money when Dickie died?"

Gert shook her head. "Nothing like that. It says he was preceded in death by his brother, Lawrence, and it doesn't say anything about a father, but it does mention his mother, Noreen Pennybaker."

I froze where I stood. "What did you just say?"

"Yeah, I think it's pretty funny, too." Gert laughed. "Dickie Dunkin must have been a stage name. Poor kid growing up must have been Dickie Pennybaker. Imagine the razzing he got for that. No wonder he turned out to be so sour."

I wasn't listening. But then, I was pretty busy thinking.

"Can you do me a favor?" I asked Gert. "Could you stay here, just for a couple minutes? I'm going to . . ." What? Somehow it didn't seem fair to tell Gert the truth and maybe involve her in breaking and entering. "I'm just going to run back to the RV and grab something to eat. I'll be back in a jiffy."

"Sure." Gert got her phone out of her pocket. "I'll give Janna a call and tell her I'll be just a few minutes longer."

"Great. Good." I headed out the door. "I'll be right back," I promised Gert.

Dickie's dressing room was locked, but really, I only tried the door for the hell of it. What I really needed to find was the storeroom where Hermosa had showed me the sum total of Dickie's worldly possessions.

It wasn't locked, thank goodness, so there was no breaking and entering involved after all. I turned on the light, scooted inside, and closed the door behind me.

The place was just as I remembered it, with metal shelves along the walls packed with props and all the stuff from Dickie's apartment piled on the floor. Hermosa had told me that Dickie's lease ran out the week before, and until they had time to get his stuff moved to her place, they'd stashed it here.

Here, not in his dressing room, which, Hermosa pointed out, was way too small.

Here, where nobody was likely to find it.

The thought sang through my bloodstream like a shot of tequila, and I scanned the mismatched suitcases, the boxes, and the trunk that Hermosa had told me had come from Dickie's.

My money was on the trunk, and I dragged the boxes out from around it and got down on my knees. The trunk was locked, but a prop rifle and a prop bow and arrow went a long way toward helping me out. I sat back on my heels and threw open the lid.

They stared up at me, all those fabric eyes.

They smiled at me, dozens of pairs of pink, bowed lips.

They twinkled, I mean what with all those pink felt dots on fabric cheeks.

My heart in my throat, I stared down at a trunk filled with Noreen Pennybaker's legendary dolls and thought about what George Jarret said about how if they were ever discovered, they'd be worth a fortune.

The dolls that had once belonged to Dickie Dunkin and had been moved to the casino along with the rest of his things.

Just to be sure, I checked the hem inside a few of the dolls' dresses. There was Noreen's looping, slanted signature embroidered into the fabric along with the block letter names of each of the dolls: Fairy Wight and Buttercup. Polly Petals and Anna Banana and Sweetheart Sue.

I was so busy looking over the dolls and the handmade storybooks that went along with each one of them, I guess I didn't hear the door of the storeroom open.

But then, I didn't hear the person in back of me, either.

And by the time that person conked me on the head and knocked me out cold . . .

Well, by that time, it was way too late.

CHAPTER 15

"Why were you messing around in there?"

"Messing?" My throat was raw from screaming. My knuckles bled from pounding. My eyes were screwed up against the light that exploded like fireworks when Nick threw open the lid of the trunk where I'd been stuffed for who-knew-how-long.

"I wasn't messing," I rasped, the emphasis on that last word because, let's face it, he deserved every ounce of sarcasm I was capable of delivering. My muscles screamed in protest when I got to my knees and unbent myself from the pretzel shape I'd been forced into. "I was trapped. In this trunk. Someone knocked me on the head and . . . ow!"

That last bit was thanks to the fact that Nick put a

hand on the back of my head and found the goose egg right about in the middle of it.

"You did get hit." He looped his arms around me and plucked me out of the trunk before I even had a chance to say *no, duh!*

"Here." With one foot, he dragged over a metal folding chair and plunked me down in it. "Who did this to you?"

Like the look I shot his way didn't speak volumes?

Apparently, not volumes Nick could read.

"Lump," I told him. "Back of the head. Obviously, I didn't . . ." My throat was raw; it hurt when I talked. I braced myself and tried again. "I didn't see who hit me."

He pulled a walkie-talkie out of his back pocket, called hotel security, and told them to send somebody over. When he was done, he paced to the other side of the storeroom (it didn't take long) and came back toward me, acting out the motions he described. "So somebody snuck up on you." He stopped right behind where I'd been kneeling by the trunk and raised his hand. "And that somebody whacked you."

When he brought his arm down, I winced.

Nick slid me a look. "And you were in this storeroom bent over that trunk to begin with . . ." He glanced around the room with its metal shelves and props, and something told me that back in the day when he was a cop and interviewing a victim, he never would have had the nerve to shrug the way he did. Like he knew that even once I told him what was going on, he'd already convinced himself he wasn't going to believe it. "Why?"

Lucky for me, I didn't have a chance to answer. A couple security guards chose that moment to show up, and Nick stepped out into the corridor to talk to them. When he came back, he had an ice pack and he pressed it (another ow!) to the back of my head and told me to hold it there.

"Explain," he said.

Though it didn't do much for the pounding behind my eyes and the aching in my neck and the fact that I was pretty sure my brain was about to pop and ooze out my ears, the cold felt heavenly on the lump on my head. I allowed myself exactly five seconds to enjoy it before I shot him a look. "You explain first. How did you—"

"Find you?" Nick crouched down in front of me so he could look me in the eye. "I heard a report over my walkie about some frantic pounding and muffled screaming coming from inside one of the storerooms. Call me crazy, but it sounded so odd, I just had this gut feeling it had something to do with you." He took my free hand in his and studied the scrapes on my knuckles. "You're lucky someone heard you."

I didn't need the reminder. If I let myself slip and allowed my mind to wander and I thought about waking up to blackness and the heart-stopping realization that someone had dumped me in that trunk and wedged the lid so I couldn't open it . . .

I sucked in a painful breath and shook away the thought, and when I did, I saw that sometime when I was lost in the panic that gripped me by the throat and refused to let go, Nick had taken a handkerchief out of his pocket and gently pressed it against my knuckles. "ER," he said.

"No. Not again. I'm fine." To prove it, I lowered the ice bag.

"Just like you were fine when that neon sign nearly cut you in half. Maxie . . ." He sat back on his heels. "You're obviously—"

"Sticking my nose where it doesn't belong. Pissing someone off. Making enemies. Yeah." I did my best to stir up some of my usual moxie, but my supply was completely drained. My shoulders drooped, and as much as I told myself it was a bad idea, I let the warmth of Nick's touch seep through the hankie and into my hand. From there it wormed its way into my bloodstream, and inch by inch, I felt relaxed, cared for, safe.

I sighed, then instantly regretted it. Sighing is for sissies. "I think I know what's going on," I told Nick. "Everything that's happened . . . everything that happened tonight . . . it's all because of those dolls."

"What dolls?" When Nick stood up, he left his handkerchief with me.

It was easier to show him than to explain so I pulled myself to my feet and walked over to the trunk. No easy thing considering that with every step I took, the room pitched. Rather than let Nick know it, I leaned against the now-open trunk lid and pointed. "Those—" My mouth fell open and memory flooded through me. My shoulders ached from where they were pressed against the sides of the trunk. My knees were red from kneeling against the hard trunk bottom. When I was locked in there in the dark, I guess I knew all along that there was nothing in there to cushion me, but thanks to my slightly scrambled brain, it had taken a while to put the pieces of the puzzle together.

Now the empty trunk brought it all home.

"The dolls are gone!" I told Nick.

At my side, he, too, peered into the trunk. "Unless they were never there to begin with."

"Are you saying—"

"Come on, Maxie, you did get hit on the head." He put a hand on my arm. "Maybe you're mixing up some memory you have of dolls you had as a kid with what really happened."

"No!" I swatted his hand away. "No, no, no! First of all, I didn't have any dolls when I was a kid. Does that surprise you? It shouldn't. Something tells me you'd be the first to admit I don't have a warm and fuzzy bone in my body. And second of all . . . I saw the dolls. Of course I saw the dolls. The dolls were what I was looking for when I came in here. And they were there!" I poked a finger toward the trunk. "I saw them. All those big felt eyes and the little mouths and the stuffed arms and legs and—"

"And so somebody conked you on the head and knocked you out. Then they took the dolls out of the trunk so they could put you in it. And the dolls are . . ." Nick scanned the storeroom. "Where?"

Getting my thoughts in line, I bit my lower lip. "The dolls aren't here. Don't you get it? The person who conked me on the head took the dolls!"

"This person assaulted you so he could take a bunch of dolls?"

I decided to play it cool, and before Nick noticed that my knees were Silly Putty, I went back over to the chair and plunked down. "Not just a bunch of dolls. Noreen Pennybaker's dolls. That's what this whole thing is about."

I didn't bother to wait for him to ask me to explain. "It's like this," I told Nick. "Noreen Pennybaker was Dickie Dunkin's mother, right? Well, of course it's right. That's what it said in Dickie's obituary. It said his mother's name was Noreen Pennybaker. And Noreen, she's famous in doll-collecting circles for making these really adorable—" I cleared my throat and gathered my wits and remembered what I'd told Nick just a minute earlier: I didn't have a warm and fuzzy bone in my body. No use making myself sound like a liar.

"Well, some people think they're adorable," I said. "Doll collectors and such. These dolls, see, they're kind of cute, and Noreen hand-made every one and then she embroidered her name and the doll's name on the inside of the doll's dress. And George Jarret, he's selling one of the dolls at the doll show at the hotel across the street."

Surprise, surprise, Nick hadn't stopped me with any lame questions. Now, his arms crossed over his chest, he leaned back against the nearest metal shelf. "Go on."

"So I thought it was kind of fishy, because Jarret's the one who was hanging around Dickie's dressing room on the night of the murder, and when I asked him what he wanted, he said he was a fan and was just looking for Dickie so he could get an autographed picture. Yeah, like he hadn't heard the news that Dickie was dead. But then the other night, he was back here at Creosote Cal's and that's when he broke into the dressing room and—"

"And you know this how?"

Since I knew he wouldn't like the answer, I took a couple moments to reapply the ice pack to the back of my head and hoped Nick would be so busy feeling sorry for me, he wouldn't have any time to get mad. "I followed him, of course," I said. "When I saw him in the hotel. Jarret went into Dickie's dressing room and he was in there about ten minutes. When he came out again, he had some autographed pictures of Dickie. If you don't believe me, take a stroll across the street. Jarret's selling the pictures as collector's items. You know, on account of how Dickie was murdered and now he figures everyone's going to want Dickie memorabilia."

"So this Jarret character—"

"Has one of Noreen Pennybaker's dolls. And he's selling it for seven hundred and fifty dollars, if you can believe that. And he's passing it off as the only one of her dolls still in existence, but I know that's not true."

"Because you saw this trunk filled with the dolls."

"Well, yeah, because of that, and because Linda Love has one of the dolls in her office. See, that's why I noticed the one Jarret's selling—Honey Bunch, that's her name—in the first place. Because when I went to the Love Chapel and talked to Reverend Love, I saw a doll just like it in her office. Tout Sweet. That's the name of Reverend Love's doll. And that's what I was thinking, you know, that maybe Jarret, being a doll collector and a doll dealer, he wasn't really lurking around Dickie's dressing room because he wanted some autographed pictures. He was in there ten minutes, Nick, and it doesn't take ten minutes to grab some pictures from Dickie's dressing table. The pictures were just a bonus and a way for Jarret to make a quick buck. He was really in there looking for something else."

"The dolls."

I nodded, then regretted it. A drum line rhythm started up inside my forehead. "Jarret told me that if there were more dolls, they'd be worth a fortune because some collector would buy all of them and he could charge out the wazoo for them."

"Then the dolls . . ." As if trying to get his bearings, Nick glanced around the storeroom. "But if Jarret was looking for the dolls, why was he looking in here?"

"He wasn't. I was looking in here. Because I knew the dolls weren't in the dressing room."

"Because you've already looked around Dickie's dressing room."

"Maybe." How's that for a great way to dodge? "But then I got to thinking about how long Jarret was in the dressing room and how maybe the pictures weren't what he was looking for. And I remembered that Hermosa told me that Dickie's stuff was stored in here. You know, on account of how the lease on his apartment was up last week and he was moving in with Hermosa. His dressing room was too small to hold all his stuff, so that's why they tucked it in here. You know, until they had time to move it all. And I thought, if Dickie did have some of his mother's dolls—"

"This is where they would be. With all the other stuff he moved out of his apartment."

I knew better than to try another nod.

Nick scraped his hands over his face. "So let me get this straight. You think this doll collector guy—"

"George Jarret."

"You think George Jarret stole the dolls that belonged to Dickie Dunkin and were made by Dickie's mother."

"Well, the fact that they're not here proves that," I pointed out even though I shouldn't have had to. "But that's not all I'm saying, Nick. I think Jarret killed Dickie. You know, to get the dolls."

Nick considered this. "Did you see him at the Devil's Breath contest?" he asked.

I had to admit I hadn't. "But he could have been in the audience," I told him. "You know, one of the people who was waiting to sample the chili."

"So how do you think he got the poison into Dickie's chili?"

I threw my hands in the air. "Don't ask me! That's what you cop types are supposed to figure out. But I do know he wanted those dolls and he wanted them bad, and now they're gone. And I know something else, Nick. I know how we can prove he really has them."

I guess Nick had learned a thing or two in the time I'd known him. Rather than tell me I was crazy, he actually shut up long enough for me to explain what I had in mind.

I would have liked to think that Sylvia was our likeliest ally, but hey, although I'd been clunked on the head, I wasn't completely out of my mind. Since I knew Sylvia would give me a song and dance about how she had to work at the Palace and how I should be helping out instead of playing around and how, if I knew better, I wouldn't get myself mixed up in things that didn't concern me and blah, blah, blah . . .

Well, I didn't even bother to ask her.

Instead, I went to the most logical choice, a person George Jarret wouldn't recognize, and if he did, one he'd never suspect was helping me out.

"You got it?" I asked Bernadette, and not for the first time. "You understand exactly what you're supposed to do?"

"All except for this silly thing." When she looked down at my phone, she made a face. "How am I supposed to carry this around and not look obvious?"

For the third time since I explained my plan to her, I took the phone away from where Bernadette was carrying it—screen out and right at her waist—and pressed it into her hand. "It's not like it's a flashlight or anything. You don't have to point it at Jarret. Just keep it in your hand. And when you stop to look at the doll, prop it against one of the other dolls. I've got the app loaded

DEATH BY DEVIL'S BREATH

and all set to go. I'm going to be watching you from . . ." Since I'd given Bernadette my smartphone to use, I was going to be using Nick's to keep an eye on her. I showed her the phone. "We'll be able to see you and hear everything," I reminded her.

"All right. Good." She drew in a long breath, then let it out slowly. "It's not that I'm a relic or anything, but this new technology . . ." Bernadette gave the phone a funny look, but this time when she was done, she kept it in her hand, just like I'd told her to.

"And don't forget . . ." Leave it to Nick to be in charge of the last-minute instructions. "You're not trying to talk Jarret into anything. Or get him to admit anything. We're not trying to trap the guy. We just want to find out about the dolls."

"The dolls. Right." Another breath, and Bernadette threw back her shoulders. She glanced at me. "You're sure about this?" she asked.

"I'm sure we need to find out what Jarret's up to, and I know he's not going to talk to me."

"But . . ." Bernadette laid a hand on my arm. "Me? I don't understand why—"

Honestly, I didn't, either, so why bother to try to explain? I only knew that I felt like I owed Bernadette something. I couldn't give her the time she wanted with Jack, but I could try and be friendly. And if being friendly helped me solve a murder?

I grinned and shooed Bernadette across the hotel lobby toward the room where the doll collectors had set up shop. "Nick and I will be in the bar," I told her with a look over my shoulder to the corner booth Nick had snagged for us. "We'll be watching everything."

I sat down across from Nick and put his phone on the table between us. I have to say, when I thought of the phone app as a way to follow Bernadette and hear what Jarret had to say, I thought it was a stroke of genius. Now I wasn't so sure.

I bent closer to the phone and pointed. "What's that—"

"It's Bernadette's hand." Nick nudged me back on my side of the table so he could see the phone, too. "This isn't going to work."

"I told her to—" Bernadette shifted the phone in her hand and I saw Jarret's face flash across the screen. "She's there. She's at his booth," I told Nick.

Who immediately told me to shut up so he could hear.

"It's a great doll," Bernadette said, admiring Honey Bunch, just like I'd told her to. "A Noreen Pennybaker, right?"

The way she was holding the phone, I couldn't see Jarret's face, but I did see him rub his hands together like he smelled a sale.

"The only one in the world," he said. "Valuable. Memorable. Distinctive. Honey Bunch here is sure to be the centerpiece of any serious doll lover's collection. Are you a serious doll lover, miss?"

"Well, I know what I like."

"That's good," I whispered and pointed to the phone. "She's doing a good job."

When Bernadette put the phone on the table, the scene jumped. The next thing I knew, we were watching her take a close look at Honey Bunch.

"She's adorable," Bernadette said. "I only wish . . ." She put a hand to her heart and sighed.

"Really?" I sat back. "That's a little over dramatic, don't you think?"

"Shh." Nick watched the screen.

"What I'd really like," Noreen said, "is an entire collection of Noreen Pennybaker dolls. Oh, I know what you're going to tell me, they're rare. And valuable. But I've come into some money, you see, and I can't think of a better way to invest it than in dolls that I know will retain their value. If you had more of these . . ."

The way the phone was set down, I couldn't see Jarret's face, but I could hear him just fine. "If only!"

I curled my hands into fists. "He's a lying sack of—"

"Maxie!" I hadn't even realized I'd gotten out of my seat until Nick's hand came down over mine, but by that time, it was too late. My head still ringing from the conk I'd taken just a few hours before, and fed up with beating around the bush, I marched out of the bar and across the hall. I was at Jarret's booth and up in his face before Bernadette realized what was going on, and long before Nick had a chance to catch up to me.

"That's a lie and you know it," I said to Jarret.

Looking back on the incident, I could understand his blank stare, but at the time, all it did was send my anger into the stratosphere.

I plucked my phone off the table and waved it in

Jarret's face. "We saw the whole thing. We heard you lie about the dolls. You know there are more of them. Dickie had them."

Spots of color rose in Jarret's cheeks. "Not in his—"

"Dressing room? Is that what you were going to say? See!" I turned to where Nick stood behind me, his fists on his hips. "I told you that's what he was doing in Dickie's dressing room. He was looking for the dolls."

"Because Dickie said he'd sell them to me." I guess Jarret thought I wasn't going to listen because he addressed this particularly interesting comment to Nick. "I found out Dickie Dunkin was in Vegas and I knew he was Noreen Pennybaker's son. I contacted him and he said there were more dolls. He said he had them and that he'd sell them to me. He gave me this one . . ." He looked at Honey Bunch. "He gave me this one to prove it. But then he was murdered and—"

"And you decided to steal the rest of the dolls."

"No!" Jarret stomped one foot. "Who are you anyway?" he asked me. "And why are you harassing me? I'm going to call hotel security, that's what I'm going to do, and I'm going to tell them to call the police. You people—"

"Are just leaving." Nick grabbed my arm and dragged me out of the ballroom. We didn't have to worry about Bernadette. Sometime while I'd been having my mini-smackdown with Jarret, she'd vamoosed.

"What did you do that for?" I jerked out of Nick's hold. "He was just talking about the dolls. He was just going to say something useful. I know he was."

Nick pointed across the lobby toward a man I'd never seen before. He gave Nick a nod, then moved toward the elevators.

"The local cops are serving a search warrant for Jarret's hotel room," Nick said. "If there's anything to find—"

"And you didn't tell me?"

He put a hand on my elbow and led me back into the bar. "What, and miss out on all the fun of you going after Jarret?" He ordered two beers and slipped back into the booth we'd gotten out of only a short while earlier, and since his hand was still clasped on my arm, I ended up sitting next to him. The adrenaline that had peaked in my confrontation with Jarret drained out of me, and the drama of the last couple hours smothered me like fog. When the beers finally arrived, I barely had the energy to lift my glass.

"Maybe we're just wasting our time," I grumbled. "Maybe I was wrong. Maybe Dickie's murder and the dolls aren't even connected. Maybe—"

The detective we'd seen earlier out in the lobby walked into the bar, looked around, and spotted Nick. He bent over and said something close to Nick's ear.

"What?" I asked when the detective was gone. "What's going on?"

He took a sip of his beer. "What's going on is that it looks like you were on to something after all. They found another one of those rag dolls in Jarret's hotel room."

"Hah!" Suddenly, I wasn't so tired anymore. I toasted

myself with my glass and drank down half my beer. "So I was right. Jarret did conk me on the head and steal the dolls."

"That's not all." Nick finished his beer. "They found something else in Jarret's room, too. A jar of what looks to be the same poison that killed Dickie Dunkin."

CHAPTER 16

"So Dickie died because of a bunch of dolls?"

We were back at the Palace, and (big surprise) Sylvia had gone back to the RV to put up her feet and relax for a while. That left me and Nick to talk over everything that had happened at the hotel across the street.

After what the cop back there had told Nick, I knew the answer to my question about Dickie and the dolls, but that didn't keep a shiver from skipping over my shoulders. "That's just . . . Any murder is creepy, but being murdered because of a bunch of dolls . . ."

"Doll." Nick had volunteered to help restock shelves and he was holding a cardboard box full of small packages of dried peppers so I could set them out. "It was one doll," he said. "That's all the police found in Jarret's

room. I mean, besides the jar of what could be desic-
cated datura. Just one more of those rag dolls."

"Impossible." I finished with the dried African Bird's
Eye peppers and moved on to the Aji Amarillo and the
Aji Panca. From there I'd restock the Aleppo peppers,
the Anaheims, and the Anchos. Yes, it was Sylvia's idea
to arrange the peppers on the shelves in alphabetical
order. No, I was never going to tell her it was a good one,
even though it did make it easier to find what we were
looking for. There are some things that are better off left
unsaid between half sisters. "There was more than just
one doll in that trunk, Nick. Plenty more. Why would
Jarret have only one?"

When he shrugged, the box in Nick's hands bounced
up and down. "He hid them? He sold them? He packed
them up and had them shipped somewhere? The local
cops will find out. You can be sure of that."

"But just one doll . . ." I turned to Nick, bags of peppers pressed to my chest, their wonderful, spicy scent
tickling my nose. "Jarret told me that selling off the
dolls individually wouldn't be as profitable as selling
them as a collection."

"So maybe he sold them as a collection."

"Except for one."

"We could speculate forever. Jarret liked that particular
doll and wanted to keep it for himself. Or maybe he promised it to his favorite niece. What's even more likely is that
he had a buyer who wanted that doll specifically and
offered him some whopping amount for it. There are a

million different reasons he might have hung on to that one doll."

"And I know someone I can ask about it." I dumped the peppers in my arms back into the box they'd come out of and marched to the door. "Sylvia will be back in a couple minutes. Why don't you—"

Nick stepped in front of me, blocking my path.

"You're not going anywhere alone."

"Don't be goofy." I would have yanked away from the hand he put on my arm, but his grip was way too tight, and besides, having Nick hang on to me wasn't the worst experience I'd had since I got to Vegas. "I'm just going to see Reverend Love," I told him. "She has one of the dolls, so if anyone knows more about them, it will be her."

"And you remember what happened last time you went to see her, right?"

My smile should have told Nick that I could easily counter his objection. "Theoretically I didn't go to see her. I went to follow Tyler and find out why he was two-timing Sylvia, only he wasn't, but I didn't know that until I talked to him. And I just talked to Reverend Love as a sort of afterthought, you know, because she was one of the Devil's Breath judges and I figured I should talk to her as long as I was there. So technically—"

"Technically . . ." Nick grabbed the *Closed* sign and propped it in the window before he walked me outside and shut the door behind us. "You're not going any-where. Not without me."

The look I gave him was more simper than smile. "Even to a wedding chapel?"

Nick rolled his gorgeous baby blues. "Heaven help me, it's the one and only time I'd ever even think of it. Yes, to a wedding chapel, Maxie. You and me."

The last time I'd been to the Love Chapel, I'd waited in the reverend's office, but when Nick and I got there, there were pieces of scaffolding and piles of tarps stacked outside the office and the smell of fresh paint wafted from behind the closed doors.

"So . . ." We sat side by side on a bench next to neat mounds of paintbrushes and rollers, drop cloths and blue painter's tape, waiting for Reverend Love to finish what her secretary called the Deluxe Renaissance Hand-Clasping (complete with a horse-drawn carriage out front). With a guy like Nick, I knew better than to pry because it wasn't going to get me anywhere. Still, I couldn't help myself. There was something about the hushed atmosphere, something about all those yards and yards of plush carpeting at our feet and the mirrors that gleamed from the walls. There was something about the chapel, something that made a weird idea pop into my head.

Maybe it was the remnants of all the promise and possibilities the place had seen over the years that still echoed within its walls.

Or maybe, like the shingles virus that never leaves the body, the leftover vibes of weddings past stick around so that they can rear their ugly heads and leave the poor suckers who suffer from them miserable.

I gave Nick a look out of the corner of my eye. "Did you ever think about getting married?"

His sidelong glance was just as fleeting. "You?"

I had. To Edik. When he was the be-all and end-all of my universe. Which was all of the two years, three months, and four days we were together and did not—in any way, shape, or form—include the last two weeks of our so-called relationship when I found out what a cheatin', lyin' weasel he was.

"Nah." When I shuddered, I hoped Nick thought it was because the very idea of marriage gave me the heebie-jeebies rather than that even four months after our epic and very ugly breakup, reliving the Edik disaster still made me feel weak in the knees and sick to my stomach. "You?"

He didn't answer right away, and that didn't surprise me. Nick is not exactly Mr. Chatty. I guess that's why I was surprised to see his shoulders rise and fall. "I have thought about it," he said. "A time or two."

"But you've never—"

"Nah. Never the right time. Never the right person."

I sighed. "Amen to that."

"But if the right person came along—"

"Really?" My nose wrinkled, I turned on the bench to get a better look at Nick. "What about the Showdown?"

Whatever he'd expected, I guess it wasn't this, because Nick raised his chin. "You can't possibly think I'd make a crucial life decision based on—"

"What?" I was already on my feet and I glared down at him. "Based on what you think is some stupid little traveling show full of stupid people who care about stupid things like making sure the people who come to the show have a good time, and buy excellent products and can show off their cooking skills and—"

"Well, I'm guessing you two aren't my next bride and groom."

I twirled around when I heard Reverend Love behind me. The way my voice bounced against the mirrors that lined the hallway and my fists on my hips told her pretty much all she needed to know about Nick and my relationship.

When she looked from one of us to the other, the reverend's smile was sleek. "Since it's obviously not a wedding, what can I do for the two of you?"

"We're here about your doll," I told her before Nick could, even though he stood up to say something. "We want to see it."

For a moment, the reverend narrowed her eyes, then a smile broke through the confused expression. "The doll in my office! The one you saw the other day when you stopped by to talk to me."

"That's the one." Nick edged in front of me. "We were hoping you could tell us something about it."

The reverend folded her hands at her waist. "If you're interested in dolls, I hear there's a collectors' convention in town. There are probably plenty of dolls there you could buy, and probably plenty of people who know far more than I do about collecting and history and such."

"We don't care about that." I stepped to my left to angle myself in front of Nick. "We care about your doll. It might be tied to a—"

"We're interested in the doll's background," Nick butted in. "We saw one that was similar at the collectors' show and the guy who's selling it claims it's valuable, but he doesn't know much about the history of the doll. We wondered if it could possibly be worth what he's asking and thought you might be able to help."

"So you're looking to buy." Reverend Love's gaze slid from Nick to me and her smile froze. "How sweet."

He put a hand on my shoulder. "Anything for Maxie," he said, and honestly, the reverend would have had to be an idiot to miss the irony in his voice.

Maybe she was. Or maybe she, too, was so overwhelmed by the happily-ever-after sense of the place that, after all these years, she couldn't think straight.

I wasn't sure if it was the idea of doll collecting or the one about being in love that bothered me more; I only knew that even when I shivered, Nick didn't remove his hand.

"Like I told you . . ." Reverend Love checked the Rolex on her left wrist. "I have another wedding starting in just a couple minutes. Cavemen." The reverend laughed. "Who am I to question what paying customers want?" She looked my way. "Like I told you the other day, Maxie, the doll was given to me by my Aunt Louise. She made it especially for me for my tenth birthday."

"We don't think so." I kept talking, even though Nick squeezed my shoulder. "We think someone else made the doll."

The reverend's expression clouded. "But I've had it all these years and . . ." She shook her head. "Are you telling me that Aunt Louise lied to me about my doll?"

"That's what we're trying to figure out," Nick said.

She inched back her shoulders. "Well, I can't see why it matters to anyone but me. If there's another doll like it over at that doll convention, maybe the person who made it used the same pattern Louise did. Or maybe both Louise and this other person saw a similar doll somewhere, and both of them decided to make a copy of it. If you love the doll you saw at the show . . ." The reverend glanced from me to Nick. "If you're looking to make Maxie happy and the doll is important to her, that's all that matters, not where it came from or who made it. Why do you care about my doll?"

Before I could tell her, Nick squeezed again.

"If we could just see it," Nick suggested.

The reverend took another look at her watch before she offered us a smile. "I wish I could help you, but I am in something of a hurry. Besides, the doll is in storage along with everything else in my office. The painters will be done in a couple days. If you'd like to come back then, I'll be happy to show you the doll."

The reverend turned and walked toward a group of people in Flinstone-esque garb who'd just entered the chapel. Honestly, if I wasn't so busy considering everything she'd just said, I would have gone over and offered my opinion of the faux saber-toothed tiger print the bride wore.

"I bet she'd be happy to show us her doll," I grumbled

and turned toward the nearest exit. "Did you catch the vibes, Nick? It took everything she had not to tell us to get lost. She doesn't want us to see that doll."

"Convenient that she just happens to be painting," he said when we stepped outside.

"But why—"

"The reverend is a smart woman. She knows it's none of our business."

"But if she has nothing to hide—"

"It's still none of our business." Nick got his phone out of his pocket. "But it might be interesting to the local cops. I'll call the detective in charge of the case."

"And maybe . . ." We stepped to the front of the chapel and I looked up at where that red neon heart once dangled over the sidewalk. Chicken? Maybe I am. Or maybe I just have the brains not to want to go somewhere I've already gone before. Like back to the ER with a needle and thread going through my arm.

I crab-stepped to the side. "While you're at it, ask that detective if there's any way I can see the doll they found in Jarret's room."

Nick held up a finger to tell me to wait while he left a message. When he was done, he swiped a finger over the screen of his phone. "I don't need to ask. I took a picture," he told me. "When they invited me to see what they'd found. Here." He angled the phone so I could see the screen. "What do you think?"

What I thought was that the doll looked mighty familiar.

Well, sort of.

She had the same skinny stuffed arms and legs I'd seen on both Tout Sweet, Reverend Love's doll, and Honey Bunch, the doll for sale in George Jarret's booth, and her pink satin dress looked to be an exact duplicate of the one I'd seen on Tout Sweet.

Except . . .

I squinted for a better look, and when that didn't work, I grabbed Nick's phone and enlarged the picture on the screen.

The pink satin dress and black felt scarf on the doll from Jarret's room did look exactly like Tout Sweet's, but unlike that doll's brown hair, this doll had black hair, and hers wasn't styled in a bob like Tout Sweet's. The long felt strips of this doll's hair were braided into pigtails that hung over her shoulders.

"What?" I didn't realize my mouth had fallen open until Nick's voice brought me back to reality. "You look like you just saw a ghost."

"Not a ghost. No. Of course not. It's just that the doll looks similar to the one I saw in Reverend Love's office and . . ." Even if I wanted to, I couldn't say anything else. For one thing, my tongue was suddenly stuck to the roof of my mouth. And for another, well, if I told Nick I'd just had an idea about who killed Dickie Dunkin—and why—something told me he wouldn't believe me anyway.

Not without a little more proof.

CHAPTER 17

If there's one thing I've learned in the years I've traveled with the Showdown, it's that a lot of the people who walk through the turnstiles consider themselves experts.

There are chili experts, of course, who want nothing more than to tell you everything they know about what kind of meat to use, and why real chili can't possibly contain beans, and how they garnish their bowls of spicy goodness with everything from sour cream to avocado, chives to cheese.

Then there are spiciness experts who most of the time don't want to talk about peppers and how they can enhance the taste of a chili as much as they want to brag about how they can tolerate more Scoville Heat Units than just about anyone else on the planet.

There are also the bean experts (kidney or pinto? great northern or black?), tomato experts, and people who insist the only way to make a really good base for their chili is to add things like beer or beef broth or (I swear, this is true, I actually met a person in Nashville who claimed it was the only way to go) clam broth.

None of this may seem like the stuff detective work is made of, but trust me, the information was always there, swimming around in my head, part of my DNA, and because of that, I got to thinking. Thinking, I arrived back at the Showdown, told Nick I had something I needed to take care of, avoided the Palace and Sylvia, and hotfooted it right across the street.

See, if there are chili experts at chili cook-offs, it stands to reason that there are doll experts at doll conventions.

Doll experts.

Doll enthusiasts.

Doll fanciers.

And the obsessed.

Exactly what I was counting on.

It didn't take me long to find exactly the expert enthusiastic fancier I was looking for. It helped that within two minutes of sitting down next to Minnie Cranston, I also knew she was obsessed.

"They're all so lovely, aren't they?" Minnie was resting her doll-weary self on a bench along the far wall of the showroom, and when she looked around at the vendor booths and the dolls displayed in them, her eyes twinkled. She was a woman of eighty or so (one of the reasons I'd chosen her), and as we spoke, she pulled a bagel out of her purse along with a can of V8 juice.

"Lunch," Minnie said, giving me a smile and a wink. "If you're smart like me, you can avoid spending money in the hotel restaurants and save a ton. That gives you more to spend on dolls. Oh, how I love the dolls!" She glanced around again and poked her chin toward the opposite side of the showroom. "There's a Just Me over there that I'm dying to get my hands on. You know, one of those sweet German character dolls made by Armand Marseille. And over there"—she turned in her seat, the better to look in the other direction—"there's a two-and-a-half-inch-tall French bisque doll for sale at that booth over there. I swear, if I had an extra one hundred and forty-five dollars, I'd snap that one right up. But I've already spent five thousand on dolls this weekend."

When my mouth dropped open, Minnie poked me in the ribs with her elbow and wagged the bagel. "Hey, kid, why do you think I swipe my lunch from the free hotel breakfast buffet? Money is money, and I need every cent I have for more dolls."

"Dolls." I hoped my thin smile didn't betray the fact that just thinking about dolls gave me the creeps and being this close to so many of them made that feeling escalate way past the creepiness stage and all the way to the point where I felt as if I were about to crawl out of my skin. "That's what I wanted to talk to you about. See, I'm pretty new to collecting."

Chewing, Minnie slapped a hand against my knee. "You'll get the hang of it, kid," she promised me.

"But there's so much I have to learn. There's a doll over at George Jarret's booth." I didn't have to look that way to know there was no one manning the booth. As far as I knew, Jarret was still in police custody. The spotlights over his booth weren't turned on; his tables were covered with cloths. "She's called Honey Bunch and she's so cute. But he's asking seven-fifty, and I don't know, I think that's pretty pricey."

"Not if Honey Bunch is the only one of Noreen Pennybaker's dolls still around," Minnie informed me. "You know the story, don't you? That's part of the reason that doll is so valuable. Noreen, see, made a bunch of those dolls, back in the seventies."

A bunch.

I liked the sound of that, mostly because *a bunch* of the dolls is what I swore I saw right before I got tossed into that steamer trunk.

"Noreen's dolls were perfect little darlings," Minnie went on. "But the whole thing . . ." She shook her head. "Well, more's the pity. That whole situation was just awful, wasn't it?"

"That's what people are saying." They weren't, at least not to me, but Minnie didn't have to know that. "But nobody's giving me any details. The dolls are so adorable, so what's the story?"

Minnie scooted closer. She was as small and as thin as a chile de árbol and I couldn't help but wonder if she packed as much of a punch. "Went crazy, you know," Minnie said, leaning in close to share the confidence.

"Noreen, that is. She went crazy making all those dolls of hers."

I had to ask because, let's face it, it's one of those catchall sorts of things that people say when they really mean something else. "Like went crazy and made a whole lot of them? Or like went crazy really crazy, crazy in the head?"

Minnie nodded. "Like went crazy really crazy in the head. See, Noreen was a stay-at-home mom. She had two little boys."

"Lawrence and Dickie."

"Those might have been their names." Another nod. "Only it hardly matters, does it?"

It did. Desperately. But I didn't want to interrupt the story so I didn't bother to mention it.

"So Noreen, she answered one of those ads. You know, at the backs of magazines. Well . . ." She gave me a look. "Maybe you don't know. You kids, you don't read like we used to back in the day. You're always on those phones of yours. Or messing with your pads or pods or whatever you call them. But back then, we women had plenty of magazines to keep us busy. Not just *Good Housekeeping* or *Life* or things like that, but romance magazines and magazines full of true confessions. And every one of them had ads at the back. You know, for women who wanted to work and still stay home with the kids."

My own mom had always worked outside the home, as the Chili Chick, of course, but later, when I was a kid, she did ten-hour-a-day shifts behind the bar at a local tavern.

"Noreen had talent," Minnie went on. "If you've seen Honey Bunch, you know that. So naturally, her interests went toward the craft ads."

"Crafts as in . . .?"

"As in assembling crafts at home." Minnie already had enough wrinkles to cover an elephant, but when she frowned, a few dozen more furrowed into her cheeks and forehead. "Bet they don't do anything like that anymore, either. But it was a big business then. You paid some small amount of money, maybe two or three dollars, and the company, they sent you the materials to put together a craft that they'd turn around and sell. You know, like a flower arrangement or a balsawood airplane."

"Or a doll?"

"You got that right." Minnie finished one half of her bagel and brushed crumbs from her hands. "Trick is, what a lot of people didn't know was that some of these work-from-home craft companies were phony balonies. See, they'd get you to spend three dollars on supplies, you'd assemble the craft, and send it back to them. The idea was that then they'd pay you a percentage of what they sold it for. But what usually happened was that they'd say what you'd sent them wasn't good enough. That you didn't paint something carefully enough. Or that your stitching wasn't any good. Or that you left off parts."

"Even though that wasn't true."

"Some of the time, I bet it was. But most of the time, no. Most of the time, what they were doing was simply getting your three dollars for a bunch of materials that probably weren't worth a quarter all told. That was their business, see, preying on people who wanted to try to earn a couple extra bucks, taking their money, then telling them that their work wasn't up to snuff."

"Is that what they did to Noreen Pennybaker?"

"Never knew the woman myself, but yeah, that's what I hear. Most people, they're burned like that, and they maybe get mad. Or embarrassed. Heck, I'd be both if I found out I was played for a sucker like that."

"And Noreen?"

Minnie twirled one finger around her ear. "Like I said, crazy. And must have been to start. I think the craft thing pushed her over the edge. You see, she paid her money and got the materials to make dolls."

I sat up. "Like Honey Bunch!"

"Like Honey Bunch." Minnie's smile was bittersweet. "You can take one look at Honey Bunch and know that Noreen's work was top-notch. Her dolls were perfect, every single one of them. But when she finished that first one and sent it back to the company that commissioned it—"

"They told her it wasn't good enough and kept her three dollars."

"Most folks would have gotten the message right off the bat. Not Noreen! Instead of realizing that those craft company folks were out to get her money, she decided to try again. She sent them more money for more supplies and she made more dolls. And every time, they told her the dolls weren't good enough and they sent them right back to her. They didn't care about the dolls, see, they only cared about the three dollars."

"But Noreen kept making dolls." This was hard to imagine, even though Minnie's nod told me it was true.

"Not only that," the old woman went on, "but she went another whole step. She named each of the dolls she made, and embroidered her name and the doll's name inside its slip. And when even that wasn't enough to impress those crooks at the craft company, Noreen started writing little stories to go with each of her dolls. She even drew the pictures in every little storybook. The more dolls she made and the more stories she wrote and the more the company took more and more of her money for supplies, then told her that her work wasn't good enough . . . well, from what I've heard, that was when Noreen really went off the deep end. Those dolls were like children to her. It's sad, isn't it? Imagine how her little sons must have suffered, what with their mother not caring about anyone or anything except those dolls. I've heard tell she had a house full of them and knew every single one of their names and stories. She ended up losing every penny she ever had, too, because she just kept buying more and more supplies so she could keep making the dolls."

I wrapped my arms around myself. "That's awful."

"It is, especially when eventually Noreen realized she had nothing left except those dolls. I hear tell that's when she went to bed one day and just never got out again. Died of a broken heart, surrounded by her dolls."

The very thought made me sick, but I told myself I

could wallow in my sympathy for Noreen another time. For now, I had more important things to worry about.

"Let me guess," I said to Minnie. "That craft company that took all of Noreen's money, it was run by a woman named Louise, right?"

"Louise?" Minnie's lips thinned. "Well, I'm not as young as I used to be and I can't say I remember everything like I did back in the day. But Louise? No. That's not the name I heard."

By the time I'd wrapped up my work at the Palace the next day and got to the auditorium, it was already chockfull of nervous couples waiting for their big moment.

Couples dressed as knights and ladies.

Couples wearing jeans and T-shirts.

Couples in vampire costumes, and couples in bathing suits, and even a few couples (obviously old-fashioned and with little imagination) wearing tuxes and white wedding gowns.

Ah, yes, it was time for Reverend Love to officiate at the largest mass wedding ceremony ever performed in Nevada at a Western-themed hotel on a Sunday afternoon.

When I saw Yancy up onstage, I waved. I was sure he saw me. I was also sure he couldn't let on so I wasn't surprised when he didn't wave back.

I squeezed between a man dressed in a weird seaweedy-looking toga and the mermaid who would soon be his missus and scurried over to the stage. "You won the contest to sell the most tickets!" I said, and I gave Yancy a quick hug. Truth be told, I wished he hadn't, but I couldn't tell him that. Something told me that before the end of the afternoon, he was going to wish he wasn't up onstage. "I knew you would. You're the only one around here with real talent."

He was dressed in a dapper gray suit and he wore a fedora with a little red feather in the band. Yancy tipped his hat to me. "I appreciate the compliment. Only now that I'm here . . ." Behind his dark glasses, I saw him glance left and right. "When are we going to get started?"

"Soon." As if he really couldn't see me, I gave his arm a squeeze before I walked away. "As soon as Reverend Love gets here."

Reverend Love, and a few other very special guests I'd made sure had been invited.

Since that was another thing Yancy couldn't know about, I kept my mouth shut, stepped into the wings, and watched and waited.

A few minutes later, the lights in the auditorium flickered to get everyone's attention and a hum of anticipation buzzed through the crowd. When the lights came up again, Creosote Cal himself stepped to the center of the stage.

"Ladies and gentlemen!" Cal glanced around at the crowd and grinned. "Brides and grooms!"

A cheer went up and Cal had to hold out his hands, palms down, to get the crowd to quiet.

"We got us somethin' here that's goin' to put all of us in the record books," Cal said.

Another cheer erupted and he waited.

"Today, you're all going to be part of Las Vegas history. Today . . ." Cal shot a grin around the room. "You are all going to be newlyweds!"

This time, the cheering lasted a minute or two, and by the time it died down, Linda Love stood center stage right next to Yancy. That afternoon, she looked like she belonged in the record books: steel gray suit, pearls at her throat, a sprinkling of white lace on the neckline of the cami that peeked from her jacket. Reverend Love was ready for her close-up, that was for sure, and when the photographer I'd seen in the bar the other night, the one from the *Review-Journal*, stepped forward, Reverend Love put an arm around Yancy's shoulders and told him to smile.

The moment captured for posterity, she stepped forward and glanced around the crowd. "Hold hands," she said, and when all those brides and all those grooms didn't pick up on the command fast enough, she motioned. "Hold hands," she said again, and couple by couple, the lords and ladies and clowns and vampires clung to one another and stepped closer together.

"Dearly beloved," the reverend said, and a hush fell over the crowd.

Ask Sylvia, there's nothing I like better than disrupting a little bit o' quiet.

I looked across the stage to where Nick waited in the wings opposite from where I stood, and on his nod, I stepped out onstage and strolled up to the reverend.

She was so intent on studying the crowd, a half smile lighting her face and reflecting back all that dewy-eyed pathetic emotion coming from the audience, it took a moment for her to notice me.

When she did, Reverend Love froze. For like half a second. Then she smiled. "Maxie, you've changed your mind! I'm so glad. You do have someone special and you've decided to tie the knot today!"

Across the stage, Nick stepped out of his place in the wings.

"I knew it." Reverend Love waved a finger, then looked from me and Nick to the audience. "These two pretend that they're not really fond of each other, but I knew it. I knew he'd be the one. Join me," she said and clapped, then raised her voice when the audience applauded, too. "Join me in congratulating them for recognizing the power of real love."

Nick's cheeks got red.

Me? I think I held it together pretty well considering what I really wanted to do was toss my hands in the air and tell these people they were so far off base, they weren't even in the ballpark.

Finally, the noise died down and Reverend Love grabbed Nick, who was standing on her left, and dragged him over to where I stood on her right.

"You can pretend all you want," she said, plopping Nick's hand in mine, "but it's hard to hide that look of love that passes between you."

"That's not all it's hard to hide," I told her.

And I guess for a second, she didn't know what I was talking about, not even when the detective in charge of

Dickie's murder investigation strolled out onstage with three burly uniformed cops.

Reverend Love's smile never wavered. "Well, I can't imagine you officers are here to get married. Unless . . ." She put a hand up to her eyes and scanned the audience. "Are there brides out there waiting for their handsome grooms?" she called.

No one answered.

The audience stirred with anticipation and a low grumble, like thunder, curled through the crowd.

"Give us a minute," I told all those brides and grooms before I turned back to Reverend Love. "We've got a couple things we need to clear up."

"Like . . .?" she wanted to know.

Thank goodness the Las Vegas cops were willing to play along. When I signaled, a cop stepped forward with an evidence bag.

"My doll!" the reverend crooned with a look at the rag doll inside the bag. Then she frowned. "No, it's not my doll. The dress is similar but the hair—"

"Yeah, the hair is different." The cop handed me the evidence bag so I could show it to Reverend Love. "This doll has black braids, and your doll, Tout Sweet, had a brown bob. That's pretty much why I didn't think anything of it the first time I saw the picture of the doll the cops took out of George Jarret's hotel room."

"Jarret!" The reverend's top lip curled. "How that man could have been so cruel and so awful! He's a murderer."

"Or not," Nick commented.

She turned to him. "Are you saying—"

"What Nick's saying," I interrupted, "is that you almost pulled it off. You almost convinced everyone that Jarret was guilty. But there's this doll." I lifted the bag so that the audience could see it, too. "See, every one of Noreen Pennybaker's dolls has a name and a story," I told them and reminded the reverend. "So this doll with the black braids should have had her own dress and her own name. But when I asked the cops to check, they confirmed what I suspected. This isn't Tout Sweet, but she's wearing Tout Sweet's dress. See." Actually, it was kind of hard, but I tipped the bag anyway, to give the reverend a look. "That's Noreen Pennybaker's signature embroidered in baby blue inside the dress. Right above the doll's name. Tout Sweet. But this . . ." I ran a finger across the bag and the doll's dark braids. "This isn't Tout Sweet. That's because you pulled the ol' switcheroo."

The reverend clasped her hands at her waist. "I don't know what you're talking about."

"Science is a wonderful thing," Nick told her, and that was okay with me; we'd already talked about this part of our little reveal and figured that if I started spouting off about forensics, nobody was going to believe it. "After Maxie presented her theory to the local police, they did a little testing and realized there was ash residue on the dress of the doll they found in George Jarret's room. That's not all they found. I won't muddy the waters with all the scientific evidence," he told the reverend and the audience. "We'll leave that for the trial.

Let's just say that there are places in the desert outside of town that have unique soil structures. The cops found that, too. Some of that unique soil. And they knew exactly where to look for it. That's when they went out to the middle of nowhere and found the charred remains of the dolls you burned."

"Me?" The reverend might have been more convincing if her voice didn't crack. "How could you possibly think that it was me?"

"Because you're the one who owns Tout Sweet," I told her. It was a no-brainer, and she should have figured it out herself, but hey, maybe she was playing dumb in the hopes of covering her reverendly ass. "See, here's the way I think it went down. You followed me the night I found all those dolls in that old trunk of Dickie's. But then," I added quickly when it looked like she was going to butt in, "that's not a surprise. You'd been following me for a while, ever since that evening I stopped at the chapel and asked if Dickie was blackmailing you. That's when you figured out that I was onto something even though . . ." I had to point it out, just to get to her. "At that point, I really wasn't. So you see, rigging that neon heart to come down and whack me really was way overboard."

She sucked in her bottom lip. "I don't know what you're talking about."

"What I am talking about are Dickie's dolls. Which were really Noreen's dolls, of course, but Dickie got them all after his mother died, and when he moved out of his apartment, he brought them over to Cal's storeroom. And that's where you followed me that night and that's when you realized you had to get rid of those dolls. That's why you conked me on the head and took them, and when you did, the cops here tell me you took them out to the desert and lit a bonfire."

The reverend stood as still as if she'd been made of stone, but that didn't stop me. I had plenty to say and, for once, the platform to say it. "That's probably when it hit you," I told Linda Love. "You could use one of the dolls and plant it as evidence. You'd seen me talking to George Jarret so he was probably the first sucker who popped into your head. He was a doll collector and a doll dealer. It would make sense that he might kill Dickie to get those dolls. But by the time you thought of all that . . ."

I put a hand to my chin. Not for any particular reason except that I'd seen detectives on TV do stuff like that, and hey, it did draw out the moment, and the drama.

"By that time, that bonfire was blazing and all those precious dolls of Noreen's were roasting like marshmallows. What did you do, pull out one of them near the edge of the fire? That would have been this one." I held up the bag. "The one with the dark braids. But her dress was ruined, right? And the cops were sure to question it if you put a doll with a burned dress in Jarret's room. So you saved the doll body and switched her dress with Tout Sweet's. You didn't imagine that anyone would know the difference because you never thought that the doll you pulled from the fire would bring along a little ash and a little soil with her. What you didn't know is that evening I was at the chapel, I got a good look at Tout Sweet. I saw the name inside her dress. That's how I knew this doll wasn't on the up-and-up."

"Charming theory." The reverend's top lip curled. "But why would I want to waste my time killing a nobody like Dickie Dunkin? And how did I do it anyway?" She glanced around the stage, the site of the Devil's Breath contest and of Dickie's way-too-ugly demise.

"Nick tells me datura, the poison you used, is easy to come by," I told her. I think that was about the same time I realized I was still hanging on to Nick's hand. I untangled my fingers from his, shook out my hand, and went on. "It grows in empty lots all over Vegas, and with the downturn in the economy, there's not nearly as much building around here these days as there used to be. It would be easy to pick some of the plants, dry them, and keep a baggie of the powder around, maybe in your purse or in your pocket. I'll bet the morning of the Devil's Breath contest you had some with you just waiting for the perfect moment to slip some to Dickie. You couldn't have possibly known that he and Osborn were going to play right into your plan. That hassle they had with each other? They had that whole thing down pat. They did it to get attention. What it also did was provide you the perfect opportunity to slip some poison into the bowls the judges would use. Once Nick jumped in and stopped the tussle, you put those bowls next to Dickie's seat. Tumbleweed . . ." He was standing in the wings and I smiled his way. Believe me, I'd already told him what I was going to say and he knew nobody was going to blame him, but I knew he felt lousy about the whole thing anyway.

"Tumbleweed grabbed the bowl and the contestant filled it with Devil's Breath and the poison did its work."

"Ingenious," the reverend purred. "And so ridiculous, I can't even begin to tell you how wrong you are."

Honestly, I didn't want to hear it, and to prove it, I turned to all those brides and grooms, who were now staring, wide-eyed and slack-jawed, at the stage. "See, Dickie," I told them, "was not only a lousy comedian, he was a blackmailer. Don't pretend it's not true." I tossed the comment over my shoulder to the reverend. "A couple other people, I won't say who . . ." And I refused to look in Yancy's direction and tip anybody off. "A couple other people have already given the cops their statements. They were being blackmailed by Dickie. And that's what he was going to do to you, too." I turned back to the reverend. "He found out. That you used to work here at Creosote Cal's. That you were one of those slick types who guess people's weight and age and pull it all off and make it look like magic. And that made Dickie think exactly what it made me think. You, Reverend Love, can be a very tricky person."

"What my background has to do with all this . . ." She spun toward the wings then changed her mind when she saw the phalanx of cops waiting there. The reverend raised her chin. "Dickie Dunkin was not blackmailing me."

"But he sure was thinking about it, wasn't he, Reverend? You doll!" I gestured toward the reverend and looked at the audience. "She's a doll, isn't she, folks? That Reverend Love, she's a real doll!"

"You sound like that ridiculous Dickie," she snorted. "The man was so stupid, he—"

"Not so stupid that he couldn't figure out about the dolls," Nick put in. He reached into the inside pocket of his suit jacket, pulled out a folded piece of paper, and flapped it open. "Linda Green," he read from the paper, "once indicted in Nebraska for running a work-at-home craft scheme." He looked over the paper at the reverend, whose face was now the same color as her suit. "You took their money, all those women who wanted to work out of their homes. You took their money and then you told them their work wasn't good enough."

"And that sent Dickie's mother over the edge." I don't think I needed to remind her, but I did anyway. With scumbags, it's always a little fun to rub it in. "She went crazy because of you. And when Dickie figured out the connection, he wanted you to pay up or he wasn't going to shut up."

"It wasn't the money!" Reverend Love stomped a foot and her voice ricocheted against the ceiling. "I didn't care about the money. But if he told anyone, if he ruined my reputation and my business . . ." I don't think she realized her hands had curled into fists until she glanced down at them, and by that time, it was already too late. There was a cop stationed on either side of the reverend, ready to escort her away.

We had lots of disappointed brides and grooms on our hands, and I guess from the point of view of true love, happily ever after, and all that other fairy tale crap, that was sad. The good news was that while some of those eager-to-be-happy couples hurried right out to find a wedding chapel to accommodate their ready-to-be-married mood, others rolled with the punches and stuck around Deadeye. The Showdown would be leaving Vegas the next morning so it was fine with me if those folks wanted to fill the Palace, to talk and to buy. The more they took away from our shelves, the less I had to pack.

"I can't believe it," Sylvia said in response to the rundown Nick and I gave her of everything that happened in the auditorium.

"It is a little disheartening," Nick mentioned. "What with her being a reverend and all. You'd think someone like that would have better ethics."

"It's not that." Sylvia shook her head. "I don't believe . . ." Her wide blue eyes swiveled my way. "Maxie, you were actually smart enough to figure it out?"

Unfortunately, two vampires, a nun and a priest, and two astronauts walked in, and I promised myself I'd set Sylvia straight later.

Those customers were just the beginning of a little mini-rush, and for the next half hour or so, Sylvia and I helped with everything from choosing spices to explaining that the myth about how eating peppers protects against poisons wasn't true. Ask Dickie. When we were done, the cash register was a little fuller (hurray!) and I was whooped. Crime fighting is hard work, and eager to relax, I scurried over to the red velvet fainting couch.

That was where I found the Chick!

"The Chick is back! The Chick is back!" Suddenly, I wasn't so tired anymore. I scooped the costume into my arms and danced around the Palace with it. Right when I kick-stepped my way to the front counter like a Rockette, Sylvia darted from behind the cash register.

"It's about time!" She yanked the costume out of my hands. "I was beginning to get really worried."

Sure, it was great that Sylvia was as excited as I was to see the Chick again, but it was also a little surreal. In all our years on the road with the Showdown, she'd never once volunteered to dance as the Chick, not even that summer back in Minneapolis when I had the chicken pox. Now she held up the costume and spun around, her eyes gleaming.

Weird.

I guess the look I shot at Nick told him what I was thinking, because he gave me a shrug.

My surprise turned to astonishment when Sylvia stepped into the costume and tugged it so that it covered her head.

"Really, Maxie." Her voice was muffled from inside the Chick. "It's a good thing those people in the costume department gave this thing a good cleaning." I heard a grunt and the Chick twitched. Sylvia's arms disappeared into the body of the costume. Another grunt, a funny half turn, and Sylvia popped the costume off and let it slide to the ground. Her nose was wrinkled when she said, "It smells like chili powder in there."

"Yeah, it's one of the reasons I love it so much and—" As if they'd been sliced by an experienced chef, my words were cut in half.

But then, that's when I saw that Sylvia was holding a folded piece of paper torn from a spiral-bound notebook.

My stomach bounced into my throat, then plummeted again and landed with a thump.

"Jack's recipe!" I darted forward, but it's not for nothing that Sylvia exists on seaweed and tofu. Turns out eating healthy foods makes her pretty darned fast.

She tucked the recipe behind her back and scooted out of my reach. "It was the one place I knew you'd never look for it," she crooned. "So who's the smart one now, Maxie?"

Fortunately, she didn't give me a chance to answer. Grinning, Sylvia slipped out of the Palace, Jack's secret recipe for the greatest chili in the world clutched in her hot little hand.

"Your mouth is open."

I'm not sure how long I'd stood there stunned before Nick came over and put a hand on my shoulder.

"She didn't," I stuttered. "She c-couldn't."

He gave me a friendly pat. "You'll get it back."

"I'll wring that perfect little neck of hers."

Since I'd already started for the door, I guess he was

justified in slipping an arm around my shoulders. "We've already had one murder here this weekend," he reminded me. "Let's not have another one."

"All right. Okay." I shook off his arm. "I'm fine. I'm not going to kill her. Promise." I looked up at Nick and grinned. "At least not until we leave Vegas."

I guess he thought I was kidding, because Nick smiled, too.

"Sorry to interrupt!"

The voice came from the doorway, and we both spun that way and saw Bernadette poke her head into the Palace. She glanced at where the Chick lay on the floor. "We're good?" she asked.

I grabbed the costume and held it to my chest. "We're good. Thanks for taking care of her."

Like it was no big deal, Bernadette waved a hand. Even so, I didn't fail to catch the look she gave the Chick. Or the fact that her eyes misted over.

"I'm going to . . ." She poked a thumb over her shoulder. "I've got to be at work in an hour, and I really need to get going."

"Except . . ." I moved forward, my arms extended. "I was kind of wondering if maybe you had a few minutes to help me out."

"This is going to completely ruin your reputation."

I ignored the tiny shiver that scooted over my shoulders and down my arms when Nick purred in my ear, and gave him a sidelong glance to prove it.

"Only if you tell."

He crossed his heart with one finger. "Your secret is safe with me."

"And if anybody asks?"

Like me, he looked out the window of the bordello to the dusty main street of Deadeye. "I'll swear I don't know a thing."

"Good enough for me," I told him.

"Really?" He pursed his lips and crossed his arms over his chest, and side by side, we watched the Chili Chick do her dance routine outside the Palace, and I'll admit it, she was plenty good. The taps, the swishes, the graceful movement of arms and legs. Honestly, I could see why Jack had fallen under her spell all those years before.

Maybe I was imagining it, I mean what with the mesh front on the costume that made it hard to see inside, I really couldn't be sure, but I swear, when the Chick whirled and looked in my direction, I saw Bernadette smile. She knew what I knew: I couldn't give her Jack. Not here, not now. But for these few moments, she could be the Chili Chick again.

TOO CHICKEN FOR DEVIL'S BREATH?

Not everyone loves hot chili as much as Maxie does. If you're looking for something kinder and gentler, give this chicken chili a try. It's especially good topped with fresh avocado, sour cream, and a sprinkling of cheddar cheese.

½ pound bacon, cut into small pieces
5 medium yellow onions, chopped
1 bulb garlic, chopped
½ bunch celery, sliced
1 red, 1 yellow, 1 orange, 1 green pepper, all diced
3 medium to hot yellow Hungarian peppers, chopped
1 (4.5-ounce) can chopped green chilies
2 (28-ounce) cans whole tomatoes, chopped
5 pounds boneless, skinless chicken breasts, cubed
salt and white pepper to taste
optional spices: garlic salt, shallot salt, and poultry
    seasoning

Fry up the bacon and drain on paper towels. Sauté the onions in the bacon grease. Add the chopped garlic to the onion and let the onion-garlic mixture cool.

Transfer to a large soup pot. Add the celery, peppers, green chilies, and tomatoes.

In the original frying pan, brown the chicken cubes in a little of the bacon grease. Transfer the chicken to the soup pot. Add salt to taste. Sprinkle in white pepper.

Taste and add other spices of your liking, including garlic salt, shallot salt, and poultry seasoning.

Simmer, uncovered, for about an hour.

Turn the page for a preview of the new
League of Literary Ladies Mystery . . .

THE LEGEND OF SLEEPY HARLOW

Coming soon from
Berkley Prime Crime!

I wish I could say that the worst thing that happened that fall was Jerry Garcia peeing on Marianne Little-john's manuscript.

Jerry Garcia? He's the cat next door, the one whose bathroom habits have always been questionable and whose attention is perpetually trained on the potted flowers on my front porch.

Except that afternoon, that is.

That day, Jerry bypassed the flowers and went straight for the wicker couch on the porch, the one on which—until the phone rang inside the B and B—I'd been read-ing Marianne's manuscript because she wanted one more set of eyes to take a look at it before she sent it off to the small academic press that specializes in local history.

Yeah, that was the couch where I'd left the pages neatly stacked and—this is vital to the telling of the story—completely dry and odor-free.

Jerry, see, had motive, means, and opportunity.

Jerry had mayhem in his kitty cat heart and at the risk of sounding just the teeniest bit paranoid, I was pretty sure Jerry had it out for me, too.

It was the perfect storm of circumstance and timing, and the results were so predictable that I shouldn't have walked back out onto the porch, taken one look at the puddle quickly soaking through Marianne's tidy manuscript pages and stood, pikestaffed, with my mouth hanging open.

Jerry, it should be pointed out, could not have cared less. In fact, I think he enjoyed watching my jaw flap in the breeze that blew from Lake Erie across the street. But then, Jerry's that kind of cat. He leapt onto the porch railing, paused to give one paw a lick, and looked over his shoulder at me with what I would call disdain if I weren't convinced it was more devious than that.

A second later, he bounded into the yard and disappeared, leaving me to watch in horror as the liquid disaster spread. From the manuscript to the purple and turquoise floral print cushions. From the cushions to the wicker couch. From the couch to the porch floor.

Oh yes, at the time, it did seem like the worst of all possible disasters.

But then, that was my first October on South Bass Island and I had yet to hear about the legend.

Or the ghost.

And there was no way I could have imagined the murder.

"Visit from Jerry?"

I didn't realize Luella Zak had walked up the steps and onto the porch until I heard her behind me. I shrieked and spun around just in time to see her eye the smelly disaster.

"I was only gone two minutes," I wailed. "I swear. It was only two minutes."

"And Jerry managed to stop by." Luella is captain of a fishing charter service that works out of Put-in-Bay, the one and only town on South Bass Island. She's short, wiry, and as crusty an old thing (don't tell her I said that about the "old") as any sailor who plied any of the Great Lakes, but when she stepped nearer to have a look at the mess, she wrinkled her nose.

"I hope those papers were nothing you planned on keeping," Luella said.

The reality of the situation dawned with all the subtlety of a dump truck *bumpety-bump*ing over railroad tracks, and I shook out of my daze and darted to the couch. Before I even thought about what it would do to my green sweatshirt and my jeans, I scooped up the pile of yellow-stained pages and shook them out.

"It's Marianne's manuscript," I groaned. "Marianne asked me to look for typos and—"

Luella didn't say a word. In fact, she ducked into the house and a minute later, she was back with a garbage bag in hand.

"We can't." Cat pee dripped off my hands and rained onto my sneakers, but still, I refused to relinquish the soggy manuscript. "We can't throw it away. I promised Marianne—"

Careful to keep it from dripping on her Carhartt bib overalls, Luella snatched the bundle away from me and deposited it in the bag. "Marianne can reprint it."

"But if I tell her to do that, I'll have to explain—"

"So what, you're going to take this back to her?" Luella hefted the garbage bag. "And you think she won't notice the stains? Or the smell?"

My shoulders drooped. "I think I need to find a way to tell her I'm really, really sorry."

"I think . . ." Luella thought about clapping a hand to my shoulder, and I could tell when she changed her mind because she made a face and backed away. But then, I was standing downwind. "I hate to tell you this, Bea, but I think that you smell really bad."

I didn't doubt it for a minute, but really, there were more important things to consider. "Poor Marianne. All that work and all that paper and now she'll need to do it all over again. Printing out an entire book takes a lot of time."

"Marianne wrote a book?" The instant I looked her way, Luella was contrite. "Oh, it's not like I'm doubting how smart she is or anything. She's a good librarian. But Marianne doesn't exactly strike me as the type who'd have enough imagination to write a book."

"It's history. Island history. I didn't get more than a couple pages into it, but I know it's about some old-timer, Charles Harlow."

"Sleepy!" Luella laughed. "Well, that explains it. Word is that Marianne's family is distantly related. I'd bet a dime to a donut she devotes at least one chapter to trying to disprove that. Sleepy has quite a reputation around here, and it's not exactly politically correct for the wife of the town magistrate to be related to an old-time gangster and bootlegger."

"I dunno." My shoulders rose and fell. "I mean about the gangster part. I never got that far. I'd just started reading and then the phone rang and then—"

"Jerry." Luella shook her head. "Chandra really needs to do something about that cat."

"I've been saying that for nearly a year."

"We'll talk to Chandra," Luella promised. "Next Monday at book discussion group. And as far as Marianne, maybe if you just explain what Jerry did—"

I dreaded the thought. "She's so proud of her book. You should have seen her when she brought the manuscript over here. She was just about bursting at the seams." My stomach swooped. "She asked for one little favor and I messed up."

"Not the end of the world. She'll reprint, you'll reread—"

"Inside the house."

"Inside the house. And then—"

And then three black SUVs slowed in front of the house and, one by one, turned into my driveway.

"You've got guests coming in today?" Luella asked.

I did, a full house, and what with the manuscript disaster and fantasizing about the ingenious (and completely untraceable) demise of a certain feline neighbor, I'd forgotten all about them.

"Go!" Luella shooed me into the house. "You go change. And a quick shower wouldn't hurt, either. I'll let your guests in and get them settled and tell them you'll be with them pronto."

Okay, so it wasn't exactly pronto, but I did manage what I hoped was a less smelly transformation in record time. When I was done, curly, dark hair damp and in a clean pair of jeans and a yellow long-sleeved top (dang, I didn't even make the Jerry Garcia and yellow connection until it was too late!), I lifted my chin, pasted a smile on my face, and strode into my parlor.

Straight into what looked like the staging for D-Day.

Two women, two guys. Another . . . I glanced out the window and counted the men on my front porch. Another four out there. Each one of them carried at least two duffel bags or a suitcase or a camera of some sort, and each one of those was plastered with bumper sticker–variety labels. Black, emblazoned with icy blue letters: *EGG*.

"Welcome!" I tried for my best innkeeper smile and thanked whatever lucky stars had made it possible for Luella to take a few moments and swab down the front porch; through the window, I saw that the floral cushions were missing from the couch and the water she'd splashed on the porch floor gleamed in the autumn afternoon sunshine. "I'm Bea, your hostess. You must be—"

"EGG." The woman closest to where I stood in the doorway was at least a half dozen years older than my thirty-four, and taller than me by six inches. She was square-jawed, dark-haired, pear-shaped, and more than equipped for whatever situation might present itself. The pockets of her camouflage pants bulged and the vest she wore over a black EGG T-shirt was one of those that fishermen sometimes sport. It had a dozen little pockets and I saw batteries, flashdrives, and other assorted gear peeking out of each one.

"Noreen Turner. I'm lead investigator for EGG, the Elkhart Ghost Getters." When Noreen pumped my hand, it felt as if my fingers had been gripped by a vise. Her dark gaze stayed steady on mine in a firm—and sort of disquieting—way. "I'm the leader of this jolly little band and—" She must have had first-class peripheral vision because though I hadn't even noticed the activity going on over in the direction of the fireplace, Noreen didn't miss a thing.

She whirled toward a young, redheaded woman and a muscle jumped at the base of Noreen's jaw.

"Thermal camera, full-spectrum camera, Mel meter, IR light." Noreen's laser gaze flashed from the redhead to the cases of equipment she was busy stacking. "Really, Fiona? Really?"

Fiona's cheeks shot through with color. She chewed her lower lip. "I thought . . ."

"Exactly your problem." Noreen marched over, unstacked the equipment, and, fists on hips, gave it all a careful look. "Thermal camera on the bottom," she said, setting that case down on the floor first. "Then the Mel meter on top of that." The case with the thermal camera in it was larger than the one that contained the Mel meter, and she set the second case on top of the first, adjusting and readjusting so that the second case was exactly in the center. "Then full spectrum, then IR light." She positioned those cases until they were just right, too, and, finished, turned her full attention on Fiona who held her breath and looked as if she was about to burst into tears. "You see what I'm getting at here, don't you?"

Fiona didn't answer fast enough, and Noreen lifted her chin and took a step toward her. "Don't you? Top to bottom, kid. Top to bottom. IR on top, then full spectrum, then Mel, then—"

The oldest of the men in the room (I'd learn later that his name was Rick) was maybe fifty, a reed-thin guy with a receding hairline and a gold stud in his right earlobe. He stood closest to Fiona and he leaned in like he wanted to share a confidence, but since he didn't lower his voice, whatever he had to say wasn't much of a secret. "She wants it alphabetical," he rasped. "She always has to have equipment stacked alphabetically."

"So it's easy to find what we need," Noreen snapped.

"Whatever." The man waved a hand and turned his back on us to look out the window.

"Well, it makes sense. And it's the right way to do things. You can see that, can't you?" She swiveled her gaze to me. "You're a businesswoman. You can see the sense of it."

Fortunately, I didn't have a chance to answer. One of the men who'd been on the front porch came into the house pushing a two-wheeler with a big rectangular box on it. He parked the two-wheeler in the hallway before he joined us in the parlor. The man was about my age, with black wavy hair and the kind of a face generally reserved for statues of Greek gods. Dimpled chin, straight nose, high cheekbones. A picture flashed through my mind: Mediterranean island, whitewashed cottage, aquamarine water. A loaf of bread, a jug of wine, and—

"I didn't ask you to bring that in."

Noreen's growl yanked me back to reality and I found her glaring at Mr. Greek God. "We're not ready for it," she said and pointed toward the box that was maybe three feet high and another couple feet wide. Like the rest of the gear, it was plastered with EGG stickers. "I told you to leave it in the truck, Dimitri. That means . . . well, duh, I dunno. I guess it means you should have left it in the truck."

"You said you wanted it in your room with you," the man sucked in a breath and shot back. "And that means—"

"What it means is that you're not listening. When I'm ready for it, that's when I'll tell you to bring it in."

"In like what, ten minutes?" Dimitri ran a hand through his mane of glorious hair. "I'll tell you what, Noreen, you want it back in the truck, you take it back to the truck. I'm not moving it another inch. Not now, not ten minutes from now. I'm not stacking anything alphabetically, either, or measuring stuff to make sure it's precisely two inches apart. You want to waste your time with your crazy organizing—"

"It's not a waste of time, it's a system." Noreen held her arms close to her sides, her fingers curled into fists. "And so far, it's worked pretty well, hasn't it? If it wasn't for me—"

Was that a collective groan I heard?

From everyone but Fiona, who was so ashen I had no doubt she wanted to fade into the woodwork.

And Noreen, of course. With a look, Noreen dared them all to say another word.

We'd been introduced like three minutes earlier and already, I knew Noreen wasn't the type of person who backed down from anyone. Or anything.

Fine by me. I wasn't, either.

And it was about time I proved it.

"I've got all your rooms set and your room keys ready," I said, deftly sidestepping their bickering. I darted into the hallway and grabbed the keys I'd left on a table at the bottom of the stairs. "Each one's marked," I said, handing them around. "All the rooms are on the second floor."

I'd received room instructions along with the group's reservations and I knew that the only two guys bunking together were Ben and Jerry (honest!). Since I had six guest rooms, that meant Noreen and Dimitri each had their own room as well as the other three men who, according to their reservation forms, were Liam McCarthy, David Ashton, and Rick Hopkins.

"I know. That leaves me with no room." Fiona watched

as the others stacked their equipment cases (alphabetically, I presumed) and headed upstairs. She scraped her palms against her jeans. "Noreen . . ." Her gaze darted across the room to where Noreen was doing another once-over of the equipment and checking off a list on a clipboard. "Noreen told me I wouldn't be staying here. That there aren't enough rooms. You don't have to apologize."

"I wasn't going to." I softened the statement with a smile and would have gotten one back if Fiona's gaze didn't shoot Noreen's way again.

"It's not like I didn't know you were coming," I told the kid. "Ms. Turner told me you'd need a room. I've got everything arranged."

Fiona squinched up her nose in a way that told me that whatever I was going to say, she had heard it all before. "I know, some little no-tell motel on the other side of the island. That's fine, really. I'm used to it. It's not always possible for me to stay with the rest of the crew. I get it." Her gaze landed on Noreen who was so busy restacking the equipment the others had just stacked, she didn't notice. "I just joined the group and I'm only the intern and I don't rate the same perks the rest of the crew gets."

"Which doesn't mean you shouldn't be comfortable." I waved a hand, directing Fiona to look out the window. "That's why I was able to arrange a room for you next door, at my friend Chandra's house."

"Right next door?" Some of the stiffness went out of Fiona's shoulders.

"And you'll be joining us here every morning," I told

Fiona, loud enough to make sure Noreen heard. After all, Noreen had made the original reservations and agreed (begrudgingly, as I remember) to pay an extra small charge for Fiona's breakfasts. "Breakfast is every morning at nine, and we've got coffee and tea available all day, too, and cookies in the afternoon. Anything you want, just stop in."

Fiona would never be described as pretty, but when she smiled, she was cute. She was taller than me (most people are) and in her early twenties, a gangly kid with wide blue eyes that were set a little too close together and a sprinkling of freckles on her nose that made her look as if she'd been dusted with cinnamon sugar. Her hair was a wonderful dark mahogany color that I suspected wasn't natural, and she wore it pulled back in a ponytail. Like the rest of the crew, she was dressed casually in jeans and an EGG T-shirt, but she'd added a filmy pea green scarf that gave a pop of color to her outfit and perfectly framed the unusual necklace she wore, a white stone about the size of a walnut that was crisscrossed with black veins. The stone was wrapped in a spiderweb mesh of silver wire and the whole thing dangled from a black leather loop that hung around Fiona's neck.

"Is that howlite?" I asked her.

Automatically, Fiona's hand went to the stone. "You recognize it? Most people have never heard of howlite." Again, she slid a look to Noreen who was now counting the equipment and acting like we didn't exist. Fiona's hand fluttered back down to her side. "It's just something I like to wear."

"Well, it's very nice. I've seen similar stones used in Native American jewelry. Is it from the Southwest?"

I don't think I imagined it; Fiona really did look Noreen's way again.

And I couldn't help but think that like my ol' buddy, Jerry Garcia, Noreen really couldn't care less.

Fiona's smile withered around the edges. "The necklace is from New Mexico. Can we stop at the truck on our way next door?" she asked, effectively changing the subject. "I'll get my suitcase."

Together, we walked out to the front porch. I was quickly finding out—and enjoying every minute of it—that October on South Bass is a feast for the senses. The wineries were in full production and farmers sold cider and pumpkins from roadside stands. Goldenrod danced in the lake breeze and the lake itself, as smooth as glass that afternoon, reflected the kaleidoscope mood swings of the sky: gray one day, sapphire the next, and when the clouds were low and the winds calm, ghostly white.

In wonderful counterpoint to it all, the trees between my house and Chandra's were a riot of rich color—golden elms, rusty oaks, fiery red maples—all of their glory like an exclamation mark to Chandra's purple house with its yellow windows, orange doors, and teal garage.

Though I hardly knew her at all, something told me Fiona appreciated all of that as much as I did. Once I ushered her down the steps and she retrieved her suitcase from the truck, we closed in on Chandra's and she caught sight of the wind chimes and the sun catchers, the gnomes that filled Chandra's garden and the gigantic pumpkin near the front door carved with wide round eyes and a huge grin. Her smile came back full force.

"Cool!" Pink shot through Fiona's cheeks. "Not that I don't like your place. It's a great house, but . . ." she stammered, looking back at my B and B. Believe me, I did not take offense. I know hulking Victorians aren't everyone's cup of tea, but this one was my pride and joy, from the teal color accented with rose, terra cotta, and purple to the distinctive chimney that caressed the outside of the house all the way from the first floor to the slate roof. I'd lived there less than a year and my business had been up and running for just one season, but already, the house and the island felt like home. After a hectic life in New York and a past I was anxious to put behind me, a home was exactly what I was looking for.

I laughed. "No worries. There's a lot to like about Chandra's and I figured being close by was better than you staying all the way downtown at the hotel." I didn't bother to explain that technically, *all the way downtown* was less than a mile. "Chandra's so excited to have a guest. She's . . ." I wondered how to explain and decided it was best just to lay things on the line. Since Fiona would know all about Chandra soon enough—Chandra would make sure of that—she might as well get the truth from me.

"Chandra's our resident crystal and tarot card reader," I warned Fiona. "If you have any problem—"

The kid actually skipped across the next few feet of lawn. "This is going to be so much fun! I read tarot, too.

And I meditate every evening. I have for years. It sounds like Chandra and I will have a lot in common."

I didn't doubt it, especially when Chandra's front door flew open and a plume of patchouli incense streamed outside. It was quickly followed by Chandra, resplendent (as always) that day in an orange turban that hid her bobbed blond hair and showed her earrings—witch hats studded with purple beads—to the best advantage. The earrings looked just right with her diaphanous purple top painted with orange jack-o'-lanterns and cute black cats.

Cats.

I couldn't help myself. I automatically looked around for my nemesis, but Jerry was nowhere to be seen. I indulged in a moment of obsessing. Where was the little dickens? And when would he leap out and ambush me?

I never had a chance to speculate further.

Chandra took one look at Fiona—and that T-shirt she wore with the icy EGG logo—and her welcoming smile vanished in a flash.

"EGG? Bea, you didn't tell me EGG was here again."

I wasn't sure who was suddenly more pale, Chandra or Fiona.

The kid backstepped away from the house. "I . . . I can stay s-somewhere else. I don't want to . . . want to inconvenience you . . . or . . . or anything . . . or . . ."

Feeling a bit as if the sidewalk had been pulled out from under me, I put a hand on the kid's shoulder to keep her from bolting. "EGG's been to South Bass before?" I asked Chandra.

Chandra is nothing if not the friendliest and the most accepting of all the people I'd met on the island. With a start, she realized she'd made Fiona uncomfortable and she smiled. Or at least she tried.

"I don't remember you from last year." Chandra stuck out a hand and, as if she wasn't sure what was going to happen when she took it, Fiona stepped forward for a quick shake. "Sorry! I was just surprised to see your shirt. That's all. Bea, you didn't tell me EGG was back."

I hoped my laugh didn't sound as phony as it felt. "I didn't know this was a return visit. Besides, EGG might have been here, but Fiona never has. She's new with EGG." Did the look I gave Chandra send the right message? That we had to make sure Fiona felt welcome and at home?

"Sorry." Chandra's weak little laugh was an echo of my own. "I just . . . oh, never mind!" She backed up a step to allow Fiona to walk in the house. "Come on in and we'll make a pot of white tea. How does that sound? It's nice and mild and fruity and—"

"I love white tea!" Fiona turned misty eyes toward me. "Thank you, Bea. I think I'm going to like it here. And sorry . . ." She turned that puppy dog look on Chandra. "I'm sorry I surprised you."

Peace.

I was grateful for it, even if I was a little confused by Chandra's reaction to her guest.

I promised myself I'd have a talk with Chandra, told them both I'd see them later, and headed back home only to find Noreen rearranging the equipment. Again.

I poked my head into the parlor. "Need anything?"

"No, we're all set. At least for now." Noreen set down her clipboard, picked it up, swiped a hand over the top of the case where she'd just deposited it, and set it down again. "We're anxious to get started, of course."

"You never told me . . ." I looked around at the equipment cases and cameras. "You've been here before. What exactly are you doing back here on the island?" I asked Noreen.

She barked out a laugh. "Elkhart Ghost Getters?" She looked at me hard. "You've never heard of us? Well, it doesn't matter," she decided even before I could tell her she was right. "We're paranormal investigators."

It all made sense now: the thermal cameras and the Mel meters and such. Though I was not a fan of reality TV shows of any kind, I didn't live under a rock. I knew cable television was fat with shows that followed the adventures of crews who were out to prove—or disprove— the existence of things that go bump in the night.

"You're filming a TV show." It never hurts to state the obvious.

Noreen nodded. "Not just a show. The first episode of our new series."

"And you're doing it here on South Bass?" I realized my mistake immediately and, with a quick smile, apologized for the skepticism in my voice. "It's not that I don't think it's great, but South Bass? I never associated South Bass with—"

"Never saw our pilot episode we filmed here last fall, did you?" Noreen wasn't just happy to show how completely out of it I was, she was downright smug. She crossed the room, flipped open one of the equipment cases, and pulled out an iPad. A few clicks of the keys and she flipped the screen around so I could see it.

Except for the glow of what looked like a gigantic camping lantern on the floor in the center of the scene, the video was dark and grainy, a mishmash of gray and black shadows, and I bent nearer, the better to focus.

"You?" I asked, looking up briefly from the shot of the woman standing just outside the eerie beam of light. "You're standing behind what looks like—"

"Wine barrels."

"And this was taken here on South Bass?" It wasn't really a surprise; there are any number of wineries on the island. "What am I supposed to be watching for?"

"You'll know it when you see it," Noreen assured me.

She was right. Fifteen seconds in, there was a movement to Noreen's left that reminded me of the wave of heat that comes off a candle. It rippled and shifted, and the shadows darkened for a moment. That giant lantern-like object in front of Noreen flashed, and a second later—

"You're kidding me, right?"

I stared at the screen for a couple seconds, then stood up straight and fastened the same sort of sucker punched look to Noreen while I repeated myself. "You're kidding me, right?"

"Want to see it again?" Before I could tell her I did, she restarted the video and this time, just like last time, I saw what I thought it was impossible to see.

In those couple seconds after the light flashed, a figure materialized out of nowhere.

It was a man. I could tell that much from the cut of his clothes. He was tall and completely transparent and he was missing—

I swallowed hard. "Where's his head?"

Noreen clicked out of the video. "No head."

"And he's a—"

"He is the best video evidence of a full-body apparition anybody anywhere has ever seen."

"And you—"

"Filmed it last fall. Right here on South Bass. This is the video we showed at a paranormal investigation conference last fall and let me tell you . . ." Noreen's eyes took on a dreamy look that told me she savored every moment of the memory. "That made the other investigators in our field stand up and take notice. Got the cable networks to finally come to their senses, too. I'd been sending them film of our investigations for years and it showed some good evidence, too. But TV producers, they aren't interested in what's good. They only want what's fantastic. This." She tapped the iPad. "This is fantastic. This is what got us our show."

"Because it's—"

"Like I said, the best video evidence of a full-body apparition anybody anywhere has ever recorded."

In an effort to clear it, I shook my head. "A ghost here on South Bass?"

Noreen tossed her head. "Not into island legends, are

you? It's why we came out to the middle of nowhere last year in the first place. You know, because of the legend."

"Of the headless ghost."

She slapped my back so hard, I nearly toppled. "You got that right, girlfriend. And that's exactly why we came back this year. You know, to get more evidence. We're headed out to find the ghost of Sleepy Harlow."

Becca Robbins is happy to help research a farmers' market and tourist trading post—until she has to switch her focus to finding a killer...

AN ALL-NEW SPECIAL
FROM NATIONAL BESTSELLING AUTHOR

PAIGE SHELTON

Red Hot Deadly Peppers

A Farmers' Market Mini Mystery

Becca is in Arizona, spending some time at Chief Buffalo's trading post and its neighboring farmers' market to check out how the two operate together. She's paired with Nera, a Native American woman who sells the most delicious pecans—right next to a booth with the hottest peppers money can buy.

When Nera asks her to deliver some beads to Graham, a talented jewelry maker inside Chief Buffalo's, Becca is grateful to get a break from the heat. Little does she realize that the heat's about to get cranked up even more—because Graham has been murdered, and she's the one who finds his body. She soon discovers that Graham was Nera's cousin, and that her uncle was recently killed, too, after receiving a threatening note. Becca begins to think the murders may have something to do with the family's hot pepper business. Now she must find the killer, before she's the one in the hot seat...

Includes a bonus recipe!

paigeshelton.com
facebook.com/TheCrimeSceneBooks
penguin.com

M1144T0813